THE
LIGHT
TO MY
DARKNESS

IVY SMOAK

This book is a work of fiction. Names, characters, places, and incidents are fictitious. Any resemblance to actual persons, living or dead, events, or locales is purely coincidental.

To my fiancé.
Because technically, I'll never be able to write a dedication with those words again. This is the last book I'm coming out with before you become my husband. And as we take that step, I'm very aware of the fact that you are my foundation.

PART 1

CHAPTER 1

Friday

I wrestled with the fabric until I was able to pull it down over my large pregnant belly. Even after the alterations, the dress pinched me uncomfortably on the sides. I blew a strand of hair out of my face and placed my hands on my stomach. In two months, my little baby boy would be born. But Bee and Mason's wedding was next week. I stared at my reflection in the mirror. And I was going to look like an elephant in their pictures. I sighed and stepped out of the changing room.

"Oh, it's perfect," Bee said.

I laughed. "You have a strange definition of perfection."

"The gray doesn't take away from your beautiful pregnancy glow at all."

It just makes me look like a huge zoo animal. "Why does everyone else get to wear blue again?" Not that it mattered. The blue would make me look like a whale instead.

"Because you're my matron of honor and I love you." She smiled at me. "Are you alright, Penny? You look a little pale."

I waved my hand through the air. "I'm fine. You'll see soon enough. Being pregnant is the freaking worst." I collapsed in the chair beside her.

Bee laughed. "Just a few weeks ago you wouldn't stop talking about how it was the best thing ever. The miracle of birth. All that jazz."

"Well, a few weeks ago it wasn't 90 degrees outside. What possessed you to get married in the middle of summer anyway?"

"If I recall, you had a wedding in June. It was hot that day too. And I love summers in the city. It always seems less crowded."

"That's because everyone leaves since it's literally hell here."

"Oh come on." She lightly tapped my arm. "Stop letting your pregnancy hormones win."

I pressed my lips together. I hated that she was right. It was like I had no control over my emotions at all recently. "It has nothing to do with hormones," I lied. "It's just so hot, Bee. How am I going to last two more months?"

"How about you go change and I'll take you out for ice cream?"

I glared at her. "Are you practicing weird parenting techniques on me or something?"

"Maybe?" She raised both eyebrows.

"Fine. You win. But water ice, not ice cream. Or else I won't be able to fit into this dress next week." I slowly stood up.

Bee laughed. "You're being too hard on yourself, Penny. You really do have that whole pregnancy glow thing going on."

Pregnancy glow my ass, I thought as I closed the dressing room door behind me. I wrestled the dress back off over my head and hung it on the hanger. I pulled on the comfortable dress I had worn in. It was stretchy and cotton, and the only thing I ever wanted to wear anymore. I glanced back in the mirror. The pregnancy glow thing really was just a myth. If anything, I looked pale like Bee had mentioned earlier. It was probably just because my makeup had melted off in the sweltering heat. After getting water ice I would need to spend the rest of the day sitting down in the air-conditioning.

"Mason is swinging by tonight to grab all of them," Bee said and took the hanger out of my hand as I exited the dressing room.

"I'm pretty sure that's the matron of honor's job," I said. "I can handle carrying a dress." Bee had slowly been taking responsibilities away from me for the past few weeks. I was starting to feel like the most useless matron of honor in the history of the title.

"No, actually the matron of honor doesn't have to do anything like that. Usually maids of honor handle it because they're never pregnant. You know...because they're maids. But you're technically my matron of honor. And matrons of honor have less tasks, especially if they're pregnant."

I laughed. "Fair enough." I watched her hand the dress back to the sales associate.

"Now, come on, big momma. Water ice time!" She linked her arm in mine.

"Please don't start calling me that."

"That's actually how we had the programs printed. They say Matron of Honor - Big Momma, all in bold."

"That's exactly what I feared," I said with a laugh. The wave of heat seemed to hit me like a brick wall when we stepped outside. "Is it possibly even hotter?" I could already feel beads of sweat on the back of my neck.

"How about we just get you home. We can stop somewhere on the way and get water ice to-go. Then we can eat it at your place." She dropped my arm and walked over to the town car parked alongside the curb.

I glanced down the sidewalk at the water ice place. "Bee, it's just a block away." I pointed at the sign. "I can manage." I walked past her before I heard her response. First the pale comment. And now she didn't think I could walk a few feet? I bit the inside of my lip.

Ow, don't kick me. I placed my hand on my stomach and tried to steady my breathing. I wasn't an idiot. Obviously James told her. He promised he wouldn't tell anyone. The baby kicked again. *Don't go agreeing with your father. You're supposed to be on my side.*

"Whoa, wait up," Bee said. "Now you're a pregnant sprinter? It's not a race. Seriously, slow down, Penny."

"He told you, didn't he?" I asked as I grabbed the door handle of the water ice place.

"Who told me what?"

I shook my head. She didn't get to play innocent. I didn't want anyone else to know. My medical history wasn't anyone else's business. I stormed into the shop.

"Really, I have no idea what you're talking about," Bee said from behind me.

I ignored her and ordered a small lemon water ice. I continued giving her the silent treatment until she sat down across from me with that sad look on her face.

"I'm sorry," we both said at the exact same time.

Bee smiled. "Just for the record, James didn't tell me. He told Mason because he was worried about you. Then Mason told me. You know how these things go."

"I know. It's fine. But there really isn't anything to worry about."

"James said it makes the pregnancy more dangerous."

"It's just a heart murmur. Two percent of the population has one or something like that." Repeating facts that the doctor told me made me feel better about it. It wasn't like mitral valve regurgitation was some uncommon thing. Tons of people had it.

"Still. James is all worried. And now he's got me worried too."

"I'm fine. Really." I ate a huge spoonful of my water ice. *God is that good.* "See." I gestured to my water ice. "I'm doing normal pregnancy things. Everything is normal."

"You said normal too many times for me to believe you."

"Miss Cowan, soon to be Mrs. Caldwell, you should be focusing on your wedding. Not me." I gave her what I hoped was an encouraging smile.

"Well, that's the thing. I know you're supposed to be on bed rest, Penny. Technically you shouldn't even be coming to my wedding."

James didn't seriously tell Mason that. I was going to kill him when I got home. We had talked about this. I could do the whole bed rest thing after Bee's wedding. She needed me right now. I wasn't going to leave her in the lurch like Melissa had done to me. I was taking my role as matron of honor very seriously.

And I felt fine. Besides, the doctor recommended bed rest. He didn't demand it. The baby kicked me again. *Ow. Traitor.* "Bed rest is just a general term for taking it easy. I think relaxing and eating water ice counts."

"You're sure you feel okay? I don't want to be the reason that something happens to the baby."

I shook my head. "Nothing is going to happen. Everything is normal."

She winced at my use of the word normal again.

"Can we please just have a conversation that doesn't have to do with the fact that I'm pregnant? Let's focus on the wedding. Have you written your vows yet?"

"Ugh. No. I can't properly express how I feel in words. I so badly want them to be perfect, you know?"

"Well, what do you have so far?"

"Um...nothing, really. I'm too in my head. Everyone's going to be staring at me and I don't know what's going to come out of my mouth. I do presentations and pitches all the time, but this is way more intimidating."

"Think about the positives, though. You could spill red wine down the front of your wedding gown and still look smoking hot next to me. I secretly think you picked me to be your matron of honor because you knew I'd be a blimp."

Bee laughed. "You're right. It has nothing to do with the fact that you're my best friend."

I swallowed hard. I had been so flattered when Bee asked me to be her matron of honor. She had made friends in the city before meeting me. But we hung out all the time now. James and Mason being best friends basically forced us to be best friends too. And I was so happy that it did. I reached for a napkin.

"Are you crying?" she asked.

I blotted the napkin under my eyes. "I can't control my emotions. I'm a mess."

"Let's get you home. I have a wedding to focus on. James can take care of you for the rest of the day."

I laughed. "I don't need a babysitter."

"You sprinted here when you're supposed to be on bed rest. You absolutely need a babysitter."

"What I need is for him to stop kicking me." I placed my hand on my stomach. *Calm down.*

"Still convinced it's going to be a boy?"

"It feels like a boy. I can't explain it. But I know it is."

"Yeah, that makes no sense to me at all."

"That's because you've never been pregnant before," I said.

"Whenever I do get pregnant, I'm going to find out the sex of the baby immediately. I don't know how you can bear not knowing when you could literally pick up the phone and find out."

"I already know. It's definitely a boy."

Bee rolled her eyes. "Come on, big momma. Let's get your crazy ass home."

"Bee!"

We both laughed as she helped me to my feet. Before we stepped out into the scorching heat I turned and gave her a hug. With all of our jokes, I could still tell she was worried. I truly did believe that there was nothing to worry about. She should be spending the next week in pre-wedding bliss, not studying my pale face.

"You can worry about me after you get back from the honeymoon. But not before, okay?"

She squeezed me back. "It's a little hard to just turn off an emotion, Penny. I do need to focus on my vows, though. Or else the whole wedding will be a disaster."

I held her at arm's length. "A disaster? As long as no one gets shot, I think we're good."

"It's still too soon to joke." But she smiled anyway. "Besides, last time I checked, Mason didn't have any crazy exes."

CHAPTER 2

Friday

"I'm home!" I called as I locked the door behind me. I was greeted by silence. "James? Ellen?" No one responded. It was rare to be home alone. I couldn't even remember the last time our apartment had been so quiet. I walked into the kitchen and scanned the counter.

"I'm sorry, little man," I said to my belly as I smoothed the fabric of my dress over my stomach. "There aren't any bananas left. How about an apple?" I shook my head as I eyed the fruit basket. "Yeah, that doesn't sound as good to me either."

I grabbed a glass of water instead and wandered into the living room. I sat down on the couch and rested my head back, staring up at the ceiling. It felt so good to sit down. Everything ached today. Silence probably comforted some people, but it made me feel unsettled. It was like this big empty void. Bed rest would be okay if there were people around all the time. But I didn't want to just sit around by myself. That sounded more like torture.

I sighed and stood back up. *Ow.* I placed my hand on my stomach. "Really, you need to stop doing that. I already told you there aren't any bananas." Another kick landed beneath my ribs. "I'll find something else. Please just stop kicking me." I walked back into the kitchen. I was about to open up the fridge when I spotted the mail on the counter.

It was foolish, but I let myself get excited when I saw a letter addressed to my pen name, Ivy Smoak. I tore open the top, unfolded the piece of paper, and held my breath as I read the words.

Dear Ms. Smoak,

Thank you for your query. We greatly appreciate your submission and have given it our careful consideration. Unfortunately, we do not feel that your project is the right fit for our agency. Please keep in mind that this is a very subjective business. Thanks for thinking of our agency and we wish you the best with your writing career.

Sincerely,

Mallory Jenson

Agent/Submissions Coordinator

Clark Henshaw Literary Group

I slowly exhaled. *Subjective business.* It was only biased in the sense that every agency in the city agreed that my writing sucked. The problem was that after this many rejections, I was starting to believe them. At first it was easy to push the rejection aside. Now though? Maybe I didn't have what it took. Maybe my manuscript really was as crappy as everyone said. I stuffed the paper back in the envelope. Or maybe they weren't reading it at all. Careful consideration probably meant straight in the trashcan. Well, two could play that game. I tore the rejection letter in half and tossed it into the trash.

"I know," I said and looked down at my stomach. "Putting Penny Hunter on the submission form is a foot in the door. But I need to do this on my own. Now please stop agreeing with your father about everything. I'm the one carrying you around for months." My words earned me another sharp kick in the ribs.

Thirteen rejection letters. I sat down on a stool in the kitchen and let my face sink into my hands. I had submitted my query to at least 50 agencies and most of them hadn't even bothered responding. I told James I was going to write instead of work, but all I had to show for it was a manuscript that I had reworked dozens of times because no one liked the story. *Our story.* Maybe I was the one being too subjective. Maybe I couldn't see that it wasn't a story worth telling because I saw it with rose-colored glasses. I lived it. James was everything to me. And I was a naive, annoying, indecisive girl that no one wanted to read about. Fiction had never been so real. And in this case, maybe fiction would have been better. I should have just written a story that someone actually wanted to read instead of my idealized notion of what my life was.

I grabbed the apple that had been taunting me ever since I got home and bit into it. *I know it's not a banana, but you can't just eat bananas and water ice all day. You have to be a grown-up.* For some reason I burst into tears. Because I wasn't talking to the baby growing in my stomach. I was talking to myself. I was living off my husband. When had I become a Stepford Wife? I was, in every sense of the word, useless.

Oh my God, I'm losing my mind. This baby was seriously making it impossible to stay sane. And every time I even thought such a thing, he kicked me so hard. He was feisty. And stubborn. And just like his father. I smiled. James would probably say that those characteristics were just like me. I placed my hand on my stomach and waited for the kick. But this time it didn't come. "Thank you for being on my side," I said into the empty kitchen.

I knew I wasn't useless. But just once I wanted to show everyone that I wasn't just some trophy wife. It wasn't like I didn't see the tabloids. I knew what people said about me. They talked about my dress at this event and my necklace at that. But damn it, I had a brain. I was more than my smile and my clothes. I could pull my own weight. No, not enough to afford a place like this. A small salary coming in off my books, though? That would make me feel so much better. Wife and mother were the two best titles. They were music to my ears. But adding author at the end of it would just make it a tad sweeter.

I took another bite of the apple. "And there's the kick. You are going to be such a handful, baby boy."

The sound of the front door opening made me jump. I quickly wiped away my tears. Bee was right, I needed to stop letting my pregnancy hormones win. An agent would call any day now. And even if one didn't, I was happy. I loved my life. I loved our story even if no one else did. Even if no one else would ever read about it. Honestly, maybe that was better. It was our story, not anyone else's. No one knowing kept it more pure somehow.

"Hey, beautiful." James kissed my temple and ran his hand along my stomach. "How are my girls today?"

I smiled up at him. "We're good, but you know perfectly well that it's your son brewing in there."

"I beg to differ. This baby is every bit you." Suddenly the smile was gone from his face as he lightly touched my chin. "What's wrong?" He ran the pad of this thumb beneath my eye even though I knew my tears were gone.

I swallowed hard. A lie was on the tip of my tongue and I wasn't even sure where it had come from. The word nothing just wanted to fall out of me. The thought of the lie left a sour taste in my mouth. That was the one thing we never did. Not now. Not after everything we'd been through. "I got another rejection letter in the mail." I bit the inside of my lip, feeling every bit the failure.

He placed a soft kiss against my forehead. "Those agencies are insane. They have no idea what they're missing out on."

I laughed. "I don't know about that. They're all saying the same thing. Which means I'm the one that's insane for thinking I had a chance."

"You know, you could let me read it. Maybe I could help." He leaned against the counter as he stared at me.

I let my eyes wander down to his lips. For some reason I was finding it hard to concentrate on his words. Probably because we were rarely alone. And by some stroke of luck it was currently just the two of us. I forced my eyes back up to his. "You can read it. Eventually. The grand plan was to get an agent, get it published, and give you a real hardback copy. I wanted you to read it when I was sure that it was perfect. I wanted to show you that I was worth something more than..." I let my voice trail off. "I just want to prove that I'm worthy of you."

"Oh, Penny." He wrapped his arms around me.

I breathed in his heavenly cologne. Wife. Mother. I didn't need the extra title. This was all I truly wanted. "I could get a thousand rejections and I'd still be happy," I mumbled into his neck.

He kept his arms wrapped around me, and didn't say a word. But his silence was louder than words. I knew exactly what he was thinking.

"I need to do this one thing on my own," I whispered.

"I didn't say anything."

"But you were thinking it."

He sighed and took a step back from me. "Honestly, it's probably good to have anonymity. Our life is already in the public eye way more than I'd like it to be. I'm getting used to the idea of you wanting to use a pen name."

"Really?" I placed my hand on my stomach. Both my boys were agreeing with me tonight.

"Really. You took my name in real life. That's what matters to me, Mrs. Penny Hunter. Now, aren't you going to ask me what's in the bag?"

I looked at the grocery bag on the counter. I hadn't even noticed that he brought one in. I smiled at him. "Fruit and chocolate?"

He laughed and slid the bag down the counter toward me. I opened it up and pulled out the bananas and Dove ice cream bars.

"This is why I love you. You're a mind reader." I pushed the apple aside and grabbed a banana instead. In two seconds flat I was biting into the food I had been desperately craving. "Mmm."

"Are you trying to torture me?" he asked.

I looked back up at James as I finished chewing. "There is no way that you're turned on right now. I'm huge." I gestured to my stomach. "And it's not like I'm sucking on this seductively. I just took the biggest bite."

"You're not huge. You're pregnant." He ran his palm along my stomach. "With my daughter. And I think you're absolutely gorgeous."

"It's a boy, James!"

A smile spread across his face. "It's definitely a girl."

"I swear it's not."

He raised his left eyebrow. "Do you want to bet?"

"Everyone else already has a wager going." I took another bite of the banana. "We might as well too. What did you have in mind?"

"Winner gets whatever they want."

I laughed. "That's rather vague. So you're saying that if it's a boy, I can have anything I want? Anything at all?"

"And if it's a girl, I can have anything I want." His eyes scanned down my body.

"Deal. But all you have to do is ask. I'll give you whatever you want right now." I glanced at the clock on the wall. "We should have a few minutes before..." my words were cut short by his lips crashing against mine. I loved that he craved me the way I craved crazy foods. And him. I certainly never stopped craving him.

I pulled on his tie to deepen the kiss. He groaned into my mouth. I loved that sound. Yes, we were rarely alone anymore. But we knew how to take advantage of those few moments in between the hectic ones.

We both jumped when we heard the front door open.

"We're home!" Ellen called from the foyer.

James ran the tip of his nose down the length of mine. "To be continued?"

"Of course." I straightened his tie. A continuation could mean anything from a few hours to several days, but neither one of us were upset. Maybe a couple years ago we would have been annoyed by the interruption. But we were a family now. "I love you."

"I love you so much." He placed a swift kiss against my lips.

"Daddy!" the sweetest little voice squealed from the doorway of the kitchen.

CHAPTER 3

Friday

I turned to see the brightest smile, the rosiest cheeks, and the curliest mop of red hair running toward us. Scarlett collided with James' leg and wrapped her little arms around it.

"Hey, pumpkin." James ruffled her hair and bent down to lift her into his arms. Scarlett easily settled onto his hip, which was probably her favorite seat in the world.

I smiled at the scene. No, I wasn't the least bit upset about the interruption. James had two girls in his life now. And I was okay with sharing him. He was the most wonderful father.

"Daddy, Ellie took me to the park!"

Ellen smiled from the doorway. Scarlett had been pronouncing Ellen's name as Ellie ever since she had learned how to talk. I was pretty sure she was able to pronounce Ellen now, but Ellen seemed to like the nickname.

"I can see that," James said and lightly tapped the tip of Scarlett's nose. There was a splatter of mud on the side of it and her dress had several grass stains.

"Let's get you in the bath before dinner," Ellen said.

"No, I want Daddy to do it!" Scarlett nestled her face into James' chest.

James laughed. "It's okay, Ellen, I can give her a bath." He placed Scarlett back on the ground. "Go say hello to your mother first."

A few months ago, Scarlett wanted me to do everything with her. Now she greatly favored James and had to be reminded of my existence. I hated how fast time was flying by.

But the beaming smile on her face as she ran toward me made my heart swell. I knelt down as she threw herself into my arms.

"Hi, Mommy. Ellie took me to the park today!"

"I heard, baby girl. Did you have fun?"

"Yes." She pulled away from me and frowned. "But I'm just girl now. This is baby." Scarlett put her hand on my stomach and leaned down so her lips were a few inches from my belly. "Hello, baby. I get to go take a bath with Daddy. You're too little, but you can come with us when you're older." She turned and ran away from me.

I put my hand on my chest. Tears were starting to well in my eyes. Scarlett was too young to be saying things like that. She would always be my baby girl. I wanted to freeze time. "I can come help too," I said as I slowly got to my feet.

"No, I've got it," James said. "You should lie down for a bit." He lightly kissed my temple and ran after our daughter who was already charging toward the stairs.

I turned to see Ellen pulling ingredients out of the fridge. "Do you want some help with dinner?" I asked.

"Oh, no, it's okay, dear. Go rest. I'll call you when it's ready." Ellen turned toward the stove.

I put my hand on my stomach. *At least you still need me, little man.* I wandered out of the kitchen. Scarlett and James' laughter drifted down the stairs. The sounds of pans clinking together echoed into the living room. I looked around at the spotless room. Everyone was busy being useful and I couldn't think of a thing to do.

I slowly wandered down the hall and opened up the door to the library. I still remembered the first day James and I moved into this apartment. We had played hide-and-go-seek and ended up in this room. Today the fireplace was off and we now had books covering every inch of shelf space. The other main difference was that there was a small desk set up in the corner. James had surprised me with it after we got back from our honeymoon. He had also dubbed this room as my office. But in reality it was just a library. I sat down at my desk and stared at the last line of the manuscript on my computer.

"I grabbed my umbrella in one hand and my coffee cup in the other and walked out into the rain."

The cursor blinked at the end. Whenever I stared at the cursor, my heart seemed to match the rhythm of its blinks. I closed my eyes and tried to picture sitting back at that coffee shop. I could feel the sense of despair from my head to the tips of my toes. It had felt like I had lost everything. Even then I knew that James was my one great love. I cried when I wrote the last chapter. I had found it hard to eat. Hard to focus. I had put myself back in that moment to the point where James was concerned about me.

I opened my eyes and stared at the blinking cursor. This story was my heart and soul. How could it not be a good fit for any agency? How could they not see my tears on the pages? How could they not understand me?

Maybe the end was too sad. There should have been hope. Or a happy ending. But I refused to change our story. It had felt like my life was over in that coffee shop. I had been numb. That's how this book had to end. The next one could end on a happy note. I pictured James proposing on one knee.

I had started the next novel, but it was harder to write. Being apart from James almost ruined me. And I didn't want to think about that night with Tyler. Mostly because I didn't want to ask Tyler if it was okay if I wrote about it. I was going to change the names, of course. But I wasn't just going to release a book and hope he never heard about it. We were friends. Friends didn't do that. I thought about his wife, Hailey. Would she read it? Would she be upset?

Just thinking about it made me close my laptop. That was the problem. I had told myself I was going to write a whole series. But I was too scared to write the second installment. I needed to talk to Tyler. He was coming over tomorrow night. I could ask him then. I thought about the things I had already written. Originally I meant to have this conversation when I first started writing. But I had chickened out. Writing about almost being with him was different than writing about our actual night together, though. It was possible that Tyler would veto the whole thing. So maybe it was better that no agency accepted it.

I hated to think I had spent the last three years of my life working on something pointless. I immediately shook away the thought. Writing hadn't been the only thing I was doing. I was raising Scarlett. I could picture her when she was a baby. She would scream bloody murder whenever we laid her down in her crib. For that first year I wasn't sure I ever slept for more than two hours at a time. But I loved every second of it. Well, maybe not the week where she couldn't keep anything down and we were in and out of the doctor's office every day. I could have done without that week.

"Don't scare me like that," I said and put my hand on my stomach. "Promise me you won't scare me the way your sister did." I waited for an answer. In a few seconds I felt the sharp kick under my ribs.

Ow. I smiled. "That'll do," I said.

"What'll do?"

I looked up to see James leaning against the doorjamb with his arms crossed. He had lost the suit and tie. He was wearing a pair of faded jeans and a white t-shirt. His hair was pushed back like he had gotten it wet with the bath water. There were wet splotches on his shirt. And I had never seen him more handsome.

"I was just talking to our son," I said.

He walked into the room. "And what were you talking to our daughter about?"

I laughed and shook my head. He was so stubborn, but he was going to be proven wrong when I gave birth to our son in a couple of months. "I was thinking about that week where Scarlett wouldn't eat anything. I was asking our son not to do that. He responded by kicking me, so I'm pretty sure we're on the same page."

"All that baby does is kick you. I don't know whether that's a yes or a no."

"It was a yes. I could tell. And you're right, he does kick me a lot. A whole lot more than Scarlett did. Just further proof that it's a little boy."

"Hmm. Time will tell."

I sighed. "Time. Time is going by too fast if you ask me. Did you hear what Scarlett said? That she wasn't my baby girl anymore. It was like a knife to my heart."

"I thought it was adorable."

"You think everything she does is adorable. Just wait until she's a teenager and she says she hates us on a daily basis."

"Did you do that with your parents?"

"No. But that's a thing that normal teenagers do I think."

"Well, there you go. She won't do that because she's just like you."

I laughed. "She is nothing like me. She's outgoing and carefree and completely like you."

James sat down on the edge of my desk and folded his arms across his chest. His eyes fixated on my face as if he was studying me.

I awkwardly tucked a loose strand of hair behind my ear. "What are you staring at?"

He didn't say anything. He just continued to stare at me intently.

"James, seriously, you're freaking me out." I laughed nervously.

He reached out and ran his hand down the side of my face. "Why after all these years do you still feel that you need to prove yourself to me?" He lowered his eyebrows slightly. "Are you not happy?" His hand fell from my face.

"What?" I stood up and slipped my hands into his. "No, it's not that. I'm so happy. You, our family, I'm so so happy, James."

"Then what is it?"

"It's just...I put everything into this book. Maybe I didn't realize how much I needed approval until this moment. But all these rejections weigh on me. This character," I said and gestured to my laptop. "She's me. It feels like they're all saying that they hate me. As a human being. That I'm not good enough. That I'm worthless."

"You are not worthless. Penny, you are the most amazing woman I have ever met. You are the most loving mother and wife. You're intelligent and stunning. And you have the most beautiful soul." He put his hand on the center of my chest. "Your heart beats with love and kindness and hope. And I don't know anyone else as worthy of everything they want in this world than you. So if what you want is for this book to be read, please, baby, let me help you get it into the right hands."

"You haven't even read it. You don't know if it's any good."

"If you wrote it with half the heart that you do everything else with, then I'm certain it's better than anything I've ever read."

I hastily wiped the tears away from my face.

"And if you shed one more tear over this book, let it be because you're celebrating hitting a bestseller list. Not fretting over a rejection letter from a company who wouldn't know what a good book was if it hit them in the face."

I laughed.

"There." He put his hands on both sides of my face. "That smile. How can you think that you're worthless when I live and breathe each day just to see that smile."

I stood up on my tiptoes and wrapped my arms around the back of his neck. He smelled like a mixture of children's berry scented shampoo and his cologne. It was the most glorious scent in the world. "Okay."

"Okay what?" His hands slid down my back, igniting this flame inside of me that I hoped would never extinguish.

"You can read it."

A smile broke over his face.

"But don't get all professorly on me and nitpick every little thing."

He laughed. "We talked about this. Professorly is not a word. So if you've used that in your novel I'm going to have to point it out."

"I've changed my mind. You can't read it now." I tried to wiggle out of his grip. I laughed as he pinned me to his chest and rotated us so that my ass was pressed against the desk.

His kiss silenced my laughter. God, I wanted to spend the rest of my life in his arms.

"Dinner time!" Ellen yelled from the kitchen.

James sighed and pressed his forehead against mine. "The timing of that woman."

I laughed. "To be continued?"

He grabbed my waist and pulled me off the desk. "To be continued."

But we both knew that our night consisted of watching a children's movie with Scarlett and falling asleep on the couch. I was usually the first one to pass out.

CHAPTER 4

Friday

Scarlett was smearing the pasta around her plate with her hand. A few months ago she had started refusing to sit in her highchair. I missed the days where she couldn't run off in the middle of dinner like a little banshee. She was giving me that look like she was eager to play tag. It was only a matter of minutes before she screamed "you're it" to no one in particular and took off. I wasn't sure if I had the energy to play tonight.

"Honey, are you all done eating?" I asked. "How about we go wash your hands and get everything ready for movie night?"

"I want Daddy to do it!" She slammed her hands back down on the pasta sending sauce flying off her plate. She giggled and smiled up at me.

The smile lifted my spirits slightly, but I wasn't sure how many times she could say she didn't want me before I burst into tears in front of her. I knew it was a phase, but it didn't mean it wasn't hurtful.

"I can help you, Scarlett," I said. "Let your father do the dishes and get the movie set up and we'll join him in a minute."

"But." She stuck her bottom lip out and it looked like she was the one that was going to start crying. "Why can't

Daddy help me?" She turned her adorable little face toward James.

"Of course I can help you clean up, pumpkin," he immediately said. He stood up and lifted her off her booster seat. "Let's go get you washed up again."

I sat there for a moment as they wandered off, wondering if that was it. That Scarlett was a Daddy's girl now and would never want my help with anything ever again. I sighed and started to clean up the mess she had left behind.

Doing dishes was one of my least favorite things to do when I was pregnant. It was hard to lean over with my hands in the sink with my huge stomach in the way. And for just a brief moment I was bitter. Because James knew that. When I had been pregnant with Scarlett I had mentioned that it hurt to do dishes once and he had been on top of it every night. Or he would at least insist that they just soak in the sink for Ellen to do in the morning. He barely let me lift a plate.

I leaned down and buried my hands in the soapy water. I was scolded with a soft kick. *I know, baby boy. But I'll do them quickly.*

There was no reason to be bitter. I rinsed off one of the pans and set it on the drying rack. James was being a good father. I understood that Scarlett came first now. And I was glad that they were two peas in a pod. I was.

Damn it, so why am I crying? The hormones were making me feel insane. I blinked hard to try and will the tears away as I rinsed off another pan. James had just told me that he lived and breathed each day to see my smile. But that wasn't even true anymore. He lived and breathed to see

Scarlett's beautiful smile. And sometimes, just sometimes, I missed having his undivided attention.

"Ow." This time my hand went to my chest. The plate I was holding made a terrible clattering noise as it hit the side of the sink, and then it plopped back into the water. I closed my eyes and willed the sharp pain to go away. Ever since the doctor had told me about my condition, I had these phantom pains. I knew they weren't real because I had never had them before. It was just in my head. But no matter how many times I told myself that, it still felt like my heart was being sliced in two.

I'm okay. We're okay. I looked down at my stomach. The pain slowly subsided and I reached back into the water and lifted up the plate. Luckily it had survived the fall. *Everything's okay.*

"What are you doing?" James grabbed the plate out of my hand. There was an icy look in his eyes and a sternness in his voice that I didn't quite understand. "We were going to do those." He plopped Scarlett down on the counter and she leaned down and picked up a spoon out of the sink.

"Daddy said we were doing dishes tonight, Mommy!" She slapped some of the bubbles in the sink with the spoon.

James turned away from me. I thought maybe I had imagined his tone and the look in his eyes, but his back seemed rigid and uninviting.

"Thank you." I lightly touched his back and leaned over and kissed the top of Scarlett's head.

Neither one of them acknowledged me.

I just knew I was a few seconds from bursting into tears and I didn't want to be seen. Tonight I wanted to disappear. I took a step back from the two most important people in my life. And I tried not to think about the fact that I wasn't sure either of them needed me anymore.

The pain was back in my chest. But it wasn't like the one I had felt moments before. This one mimicked the way I had felt in the last few pages of my manuscript. Like I had just lost everything. And I didn't understand the feeling. My family was right in the other room. So why did I feel so far away?

"You're hurting me," I whispered. I placed my hand on my stomach as I made my way up the stairs. It felt like the baby was doing a summersault in my belly. My hand gripped the railing tighter. It was like he was trying to tell me I should go into the family room and get the movie set up. But I just couldn't tonight. I didn't want Scarlett to see me cry. That was one thing I never wanted to do in front of my daughter. I wanted her to think I was strong. Even on the days where I felt weak.

I knelt down before I even reached the bed and let myself cry. Maybe it was the hormones. Maybe it was the feeling of not being needed. Maybe it was the rejection letter. Or maybe it was the fact that James had snapped at me when what I really needed was a hug. I had no idea. I just felt so defeated.

"Penny, we're starting the movie!" James called from downstairs.

I wanted my daughter to think that I was strong, but maybe that was a lie. Because right now I just needed James' arms around me. "James," I whispered. *Ow.* He could take away the pain. He'd know what to do. He always made me feel better.

"Penny?" he called again.

I waited for his footsteps on the stairs, but they didn't come. I lay down in the middle of the carpet. James didn't come to see if I was okay. He left me completely alone. I used to think he could feel when I needed him. He always just showed up. When had he stopped feeling my pain?

Scarlett's ecstatic giggle and James' deep laugh drifted into the room from downstairs.

It made everything hurt even more. How could he tell Mason about being worried about my health and then act this way? He could read me like the back of his hand. He knew I was about to cry downstairs. And he took my silence as me being upset with him. *I need you, James.*

This wasn't concern. This was something else. I closed my eyes tight. Were we falling apart?

***

The sun streaming across my face made me open my eyes. I wiped the drool off the side of my face as I slowly sat up. For a moment I was disoriented. But then I remembered falling asleep on the floor. I remembered the pain in my chest and my son fighting my poor decisions. I put my hand on my stomach. The pain was gone. But now my side ached from sleeping on the hard floor. Why hadn't James moved me? Why hadn't he asked if I was okay when he found me like this?

I turned to look at the bed. It was still made. I swallowed hard. *James never came to bed?* I pushed myself up off the floor. I would have started calling his name, but I didn't want to disturb Scarlett sleeping in the other room. *God, where was he?*

My heart felt like it was slamming against my ribcage. Had he left? I knew he was mad at me, but that was no reason to leave in the middle of the night. We hadn't even talked about what had happened. Why would he just leave? I went down the stairs as quickly as I could. Panic was starting to set in. There was always this thought in the back of my head. What if he started using again? Would I even be able to notice the signs? I grabbed my phone off the kitchen counter and clicked on his name in my contact list. I was just about to call him when I walked into the living room.

I froze when I saw them on the couch. Scarlett's head was nestled on James' lap. She had her arms wrapped around his hand like it was one of her stuffed animals. James' head was leaning against the back of the couch. He looked ridiculously uncomfortable, but he was sleeping peacefully.

All my worry and anger dissipated, replaced by this warm fuzzy feeling. I shouldn't have run off last night. I should have talked to him about the way his tone had upset me. But none of that really mattered. I knew he had snapped at me because he didn't want me doing dishes. He wanted me to be more closely following the doctors recommendations. How could I be mad at him for caring about my wellbeing?

"I'm sorry," I whispered and sat down in front of them on the couch. I rested my head against James' thigh.

He made a soft moaning noise, but didn't stir.

James was the most caring husband, the sweetest father, and the best friend I could possibly ask for. If he wanted me to take it easy, I'd take it easy. Why would I hide in my room in pain when my whole life was in this room? We weren't falling apart at all. Our relationship had changed, yes. But change was a good thing.

The problem was that I had never really been good at change. And soon our three would be four. James and I would have even less time together. I just needed to hold on to those moments in between. I needed to remember that our family was better when it wasn't just us. Sometimes the messiest moments were the most fun. I eyed the bowl of popcorn that had fallen on the floor. I smiled and closed my eyes. James would never slip. Scarlett and my smiles were enough to make him happy. *And yours, baby boy.* I placed my hand on my stomach. *He's going to love your smile too.*

CHAPTER 5

Saturday

"Penny, what are you doing on the floor?" James whispered.

I smiled. His breath was warm in my ear. I loved the feeling of him being close, even though I knew he was just trying not to wake Scarlett. I slowly opened my eyes. James was sitting next to me on the ground, his back against the sofa. Concern was etched on his face.

"You never came to bed," I said quietly.

He gestured toward Scarlett sleeping peacefully behind us. "We fell asleep watching the movie. Here, let me help you up." He put his hand out for me and pulled me to my feet.

My back was stiff and my side was still sore from lying on the carpet for most of the night. But I hid my grimace. Today was a new day. And today, I didn't want there to be any hostility between us. I was going to start taking things a little more slowly like he wanted. If getting the cold shoulder last night was his plan for making me behave, it had certainly worked.

I looked down at Scarlett. She had grabbed a pillow and was hugging it where James' hand had been a few minutes ago. She really was the most adorable little girl. I looked back up at James. He was staring at me, like he was waiting for me to say something. He was probably waiting for me to apologize. But before I could say anything, he grabbed my hand and led me out of the room.

I hoped that didn't mean he wanted to argue with me. Heated words would surely awaken Scarlett no matter where we were in the house. That was the problem with open floor plans. I studied James as he pulled me into the kitchen. His posture didn't seem stiff and uninviting anymore. It was possible sleeping in an awkward position on the couch made it hard for him to look angry, though.

"James, before you say anything, I just want you to know that I'm sorry about last night. But I thought when you took Scarlett to wash up that it meant I needed to clear the dishes. And it got me thinking about when I was pregnant with her and you barely let me lift a pillow, let alone do any cleaning. After the doctor told us about my heart murmur, I thought you'd be even more concerned. But honestly, it seems like you don't care." I was trying to fix the problem, but apparently my mouth just wanted to make it worse. "We barely even talked about it. We just agreed that we'd keep it between us and that I'd start taking it easy after Bee and Mason's wedding. That was it. You never asked if I was okay. Or if I was scared." I felt my lip trembling. "And then I had to find out from Bee that you told Mason and who knows who else. Which was embarrassing for me. I really didn't want anyone else to know about my health problems. I don't want anyone worrying about me, especially when it seems like the person I'm closest to doesn't even care." I wanted to poke him in the middle of the chest but I didn't want to make him any angrier. Instead, I placed my hand on the counter to steady myself. "It doesn't even seem like Scarlett needs me anymore. She only ever wants you." I started to cry big, ugly tears. "And, God, James, I'm not okay. I'm so scared." I put my hand over my mouth, effectively silencing myself from the words that wouldn't seem to stop.

He immediately wrapped his arms around me and didn't say a word.

"Say something," I sobbed into his chest.

He ran his hand up and down my back.

"Say anything, James."

"I don't want you to give Scarlett a bath because I don't want you to strain when you pick her up to put her into the tub. And I don't want you doing dishes or lifting pillows."

My laugh was muffled by his shirt.

"And I didn't want to talk to you about any of this because I didn't want you to worry about me being worried. I was trying to be strong for you. But I'm scared too. Does that help? I'm terrified every day that the baby I put inside of you is going to kill you."

Those were the words that I needed to hear. They were morbid. And horrible. I swallowed hard. But that was the truth I needed to hear.

"And I'm mad at you for not following Dr. Nelson's advice. He didn't say to start bed rest in a week. He said now, Penny."

I leaned back and put my hands on either side of his face. "And Dr. Nelson also said that he didn't necessarily mean I needed to lie in bed all day. He said to take it slow. Relax. No stress." I stared into his eyes.

He lowered both eyebrows. "Are you saying that I'm causing you extra stress?"

"By not talking to me? By snapping at me instead of saying what's actually bothering you? By pushing me away? Yes. I'm already worried about losing my son, I don't want to have to worry about losing you too."

He pulled my face back into his chest. "We're not going to lose this baby. And you're not going to lose me. And Scarlett does need you. She's just going through a phase."

I knew he was sorry. I could feel it in the way he was holding me. "I know, I'm sorry. And the baby and I are both fine," I said into his shirt. "We just had a checkup. We're both healthy." I said the words for myself as much as I did for him.

"Your heart is leaking." James' voice sounded strained.

"My very healthy heart is leaking." I could feel him shaking his head above me.

"How about we cancel our plans tonight," he said. "We can get my dad to take Scarlett for the rest of the day. Then we can spend some time relaxing, just us."

"Scarlett will crash after hanging out with her friends all evening anyway. Then we can have some much needed alone time."

"If we can get everyone out of here. Why does it seem like whenever we have company they never leave?"

"Because we're so much fun to hang out with," I said.

He laughed and pulled back so he could look down at me. "How about you spend the day in bed until our company comes? It'll make me feel a lot better."

"I swear, James. I'll go crazy sitting in bed alone all day."

"Who said anything about being alone? Maybe you and Scarlett can draw or something while I read your manuscript?"

My stomach felt like it flipped over, and for once it wasn't because my son was being poorly behaved. I had forgotten I told James he could read my novel. Now that he was actually going to, I was incredibly nervous. "You want to read it today?"

"I want to at least start reading it today."

"Maybe we should all draw together? You know how much Scarlett loves your stick figures."

James laughed. "No, I know how much you love making fun of them."

"That's because you're so good at everything except for drawing. Your stick figure proportions are completely ridiculous. I can't not make fun of you."

"You're trying to change the subject."

"No, I'm not. But I am going to casually walk away and go wake Scarlett." I smiled at him and turned to leave the kitchen.

"And Penny?"

I glanced at him over my shoulder.

"I'm sorry I told my friends about your heart murmur. I just needed to vent because I was going crazy. It won't happen again. I'll talk to you next time instead of being compelled to talk about you. I'm really sorry." He looked so sincere. It made any other resentment I was holding on to completely evaporate.

"It's okay. I understand. Let's just not start telling everyone else we know, okay?"

"My lips are sealed."

I smiled, remembering once when Rob had promised that exact same thing. He had pretended to lock his mouth closed and throw away the key. But he had immediately started talking again.

"What?" James said. Apparently my smile was contagious because he was smiling now too.

"Nothing. I was just thinking about how similar you and your brother are."

James made a face. "Rob and I are nothing alike."

"Oh really? How about the fact that you both care so much but are awful at expressing it? Or the fact that you're both still kids at heart? Or that neither of you can stop getting your wives pregnant?"

James shook his head and laughed. "Go wake up Scarlett and tell her we get to eat breakfast in bed." He opened up the fridge and started rummaging through the options for what would probably end up being Eggo waffles. Ellen really did spoil us during the week. But I never minded Eggo waffles in bed. Actually, it sounded kind of perfect. I can't believe I was upset with him last night. He was the absolute sweetest. I wandered into the family room and knelt down in front of Scarlett.

"Hey, Scar." I ran my hands down her arm. "Guess what we get to do today?"

She yawned, but didn't open her eyes. "Zoo?" She immediately sat up, perfectly alert now, and started clapping her hands. "Zoo!"

I laughed. "We get to eat breakfast in bed!" Saying no was never the best plan of action around Scarlett. She'd do that thing where her lower lip trembled and tears welled in her eyes. Then we'd have to say yes to whatever ridiculous thing she came up with. James was an even worse pushover than me. If he had been in here, he probably would have just said okay and we'd be spending the day walking around in the God forsaken heat.

She blinked as she stared up at me. "In bed? But I want to eat with you and Daddy. Mommy, please. Why do I have to eat alone?"

"Not alone. You get to eat with us in our bed. And we can spend the day drawing zoo animals. Lots and lots of panda bears."

Her eyes seemed to grow with each thing I added to our list of activities. "I'll get the paper and crayons."

I smiled as she ran off. One day she'd stop pronouncing crayons as "crowns." I thought my heart might break into a million pieces when that happened. Scarlett might not realize it, but she'd always be my baby girl.

This time as I walked up the stairs, I was happy knowing that my family was coming up right behind me. I needed to count my lucky stars more often. I settled onto our bed.

Scarlett ran into the room a minute later. She came to the edge of the bed and tossed her box of crayons and the biggest stack of paper up onto it. Then she reached out her little hands and made the grabbing motion that meant she needed help getting up. I leaned down and lifted her onto the bed.

She crawled into the middle and plopped down right next to me. "Mommy, we have to draw four pandas. A mommy, a daddy, a little girl, and then a baby girl." She shoved a stack of paper on my lap.

"You know, this could be a little boy." I pointed to my stomach.

"Nuh-uh, Daddy said I'm going to get a baby sister." She grabbed a green crayon from the box and started drawing something that sort of resembled a bear. The green color really made me need to use my imagination.

James laughed from the door.

I looked up so that I could shake my head at him. He was starting to make Scarlett believe it was a girl too, which was ridiculous. But before I could say anything, I saw the tray of waffles in his hands. They were topped with chocolate ice cream and slices of banana.

"That looks so good," I said instead of scolding him for spreading lies to our daughter.

"I thought you'd approved." He joined us on the bed and handed me one of the plates.

"Don't tell Bee I was eating this. I already had to get my dress resized."

"What's resized?" Scarlett asked with her mouth full of ice cream.

"It's when you grow, pumpkin," James said.

"I'm resized too, Daddy. I used to be like that." She poked my stomach. "Right? Before the stork stole me?"

I pressed my lips together to prevent myself from laughing. We'd had a brief conversation with Scarlett about where babies came from. But we hadn't exactly talked about what to say beforehand. She had asked so many questions that we weren't prepared for. Unfortunately, it ended up sounding like storks came in the middle of the night and stole babies and then eventually returned them when they were finished baking. Or something along those lines. I hoped we hadn't done too much damage.

"He'll probably come soon to take the baby," Scarlett said. "Draw the stork stealing the baby panda and putting it in the oven." She placed a neon pink crayon on my piece of paper. "What happens if the baby bakes too long? Does it become a grown-up?"

James stifled a laugh.

I looked up at him. His eyes danced with so much warmth. God, we really had messed up our story. What if Scarlett went her whole life thinking that was how babies were born?

"There's a timer that lets you know when the baby is done," James said. "You know what, I'd like to draw the oven."

"Okay." Scarlett put a purple crayon and a piece of paper on his lap. "But what if the stork is in the bathroom when the timer goes off?"

"Then another stork will get the baby."

She paused in her drawing of the green pandas. Her eyes got really round. "How many storks are there, Daddy?"

"Not that many. Just a couple for each baby." He ruffled her hair.

I put my chin in my hand as I watched James fumbling for the right words for this crazy story. For the first time, I realized that he hadn't brought in my computer. I felt this small feeling of relief. I wasn't sure if I was ready for him to read my book yet. I wasn't sure it would ever be ready for his eyes. What if he hated how I portrayed him? What if he didn't want me to get it published?

I looked down at James' terrible drawing of an oven, one that was apparently going to cook our baby. Maybe my book needed some more imagination. I took a bite of chocolaty waffle goodness. What it needed was some help from Scarlett. I shook my head at the thought. My beautiful sweet girl would never be allowed to read my books. I lifted up my crayon and started to draw a neon pink stork. And I started to wonder if maybe one day I'd be writing about this moment. My life was no longer filled with illicit scandals or excitement at every turn. But it certainly seemed perfect from where I was sitting.

CHAPTER 6

Saturday

"You sure you're up to this?" James asked as he finished cutting up the celery sticks.

"Yes. Besides, they'll be arriving any minute. It's too late to cancel now." I grabbed a celery stick and dipped it into the hummus.

"A bunch of little kids running around our house all night isn't exactly relaxing," he said and slid the bowl closer to me.

"But talking to our friends is definitely relaxing." I slowly finished chewing. "So...do they all know?"

"I told Rob, Mason, and Matt. And I guess Mason told Bee. Rob may have told Daphne, but I really don't know. I asked them not to tell anyone. I'm sorry, baby."

"It's okay. I just wanted to know ahead of time in case everyone's acting weird around me. Rob is actually really good at keeping secrets though. Daphne probably doesn't know."

"I don't know about that. When we were little, Rob always tattled on me whenever I fucked up."

I laughed. "That was sibling rivalry or something. It had nothing to do with his ability to keep a secret. Besides, he said he accidentally saw the sex of our baby at that appointment you couldn't come to. And he hasn't told us."

James laughed. "He was probably lying about seeing it. And if he did see it, it wasn't by accident. He was most likely snooping. But it was better that he was doing that than staring at you during your exam."

I swatted James' arm. "It was sweet of him to offer to come with me. I was all nervous that day because I had never been to an appointment without you. And our baby had just started kicking me like a little monster." I put my hand on my stomach. "I thought something might be wrong."

"Something was wrong. You had a heart murmur and no one was competent enough to catch it. If you ask me, they should have discovered it a long time ago. We should probably switch doctors."

"Dr. Nelson is a well respected OB-GYN. He's not a cardiologist. We're lucky that he did find my heart murmur. And I'm used to him now. I don't want another doctor."

James shrugged.

"I'm serious, James. If the doctor that delivered Scarlett hadn't retired, I'd still be going to him. But at this stage there isn't anyone else I'd consider seeing. You know how bad I am at change."

"You don't have to tell me." He stepped forward and ran his hand along my stomach. "But change is coming. Best start preparing." He winked at me.

"I wasn't referring to our son. I'm just excited to meet him. Although, I do wish he would stop kicking me so hard. I swear he's going to hit something loose in there."

James frowned. "Maybe you should lie down."

"That won't make him stop. I think he's going to be a hyper child."

"He probably has so much energy because he's stealing all of yours. Are you sure you're feeling okay?"

"If you say I look pale, I swear I'm going to slap you." I pointed a celery stick at him.

James laughed. "I was actually going to say you look tired."

"That's not much better," I said.

"I didn't say you don't look beautiful." He kissed my forehead. "You're always gorgeous." He kissed the tip of my nose. "Gorgeous and a tiny bit tired."

I laughed as his lips landed on my mouth.

A ringing noise sounded through the apartment.

"You have got to be kidding me," he sighed against my lips. "It's like every time we kiss someone interrupts us."

I ran my palm along the scruff on his face. "I'll answer the door."

"Axel!" Scarlett squealed from the foyer.

James frowned. "When did Scarlett figure out how to break through the child locks on the front door?"

I shrugged my shoulders. "She's always been mischievous like her father."

"I can barely open the door with those freaking locks on. So she certainly didn't learn it from me."

We walked into the foyer. Scarlett had grabbed Axel's hand and was already pulling him over to her drawings from this morning that were spread out on the floor.

"They're so adorable together," Hailey said and put her hand on her chest.

"I'm pretty sure it was love at first sight for Scarlett," I said and gave her a hug.

"Love at first sight?" James said from behind me. "I don't think so."

Tyler laughed.

"Hey, Tyler." I gave him a quick hug.

"Would it really be so bad if your daughter was in love with my son?" Tyler asked and patted James on the shoulder.

"No, that's not what I meant," James said and looked over at our children playing. "But they're just friends."

"Aw, I don't know," Hailey said. "They seem pretty smitten to me."

James lowered his eyebrows slightly.

I wasn't sure why it bothered him so much to think that Scarlett had a crush on Axel. They weren't even four years old yet. It was harmless enough. And I thought it was cute how much Scarlett adored Axel. A Hunter ending up with a Stevens wasn't such a horrible thing. I smiled at the two of them playing together. Axel looked so much like his father. He had the same shaggy blonde hair and blue eyes, but his skin was a little tanner like his mother's. He was going to be a heartbreaker when he was older.

"Do either of you want something to drink?" James asked, not at all subtly changing the subject.

"The idea of our kids being in love really bothers you, doesn't it?" I heard Tyler say as the two of them disappeared into the kitchen.

Hailey laughed. "Men," she said and rolled her eyes. "Honestly, how cute would it be if they did fall in love one day?"

"What a story that would be."

We silently watched Scarlett holding up the drawings to Axel.

I think I understood why James had gotten a little defensive. I couldn't even imagine Scarlett going to school in a few years. Stupid time flying by. God, and her dating? Just the thought made my stomach twist into knots.

"But right now they're our babies," Hailey said.

I laughed. "Did you just think about them growing up and going off to school and sneaking around our backs and getting into all sorts of trouble?"

She laughed. "My mind immediately went there. Maybe I need to hop on the train of having another kid so I'm not thoroughly depressed when Axel goes off to kindergarten."

I put my hand on my stomach.

"You definitely should," Rob said from behind us. "We always just get pregnant again whenever Penny and James do. Hello, you gorgeous, pregnant specimen of a woman." He kissed me on the cheek.

I laughed. "You did that thing again where you let yourself in instead of ringing the bell."

"You gave me a key for just that reason." He held up his keychain and jingled it in front of me.

"It's for emergencies only."

"Well, I was in serious need of a drink. Crisis averted." He winked at me.

"Where are Daphne and Sophie?"

"Daphne had to pee so she stopped at the bathroom downstairs. Pregnant women, am I right?" He elbowed Hailey in the side. "How are you doing, Hails?"

"Good. I'm just enjoying the show." She looked back and forth between us.

"Rob, you didn't wait for your wife and child?" I asked. "You just ran up here and abandoned them?"

"In the most prestigious apartment complex in the city. You're acting like I left them somewhere horrid. Besides, I had to come up. Someone had to get this party going. Am I right, Hails?"

"Does me not being pregnant somehow make me one of the guys? Stop elbowing me," she said with a laugh and lightly shoved Rob's arm.

"No, but you still get to have fun while Penny and Daphne are total party poopers. Especially now," he said and turned back to me. "Shouldn't you be lying down?"

I had just defended his ability at keeping a secret to James. Was he seriously going to talk about my heart murmur in front of one of the only people that didn't know?

"Why especially now?" Hailey asked.

Rob cleared his throat. "Because James Junior in there is going to be a kicker in the NFL. He's practically abusive already. He'll fit into the league perfectly."

I laughed. "He's just a little hyper is all. He's not a monster."

"I never called him a monster," Rob said. "Junior will be one of the good ones."

"First of all, we're having a girl," James said and handed Rob a drink. "And second of all, if it's a boy, we're not naming him James Junior."

"Oh, come on. I'm going to name my son Rob Junior. RJ for short. And we can call your son JJ. It'll be adorable.

They'll basically be twins like how we're basically twins. Penny's always saying how similar we are." He glanced back at me as if he was waiting for me to agree with him.

I looked at the two brothers. Rob was little shorter than James. And Rob almost always had a smile on his face, whereas James was currently sporting a scowl. James was more carefree now than he used to be. But he still tended to be more serious than Rob. "Similar, yes," I said. "But not twins."

Rob stuck his tongue out at me.

The doorbell rang. Rob turned around and answered it. Matt walked in with Sophie on his hip and Daphne stood there with her arms crossed above her large pregnant stomach.

"You left me," she said sternly, but the curves at the corners of her mouth gave her good humor away.

"I would never." Rob wrapped his arm around her shoulders.

Daphne laughed. "Sophie started throwing a tantrum in the middle of the lobby because she wanted you, though. Luckily Matt was there to save the day. Apparently he's a good substitute for you. She immediately calmed down when he picked her up."

"I don't know about that," Matt said with a laugh. "But I don't think my niece minds hanging out with me, do you Soph?"

Sophie shook her head. She was nestled into Matt's side with her thumb in her mouth. Her eyes were red and watery like she had indeed just been crying.

"I'm sorry, Soph," Rob said and peeled Sophie out of Matt's arms. "No need to be upset." He peppered her face in kisses until she was smiling again. "Do you want to go play with Scarlett and Axel?"

"And you too, Daddy," she said.

"Okay, princess. Which way to your friends?"

Sophie pointed toward the living room.

"This way?" Rob said and walked in the opposite direction.

"No, Daddy. That way."

Rob started walking toward the kitchen instead of the living room. "Is this the way?"

"No, Daddy! It's that way!" She pointed to where Scarlett and Axel were playing. Sophie was giggling again before they even left the room.

"He's such a good father," I said.

"Yes he is. Hopefully two won't drive our husbands insane. Hi, James," Daphne said and gave James a hug. She did all of her introductions and then stood next to me. "How are you feeling?"

"Honestly, it feels like he's going to kick right through my stomach."

Daphne laughed. "Fortunately little RJ isn't quite as hyper. Was Scarlett like that too?"

"No, not at all. It's part of the reason I'm convinced it's a boy this time."

"You're insane for not knowing ahead of time," Daphne said. "We've been having so much fun transforming everything in the nursery to blue instead of pink."

"We actually let Scarlett pick the color of the nursery," James said. "She had a blast at the paint store. Hopefully the baby likes orange. Do you guys want to come in? We're all just standing around. Let's go sit." He looped his arm behind my back. "Drinks are in the kitchen and snacks are on the coffee table in the living room. Dinner will be coming in a bit." He tilted his lips down to my ear. "How are you feeling?" he whispered.

"I'm fine, James. I promise." I smiled up at him. I had thought he wasn't being attentive enough before. He had done a complete reversal between our conversation this morning and now. Maybe we had just needed a fun day in bed for us to go back to normal. There was nothing that made me happier than knowing that he cared. I needed that. I needed him.

Just when I was about to sit down, the bell rang again.

"I'll get it," James said. He smiled and let go of my waist.

I ungracefully sat down. Matt plopped down next to me.

"How's the baby?" he asked.

"We just went for a checkup. He's very healthy."

"Can I?" He looked down at my stomach.

I nodded.

He gently put his hand on my belly. A smile spread over his face. "I can feel him kicking."

Matt was so cute with all of our kids. I could tell he would be a wonderful father. But he hadn't found the right girl to settle down with. Melissa and Matt had dated for about a month. Their personalities were both too strong, though. Now Melissa and her college sweetheart, Josh, were giving it another go. She had moved to Texas last year. I missed her, but she seemed happy and I was happy for them. James and I had talked about visiting them right before we found out we were expecting again. He had this fear that I'd go into labor on the plane. Even when I was only one month along. So our trip had been postponed indefinitely. I really needed to call her.

"And how are you feeling?" Matt asked. He kept his eyes on my stomach. He was much more discreet than Rob.

I slowly exhaled. "I'm good."

"Yeah?" He looked up at my face.

Yes, one day Matt would be a great father. He was looking at me like my dad would whenever I'd cry. "Yeah." I tried to give him a reassuring smile.

"Stop feeling her up, man," Mason said. "She's basically your sister."

"Oh, no, I wasn't." Matt immediately dropped his hand from my stomach.

"I'm just messing with you." Mason punched his brother's arm and leaned down to hug me. "How you feeling, Penny?"

The Caldwell brothers were so sweet. Which was hilarious because when I met them I never thought I'd use that adjective to describe them. "I'm good," I said as Mason released me from his embrace. "Matt just wanted to feel the baby kick."

"Oh." Mason sat down on the other side of me. "In that case, do you mind if I feel it too?"

"That's fine."

He put his hand on my stomach. I felt the baby kick and Mason smiled.

Bee laughed. "Well, I never thought I'd see the day. For someone who claims to be terrified of children, you sure are excited about this one."

"I'm not terrified of children. I'm terrified of having children. So many things could go wrong." Mason immediately dropped his hand. "I mean, the odds are small. Medicine and technology are so good now. It's very rare for pregnancies to be dangerous."

"And I'm the one harassing her?" Matt said. "Nice one."

"I just meant...Penny, you know what I meant," Mason said. "I'm sorry. Of course everything will be fine with your pregnancy."

"Mason," Bee hissed.

God, everyone was being so weird.

"I feel like I'm missing something," Hailey said. Tyler, Daphne, and her were sitting on the couch on the other side of us. It didn't look like any of them knew what we were talking about.

Daphne put her hand protectively on her stomach as she stared at me. She looked as confused as Hailey and Tyler. It definitely didn't seem like Rob had told her. The Caldwell brothers may have been sweet, but they were way worse at keeping secrets than the Hunters. I couldn't fault them for that, though. It was probably a good thing.

"Seriously, Penny, is everything okay with the baby?" Daphne asked.

What was the point of keeping a secret from half of my friends? Now I just felt guilty for thinking they shouldn't know.

"Of course everything's fine," Rob said from behind me and put his hands on my shoulders. "Don't you dare say anything, you're going to get me in so much trouble for keeping it from her," he whispered under his breath.

I awkwardly cleared my throat. "Everything's fine."

"You're lying," Tyler said.

Hails gave him a sideways glance.

Tyler shrugged. "I can tell when she's lying. She's always been a terrible liar." He took a sip from his drink.

Hailey laughed. "I guess that's true."

"It really is true," Matt said.

You are not helping.

"Are you going to tell us or are you going to make us guess?" Tyler asked. "I've found that ripping the Band-Aid off is a lot easier than slowly pulling it off."

I bit the inside of my lip.

"Really, Penny. You have to tell us now," Hailey said. She shifted slightly forward on the couch.

God, I really don't want to have this conversation. "It's not a big deal whatsoever. At my last checkup the doctor found out that I had a heart murmur. Which is pretty common. It's moderate so it's not mild but it's not severe either. So, I mean, it's okay. Everything's okay."

"Damn it, Penny," Rob said from behind me.

"Wait, you knew?" Daphne said to him. "You knew and you didn't tell me?"

"James asked me not to tell anyone."

"Who else knew?" she asked.

Matt, Mason, and Bee all awkwardly raised their hands.

"Robert Hunter," Daphne said. "She's basically my sister. How could you not tell me? And here I was going on and on about nurseries and names." She had a horrified look on her face. "Penny, I'm so sorry. Why didn't anyone tell me to shut up?"

"How serious is it?" Hailey asked. "Is the baby okay?"

"The baby's fine," I said. "He's perfectly healthy."

"Are you okay?" Tyler asked.

I don't know anymore. Talking about this made my chest hurt. *It's just in my head. It's just in my head.* "Yeah. I'm fine." I smiled and waved my hand through the air.

Tyler didn't say anything this time, but he gave me that look like he knew I was lying again.

Everyone was awkwardly quiet.

"Dinner just arrived," James said as he came in from the kitchen. The smile on his face disappeared as he looked around. His eyes landed on me and he gave me a sympathetic smile. "So, you told them?"

The idea of a relaxing night with my friends had just been thrown out the window. "Yes, and can you all please stop staring at me like I'm dying? I just want to have a normal night." I cringed and looked at Bee.

"Normal?" she mouthed silently at me and shook her head.

And I knew she was right. Just like she had been right when she said the same thing to me yesterday. Whenever I said normal, nothing was at all normal.

CHAPTER 7

Saturday

The dinner conversation was filled with everyone talking about my health. And what it meant for the baby. If I saw one more sympathetic look I was going to scream. I opened up the door to the freezer and let the cold air hit my face. I had wandered out of the dining room with the excuse of going to the bathroom. Now I didn't want to go back.

"Craving ice cream and comfy sweatpants?" Tyler asked.

I laughed and closed the fridge door. "I do miss our Friday nights."

"Me too." He smiled and leaned against the refrigerator next to me. "Tell it to me straight, Penny."

I shrugged my shoulders. "The doctor said if I take it easy everything should be fine."

"But?"

"I'm terrified that I'm going to lose him."

"You know, I remember you feeling like Scarlett was a boy too."

I smiled. "But she was my first kid. I had nothing to go off of." I put my hand on my stomach. "It already feels like he's a part of me. If I lost him..." my voice trailed off. "I don't know what I would do."

"You're stronger than you realize, Penny. I mean, look around you. You set your mind on a goal and go for it. If you let any old obstacle get in your way, you wouldn't be here right now."

I had certainly pursued James despite all the opposition. Giving up on us had never really seemed like an option. But that wasn't exactly the same as my heart not being strong enough. I had never had that issue before. I loved too hard if anything. I gave too many second chances. My heart always seemed capable of anything.

"And I don't think it's an issue of losing your son," Tyler said. "You said yourself that the doctor deemed him healthy. I know the conversation tonight has been focused on your baby, but everyone in there isn't talking about the real issue. You."

I laughed. "I'm not an issue."

"But what if something happens to you?"

"Nothing is going to happen to me." My chest was hurting again.

"You shouldn't even be standing here right now. You should be in bed resting. I know you're strong enough to handle all of this. But your body isn't on the same page as your mind on this one. We don't want anything to happen to the baby. But we don't want anything to happen to you either."

I knew he was right. And if I wasn't careful he was going to make me start crying. He was still one of my best friends, but we didn't spend nearly as much time together anymore. I probably ended up hanging out with his wife more than I did with him now. Time changed things. Fortunately for us, time healed things too.

"Just don't let your stubbornness get in the way of your health." Tyler stuffed his hands into his pockets. "You should probably go sit back down." He nodded toward the dining room.

He had talked so much about being strong. I needed to muster a little bit of that strength in order to tell him about my books. Or rather, ask him if it was okay. "Tyler?"

"Yeah?"

"I'm writing a book."

He smiled. "I know. You've told me numerous times."

Right. I had told him. I just hadn't gone into any details. "It's about James and my story. How we met. All of that. I mean, I changed the names and it's fiction. But I pulled a lot of truth out of my time at the University of New Castle."

"Does that mean I'm in it?"

"That's what I wanted to talk to you about. I wrote about meeting you and everything. Hanging out. Kind of dating. That sort of thing."

"You made me look like a complete dick, didn't you?"

I laughed. "No. You're sweet and charming."

He shook his head. "Just promise me that one day you'll tell my real story? Redeem me in some way. If that's possible."

"A Tyler Stevens redemption story? I think I can handle that."

"I'm going to look like such an idiot in your books. Chasing after a girl who was so obviously in love with someone else." He shook his head.

"You don't look like an idiot, I promise." I hesitated as I stared at him. "So, it's really okay? For me to write about everything?"

"All the ups and downs brought me here. I can't be upset about what did and didn't happen back then. The past is in the past, and I'm pretty damn happy about how everything turned out."

I slowly exhaled a breath that I didn't know I had been holding. "Me too."

"Then write it. Just don't forget that redemption story."

"I wouldn't dream of it."

"And please come sit down." He linked his arm through mine. "I'll try to steer the conversation away from your health as best I can."

"Thanks, Tyler."

James looked up at us as we walked arm and arm into the room. A few years ago, something like this would have made him furious. Instead he flashed me a smile, like he was just happy I had come back into the room. I settled into my seat next to him.

I watched as Tyler sat down next to Hailey. He put his arm around her shoulders and squeezed her tight. There was a smile on her face and she didn't seem in the least perturbed about Tyler and my chat. I wasn't sure I had ever met someone as accepting as Hailey. I remember when Melissa had dated Tyler. She wouldn't even let me speak to him. Hailey on the other hand had accepted me with opened arms. And I knew she knew about my history with Tyler. But she never even questioned me about it. She was confident enough in their relationship that it didn't matter. And that was why she was so great for Tyler. He thought I was strong, but his wife was a rock. She was perfect for him.

I leaned my head against James' shoulder. And he was my rock.

"Are you tired?" James whispered.

I tilted my head to look up at him. "No. I'm just happy."

He brushed a strand of hair out of my face and rested his head against mine.

The conversation had taken a sudden turn to real-estate. Normally I'd be bored and want to change the topic. But tonight any conversation that wasn't centered around me was what I wanted. The only strange part about it was that James was completely silent. He'd usually be jumping in to talk about something that I knew nothing about. I knew what his silence meant, though. He was tuning everything out besides for me. And I loved when he did that. I loved that he could make it feel like just the two of us in a crowded room.

"Daddy, Daddy!" Scarlett came running into the dining room at full speed. "We want to play hide-and-go-seek!"

James lifted his head off of mine and leaned down to lift Scarlett onto his lap. "Pumpkin, the grown-ups are talking. How about you play with Axel and Sophie?"

"But we all want to play together. Please, Daddy?" She wiggled out of his grip so that she could stand on his lap. She put her hands on his shoulders and looked him square in the face. "The grown-ups will hide. And we'll find them."

"I'll play," Matt said.

Mason laughed. "Count me in too. I bet he'll be found way before I will."

"Yeah, it'll be fun," Hailey said. "How long do we have to hide, Scarlett?"

"Five seconds," Scarlett said matter-of-factly.

"Scar, it's not just Daddy and I hiding," I said. "We'll need a little more time than that to find hiding spots."

She held up ten fingers. And then dropped one.

"We better go," James said and lifted her off his lap.

Chairs squeaked against the floor as our friends started running in every direction.

James grabbed my hand and helped me to my feet. "We're going to have to move a little faster than that," he said as he picked me up into his arms.

I laughed as he carried me out of the dining room and down the hallway.

"This'll do." He kicked open the door to the laundry room and then hit it closed with his foot.

We were bathed in darkness as he put me back down on my feet.

"You know that Scarlett is scared of the laundry room," I said as I clasped my hands behind his neck. "She thinks the machines are going to eat her."

"Yes, I'm fully aware of that." His breath was hot against my lips. It felt like we had been trying to get a moment alone for days. But I wouldn't have thought we'd find one during a session of hide-and-go-seek with our friends over.

"I want to freeze time. For just a few minutes." I let my fingers wander into his thick hair. I didn't think I'd ever tire of running my hands through his hair.

"And if you could freeze time, what would you do?"

My eyes were starting to adjust to the darkness and I could clearly see the fire in his. "Oh, I think I'd probably do you."

"Such an eloquent use of words for an author."

I laughed. "I'm not an author. I'm just a girl that wrote a book that no one wants to read."

"And once upon a time I was a man that had given up on life. But then I met you." He cupped the side of my face in his hand. "Look at what a few years can do to someone's life. So tonight let's freeze time. Tomorrow we can start to embrace all the change that's about to happen. Like you becoming a real author."

"Your optimism is endearing."

He smiled. "I think you find everything I do endearing." He reached behind him and locked the door.

"James, the kids have probably already found everyone else. They'll be banging on the door in just a few seconds."

"Time is frozen. And there are no worries when time is still. Besides, I wasn't going to seduce you. I just want to kiss you."

"You want to make out?" I smiled up at him. "What are we, two kids playing spin the bottle?"

"You've always made me feel young, Penny." He kissed the side of my neck. "And alive." He kissed my clavicle.

Jesus.

"I'm lucky the bottle landed on you," he said against my lips.

I grabbed the back of his neck and kissed him. And we did make out like two teenagers who had gotten paired up in spin the bottle. Not that I would really know. I was never cool enough to play that game at a party. Let alone be invited to the party in the first place. Besides, kisses with a stranger in a basement closet wouldn't have been nearly this amazing. James made me feel young and desired. He made me feel like I wasn't a mammoth trying to pass as a woman in a dress.

"When was the last time we had sex?" His hands drifted to my ass.

"I don't know. Monday?"

"Monday? No, we were going to, but you fell asleep while I was in the shower."

"Oh, yeah. I'm sorry about that." I let my lips brush against his again.

"It's been at least a week, Penny. And you've been doing nothing but driving me crazy."

I laughed. "James, I'm practically a blimp." I put my hands on his chest so I could look up at him. "I certainly haven't been driving anyone crazy recently. It's not like I'm 19 years old and trying to seduce my professor anymore."

He opened his mouth like he was about to say something, when a light knock sounded on the door.

"Daddy?" Scarlett's apprehensive voice sounded from the other side of the door. "Are you in there?"

James put his hand over my mouth and his finger up to his, silencing me.

The doorknob jiggled.

If he thought us being quiet was going to make the kids go away, he was sorely mistaken. But I wasn't going to deny that him holding me like this didn't turn me on just a little. Maybe I was still more like my 19 year self than I realized.

"Uncle James?" Axel said a little more confidently and knocked on the door.

I pulled James' hand down from my face. "You're scaring the children."

"You still drive me crazy," he said as I slipped away from him.

I looked over my shoulder at him as I unlocked the door. "You still drive me crazy too, James. To be continued?"

He nodded and ran his hand through his hair.

I opened the door and Scarlett screamed. But then she ran right toward me and embraced my leg like it was her favorite thing in the world.

"I found you, Mommy," she mumbled into the fabric of my dress.

My baby girl still needed me. I looked back over my shoulder at James. He still needed me too. I had already known that. But seeing him with lust in his eyes was something I understood so well. I couldn't believe that I thought we were falling apart last night. We were stronger than ever. We needed to start getting better at carving out time for just the two of us, though. Especially with another kid on the way. If this baby was anything like his older sister, we'd only be getting a few hours of sleep a night for months.

CHAPTER 8

Saturday

Scarlett's head was resting on my lap as the party drew to a close. She had fallen asleep over an hour ago, but whenever I'd try to carry her to bed, she'd gotten those really big puppy dog eyes and said she didn't want to miss out on anything. How could I deny her? Especially when I was tired anyway. A little nap before bed sounded heavenly. Besides, Daphne and Sophie were already curled up on the couch. And it was way past my bedtime.

Right when I was about to drift off to sleep, hushed voices startled me awake. I was about to slip out from underneath of Scarlett's head to join the conversation when I picked up on a small piece of the discussion.

"I have every mind to sue him," James said. "It has to be malpractice."

"I'm sure you could sue him if you wanted to," Rob said calmly.

James sighed. "Spit it out. I know that there's a but coming."

I looked down at my daughter. She was still sleeping peacefully. And so were Daphne and Sophie. James and Rob thought I was asleep too. Or I was certain they wouldn't be talking about this. I should have gone into the kitchen and joined their discussion. I should have at least let them know I was awake. But instead, I closed my eyes and stayed perfectly still.

"I was looking it up the other day," Rob said. "Pregnant women get heart murmurs all the time. Something about extra blood flow or something. They usually go away after the birth."

"Yeah, I know. And if that was the case it'd be fine. The cardiologist we went to for a second opinion said she'd eventually need surgery, though. That if it got any worse she'd need medical intervention if she wanted to live a long life."

"Shit."

They were both silent for a moment. Yeah. Shit. That was the best way to describe it. I ran my palm along my stomach. The doctor had said that extra stress on my heart would make it worse. That maybe I'd had a mild heart murmur my whole life that went undetected. But that my pregnancy made it worse. That my heart was beating faster and working harder to make up for the leak. And that the wear and tear were now irreversible.

"Suing him won't help, though," Rob said. "Him losing his license won't mean anything."

Of course it would mean something. Dr. Nelson would lose his job. He had a family. This conversation was ridiculous. James could not blame an OB-GYN for not finding my heart murmur. That wasn't his specialty. Maybe he could freak out if our son had a heart murmur and he didn't find it. But this wasn't Dr. Nelson's fault.

"What am I supposed to do? Sit here and continue to blame myself? I can't...I can't do that. I'm going fucking insane." James was quiet for a moment. "I brought up the idea of having another kid. It's my fault. If she dies, it's my fault. That baby effectively turned her into a ticking time bomb."

I swallowed hard. No, James shouldn't blame Dr. Nelson. He shouldn't blame himself. But he most certainly shouldn't blame our baby. Our son was good and pure and perfect. I quietly slipped out from underneath Scarlett's head. She moaned peacefully in her sleep.

James and Rob both turned toward me when I entered the kitchen. James looked guilty, like he knew he had been caught talking about me behind my back again. But Rob plastered a smile on his face.

Yup, I was right about Rob. He was great at keeping secrets when he needed to be. "Cut the crap, Rob. I know you two were talking about me. James, you can't sue Dr. Nelson," I said and turned to him. "And you can't blame yourself for wanting another kid. I wanted another kid too. If you hadn't brought it up, I would have soon. And you most certainly can't blame our beautiful baby."

"I'm not blaming any of them."

"What? You just said you were going to sue Dr. Nelson."

"No one said anything about Dr. Nelson. I want to sue Dr. Jones."

"My last OB-GYN? Why on earth would you sue him?" James' brilliant plan was to sue the doctor that delivered Scarlett. Flawlessly. A retired doctor with one of the highest successful delivery rates in the state. The practice that Dr. Jones started was still the most prestigious one in the city. The only reason I had gone to a new OB-GYN from a different practice was because after Dr. Jones retired, Dr. Nelson was the best doctor left in New York. The two had even had the same graduate and post-doctorate training. What was James thinking? He'd never win that lawsuit. Truly, he'd never win a lawsuit against either of them.

"Because apparently Dr. Jones had notes about you developing a heart murmur while you were pregnant with Scarlett. And he didn't tell us. The only reason I even know about it is because it was in the health records I requested from Dr. Nelson so I could look at everything for myself."

"What do you mean?" There was no way that Dr. Jones knew. He would have told us. I shook my head. That didn't make any sense.

"That's why Dr. Nelson didn't deliver the news with any tact. He thought we were already aware of the risk. He probably thought we were being incredibly irresponsible. If Dr. Jones had told us about it in the first place, you'd still be healthy. We could have seen a cardiologist sooner and discussed the risks of getting pregnant again. None of this would have ever happened. Your heart murmur would still be mild. You'd still be healthy."

I put my hand on my stomach. "None of this would have happened? Are you saying you regret getting pregnant again?"

"That's not..." his voice trailed off as his eyes landed on my belly. "I'm saying that if we knew ahead of time, we never would have tried for another kid. It's just making it worse."

"It? It? Are you serious right now?" My heart felt like it was beating out of my chest. I wanted to slap him, but my body was frozen. How could he say that about our son? How dare he?

Rob cleared his throat. "Tread lightly, man. You don't want to upset a pregnant woman. Hormones and everything."

I was going to kill both of them. "Do you regret having Scarlett too? For possibly giving me the heart murmur in the first place?"

"I never said..."

"How could you?" I was having trouble keeping my voice low. Scarlett was sleeping in the next room. We still had company over. But I couldn't seem to control myself. And the thought that Rob was right and that my hormones were taking over made me even madder. Screw both of them.

"I didn't..."

"You're lucky that our couch is comfortable. Because you're going to be sleeping on it." I stormed out of the room and almost ran straight into Daphne.

"Is everything okay in here? You're going to wake the girls."

"Everything is fine minus the fact that we're married to assholes."

Daphne laughed.

"Daphne, you're supposed to be on my side."

"I have no idea what the three of you are arguing about. But if you ask me, they look very sorry." She looped her arm through mine and made me turn around.

Rob had his bottom lip out like he was the saddest man on earth. James, on the other hand, was just staring at me with an expression I was all too familiar with. Those same sad big brown eyes that Scarlett flashed me whenever she was upset. Everyone said that Scarlett looked exactly like me. But I knew better. Those damn eyes. The eyes I could never say no to. He looked so dejected. And he should have been. He had said he never wanted our son. What was he expecting me to say? That I wanted to turn back time and never get pregnant? I loved our son with every ounce of my being. I was, after all, risking my life for his. I was aware of that. I wasn't an idiot.

"Well, maybe you can take both of them home with you tonight. I want nothing to do with them." I walked past Daphne into the living room and scooped Scarlett up into my arms. God, my baby girl was getting so heavy. I ignored the fact that she was definitely over the weight limit of things I was allowed to lift now. I carried her up the stairs without looking back.

James could sue whoever he wanted. I didn't care what he did with our money. Honestly, I couldn't care less. But he couldn't say he didn't want our son. Or Scarlett. I kicked the door shut with my foot. It slammed hard, waking Scarlett.

"Mommy, where's Daddy?" she said and yawned.

"You and I are having a slumber party tonight." I kissed her forehead and tucked her into the bed where James usually slept. I couldn't sleep alone tonight. And I didn't want James climbing into the bed in a minute saying he was sorry. I wasn't ready to forgive him yet.

"Slumber party? What is slumber?" She curled up to me as soon as I climbed into bed.

"It means to sleep. It's where best friends spend the night. And have fun hanging out."

"Best friends?"

"The people you want to spend the most time with in the whole wide world. Because you're happiest when you're together."

"You're my best friend, Mommy." She grabbed my hand and held it to her chest like she was hugging one of her stuffed animals.

Tears pooled in my eyes. That had to be the sweetest thing she had ever said to me.

"You're my best friend too, baby girl." I kissed her forehead. "Now get some sleep."

She sighed lightly and her eyelids drooped shut again.

I watched her drift asleep in just a few seconds. She was so energetic all day. But as soon as her head hit a pillow, she was always out cold. Maybe when you had no worries in the world, sleep came easily. I hadn't been sleeping well ever since Dr. Nelson had delivered the news. The more I thought about it, the more I realized that he had been rather tactless, just like James had said. None of it mattered, though. I didn't regret getting pregnant again for a second.

I felt a sharp kick in my ribs.

I'm on your side, baby boy.

He kicked me again.

Ow. I winced. Every day he was getting stronger. It wasn't like I wasn't aware of what was happening. Because every day I felt just a tiny bit weaker. It terrified me. But I was not angry at him. How could I possibly be angry at him?

***

"Baby?"

I slowly opened my eyes. The most handsome face in the world was just a few inches from mine. With those sad brown eyes. I had put the sadness there. The thought made my chest ache. Why couldn't I have a normal conversation with him? One where one of us didn't end up getting upset. Did my hormones really make me that insane? I felt like I had an anger hangover. I blinked, helping the room come into better focus. He was kneeling on the ground next to the bed. He was literally on his knees begging for forgiveness, when it should have been me groveling. "James, I'm so sorry."

He put his index finger against my lips. "You and Scarlett are my whole world. There's not a day that goes by that I don't realize how blessed my life is. My life revolves around my girls."

"James..."

"And I do not, for one second, wish anything had gone any differently. But I can't pretend that I'm not..." his voice trailed off, like he was searching for the right word.

"Scared?" I stared into his eyes. James always had trouble admitting his weaknesses. I knew how hard that was. How vulnerable he felt.

He nodded. "I'm utterly terrified."

"I'm scared too. And I'm sorry I freaked out. I just can't believe you said you wished we never got pregnant."

"I never said that." He shook his head. "I said if we had known, we probably would have done things differently. But we didn't know. And now this baby is a part of our lives. I don't regret that. I'm sorry if I made you feel any differently. I was upset, but I do love this baby. I love every piece of you." He put his hand on my stomach. "And now I feel like I need to ask our baby for forgiveness too."

He pushed the sheets off of me and put both his hands on my stomach. "Hey, beautiful girl," he whispered.

"Boy."

James looked up at me. "I'm trying to have a private conversation."

I smiled. "By all means, please continue."

"Hey, beautiful girl," he said again.

I shook my head and stared down at the side of his face.

"I love you," he whispered. "With all my heart. I know you already know that." He kissed my belly. "But I need to ask you a favor. Please calm down with the kicking. You're hurting your mother."

I laughed.

James kissed my stomach again. "I can't wait to meet you," he said and ran his hand across my stomach. He looked up at me again. "Do you forgive me?"

"I'd already forgiven you." I reached down and ran my fingers along the scruff on his jaw line. "Do you forgive me?"

"I was never upset with you. Maybe I'll be a little upset if you really do force me to sleep on the couch though. May I come to bed now?"

I patted the bed beside me. He climbed up and wrapped his arm around me.

"She's the best thing we ever did." He reached behind me and pushed a strand of Scarlett's hair off her face.

"Yes. She is. And just think." My eyes wandered back up to his face. "If I had been a second earlier to that door in the coffee shop, you never would have run into me. We never would have started dating. We never would have had that beautiful little girl. Everything happens for a reason, James. And we're going to get through whatever happens next together. I promise."

Something flashed across his eyes. Pain maybe. It was too fast for me to be able to read him.

"I told you I didn't want to change a thing," he said. He put his hand on the side of my face and took a deep breath, like he was breathing me in. "But if you think me hitting you with that door was our only chance at starting this, you're crazy." A playful smile formed on his face. "I thought you were a believer in fate?"

"That doesn't mean I don't realize how lucky we are."

"Hmm." He shifted even closer to me. "Never in my wildest dreams did I think I'd be this lucky."

CHAPTER 9

Sunday

"Mommy."

A little finger repeatedly jabbing me in the side made me open my eyes.

"Mommy," Scarlett said and continued to poke me.

"Good morning, Scar." She was standing up on the bed looking down at me.

"I want in." She pointed between me and James.

"Did you have a bad dream?" Usually Scarlett insisted on sleeping directly between me and James whenever she was scared.

She nodded her head.

"Come here, baby girl." I scooted over and tapped the bed beside me.

Scarlett ungracefully jumped over me so she could nestle between us.

James made a noise like he'd just gotten punched in the gut. Sure enough, Scarlett had kneed him right in the stomach.

"Good morning, pumpkin," he said and kissed her forehead. "Good morning." He reached over and put his hand on the side of my face.

I turned my face and kissed his palm.

"Daddy, I had a bad dream." She nestled her face into his chest. "The snake monster talked to me."

Snake monster? "What movie did you two watch the other night?"

"She wanted to watch Harry Potter and the Chamber of Secrets again. I think I may have fallen asleep before her."

I shook my head. We'd pretty much allow Scarlett to watch anything she wanted. But we usually turned it off at a certain point if we didn't think it was appropriate. Apparently seeing a gigantic snake was one of those things.

"Scar, there are no snake monsters. It was just a movie."

"Yes there are, Mommy." She turned to look at me. "I saw him. And he talked to me." She frowned, like she was waiting for me to question her. "Can storks eat snakes?"

James laughed. "Time to get up, Scarlett. Grandpa is coming over today to hang out with you. He should be here any minute."

"Grandpa!" Scarlett immediately dropped her question about storks.

"He is?" I asked.

"Yes, I figured while they're playing you and I could go get breakfast?" James climbed out of bed and looked down at me. There was a question in his gaze that I didn't quite understand.

Did he think I was going to say no? "That sounds wonderful," I said.

"Great. Let's go make you breakfast okay, pumpkin?" He squeezed Scarlett's shoulder.

She jumped off the bed and fell on her knees. For a second it looked like she was going to cry.

"You're okay." James picked her up and draped her over one shoulder.

"Daddy!" she squealed with delight. There was no longer any trace of her impending tears.

I sat there for a moment as I watched them disappear out the door. Sometimes Scarlett would get upset if she felt excluded. Maybe that was why James had looked worried after he asked me to go to breakfast. Or maybe he wanted to talk about something important. I certainly hadn't been acting like myself recently. I shook my head and climbed out of bed. Why was I analyzing how James had asked me? He was just being sweet. He wanted to spend more time with me. I didn't need to read between any lines.

I quickly washed up and walked into the closet. There was a new dress hanging in front of the others. It was just like my favorite stretchy cotton dress, except it was a brilliant shade of blue instead of gray. James knew it was the only article of clothing that I felt comfortable in anymore. I smiled as I pulled it off the hanger. There was no reason to analyze his expressions or his words. Everything he did was out of love. I was ready to have a romantic day with him.

I walked out of our room and down the stairs. James' father, Jon, was already there. Scarlett was sitting in his lap at the kitchen counter completely transfixed on her bowl of oatmeal, but not eating it.

"Hello, darling," Jon said as I walked into the room.

I leaned down and gave him a hug. "Hi, Jon. I see you two are already busy. What are you up to?" Scarlett was still staring at her bowl of oatmeal in the most unusual way.

"Grandpa said I could make a design with the raisins," she said. "I can't decide if I should do a snake or a stork."

I laughed. "It's going to get cold, Scar." I looked back at Jon and smiled.

"She's a perfectionist," James said as he placed a bowl down for Jon. "Remind you of someone we know?" He nodded toward me.

Jon laughed. "I was going to say you, son."

"And I was going to say Jon," I said.

The three of us all laughed.

"I have an idea," Jon said to Scarlett. "How about you make a snake with your raisins and I'll make a stork with mine."

"No, I want to make the stork. I'm scared of snakes, Grandpa."

"But didn't you just say..."

"I thought if I made a snake and ate it then I wouldn't be scared. But I don't want him inside of me forever."

Jon raised his eyebrow, just like James so often did, and looked up at us.

James shrugged.

"Well, okay, sweetheart," Jon said. "How about we both make storks then?"

She nodded and put her hand into the bag of raisins. "Don't forget the oven," she said and handed him a sticky fistful of raisins.

Jon looked back up at us. "What is all this about snakes, storks, and ovens?"

"You don't know about babies, Grandpa? I can teach you." Scarlett launched into the story James and I had spun.

Jon shook his head and looked up at us.

"We have to get going," James said and looped his arm behind my back. "We'll see you two later."

"Okay, Daddy." She turned back to Jon. "But there's a timer, so the babies don't burn. And each oven has two storks just in case one misses the timer. And they're not allowed to potty at the same time."

I tried not to giggle at Jon's expression as we left them in the kitchen. "He's going to think we're awful parents." We stepped onto the elevator.

"He was just telling me the other day how lovely Scarlett is. Maybe he'll think she made the story up herself and that he'd completely misjudged her."

I slapped James' arm. "Oh, geez, what if he tells her the truth? An innocent story about storks is so much better than an explanation of sex. She's much too young."

"I should probably text him?" He raised both eyebrows.

"Absolutely."

James pulled out his phone and sent his father a text. His phone bleeped a minute later with a response. "Yup, he said we're awful parents."

"He did not." I grabbed his phone from him. The text read, "I'm not going to explain sex to a child. What do you think I am, a snake monster?"

I laughed and handed James his phone back.

The elevator doors opened. William was already standing by the car. He opened up the door when he saw us.

I missed our old driver, Ian. It had been over a year since he had moved, but I still always expected to see his smiling face opening the door. Ian was practically family now. He had been dating James' sister, Jen, ever since our wedding. And he had quit so he could move across the country to live with her. It was romantic and wonderful. It didn't mean I didn't miss him though. Not that William wasn't great. He was. But he wasn't Ian.

"Good morning, Mr. and Mrs. Hunter," William said.

That's what it was. It was the whole formal thing that bothered me. I couldn't break past that barrier with him. "Good morning, William," I said as he took my hand and helped me into the car behind James. One time I had called him Will and he had made such a horrendous face that a passerby would have thought I had spit on him. I had called him William ever since.

He closed the door behind us.

"We should give Jen and Ian a call," I said. "I think it's been a few weeks since we've talked to them. Really we should convince them to come early for Bee and Mason's wedding. Maybe they can stay at our place the whole week?"

"We can call them as soon as we get home." James wrapped his arm around my shoulders. "You miss Ian, huh?"

I laughed. "It's the whole being bad at change thing. I miss both of them. I kinda thought Jen would move back here once they got together."

"Yeah, me too."

I rested my head on James' shoulder as the car started to move. Silence settled around us. For some reason it put a nervous pit in my stomach. The baby kicked me like he was annoyed by my feelings. I lifted my head off of James' shoulder. "James?"

"Yes? You look beautiful today, by the way." He smiled.

"Oh my God. I'm the absolute worst. I walked into the closet this morning and found this dress and was so excited. It was such a sweet gesture because you know how much I love the other one. And then I immediately forgot to thank you. That's probably what you want to have breakfast together to talk about right? How awful I've been? I think your brother is right. I have crazy pregnancy hormones. I swear I can't even think straight anymore. I'm sorry about the past few days. I'm sorry that I keep assuming the worst and arguing with you and acting insane. And by the way, you can sue everyone we know for all I care. I don't want to fight about that. It's fine with me."

William cleared his throat from the front seat. "I'm just going to..." he let his voice trail off as he raised the partition.

"Ugh." I put my face in my hands. "See. I'm the worst. Now William thinks we're going to sue him."

"Penny?"

I lifted my head. "I know I've been impossible to please. First I was upset because we weren't talking. And then I got upset because you did open up. And you're allowed to talk to Rob about stuff. I want you to feel like you can talk to your brother. I shouldn't have been eavesdropping. And I way overreacted. Like a freaking lunatic. And I'm so hungry. Where are you taking me?"

"Baby." He wiped away the tears that I hadn't known I had shed. "Do you mind if I say something now?"

I shook my head.

"We're going to that brunch place you like so much. We should be there any minute. And I'm not taking you out to breakfast because I'm upset with you. I'm taking you out to breakfast because I love you."

"Oh." I exhaled slowly. "Yeah, I mean, I thought that was a possibility too."

He shook his head. "What am I going to do with you two?" He put his hand on my stomach and leaned toward me. His lips gently brushed against mine.

"This baby is making me insane."

"No." His breath was hot against my lips.

"I'm definitely insane."

"You're not insane. What would be insane is if you didn't kiss me back."

I laughed and stared into his eyes. "I'm so sorry."

"If you're apologizing for not kissing me, I don't accept your apology. There's only one way I'll forgive you."

The car pulled to a stop.

"Damn it," James said under his breath.

"It's fine. You couldn't possibly want me right now. I look like the entire Atlantic ocean." I gave him a chaste kiss.

His hand slid to my hip. "If anything you're more of a sexy, very slender river."

"Tell that to my ass."

"I'd be happy to." The car door opened and James sighed.

"Mrs. Hunter." William put his hand out for me as I undid my seatbelt. I grabbed William's hand and let him help me to my feet. I really did feel as big as the ocean.

"I'm holding you to that," James said as he joined me on the sidewalk. He wrapped his arm around my back. As we walked up to the restaurant his hand slowly slid down to my ass. He squeezed it despite the fact that we were not the only people on the sidewalk.

"James." I laughed and grabbed his hand, pulling it back to my waist.

He opened up the door for me with a grin. "After you."

I shook my head as I walked into the restaurant. "Daphne? Rob? Hi." I had not been expecting to see them. But it made sense. We came here together all the time. It was a Sunday morning after all.

Daphne smiled as she gave me a hug. "Glad to see you two made up."

"Me too," I said. "I'm so sorry about last night."

"It was just the hormones," Rob loudly whispered and then gave me a hug. "You're mean when you're angry. I did the whole pouty lip thing and everything." He did it again to remind me.

"I really am sorry."

"All is forgiven." He turned back to the hostess. "Actually, can we all just sit together if that's okay?"

The hostess smiled politely. "Of course. Right this way."

I was a little disappointed. I loved hanging out with Rob and Daphne, but the whole point of this breakfast was to have some alone time with James. I was even more disappointed as she lead us past the window seats where we usually sat. They were the best tables in the whole restaurant. And there were a few vacant tables for four. I was just about to say something to James when we stepped into the private room of the restaurant.

"Surprise!" everyone yelled.

My eyes landed on the banner strung along the wall. It read, "Welcome Hunter Babies!" I laughed and glanced at Daphne. "Did you know?"

She shook her head and glanced around the room. "I had no clue." She pointed to the banner. "But a joint baby shower was a really cute idea."

"Right?" said Rob. "Because they'll basically be twins." He gestured back and forth between Daphne and my bellies. "It was actually James' idea. Because obviously he agrees you're having a boy."

"Really?" I looked up at James.

He laughed. "No." He leaned closer to me. "I just figured kill two birds with one stone. Less things you need to do if you and Daphne had this together. More time spent resting in bed with me."

I looked up at him. "That's not a cute reason at all."

"No. I believe you know me well enough to know my ulterior motives." His voice had dropped an octave, the innuendo dripping from his words.

Something about the way he said it and the fact that we were in front of a crowded room made me press my thighs together. Maybe he really did see a sexy river instead of a gigantic ocean.

"Rob and I should get lost," said James. "I'll see you in a few hours."

"But..."

He smiled and pulled me in close. "I'll be hanging out with Rob down the street. Call me when you're ready to go home. Sorry about the white lie." He placed a peck against my lips.

"You owe me a romantic breakfast. Just the two of us."

"That I can do. Oh, and..." He grabbed my shoulders and turned me back to the party. Jen waved at me. "No need to call her now. Have fun." He kissed my temple and followed his brother out of the restaurant.

CHAPTER 10

Sunday

"I kinda thought baby showers were only for the first baby," Daphne whispered.

I laughed. "Me too. But I guess our friends thought it would be fun to honor us all over again."

"You mean torture us?" She pushed the diaper with the Snickers bar away from her. "I'm about to change enough diapers as it is. Soph only just started using the toilet. I have a few months of freedom."

Jen sat down across from us and pulled the Snickers bar out of the diaper. "If only baby poop was this delicious." She took a bite of the candy.

"You do realize that makes it sound like you've tasted baby poop," I said.

"Don't be ridiculous. Are you guys ready for the next game?"

"That depends on what it is."

Jen sighed. "You're acting like you're not having fun."

"It's not that we're not having fun," Daphne said. "Just imagine doing all this crap with a huge stomach and feeling like you have to pee every five minutes. I'm so tired all the time. I thought I was walking into a brunch with Rob, not all this."

"You're acting completely ungrateful. I went out of my way to plan all this..."

"I knew you were behind this," I said cutting her off. "Jen, you didn't have to throw us a joint baby shower. We've both already had one of these."

"But I needed an excuse to come visit my sisters." She reached out and grabbed one of each of our hands. "I miss you guys. Skype sessions filled with snotty little kids aren't the same as girl time."

"I'm sure your nieces would very much appreciate your description of them," Daphne said.

She squeezed our hands and let go. "I'm sorry, but you know what I mean. It's hard living across the country and missing out on everything."

"You and Ian could just move back to New York," I said. "You both grew up here. Isn't this home?"

Jen pushed her lips to the side as she thought over what I said. "You know what? I think you're right. Done!"

Daphne and I looked at each other. "What's done?" I asked.

"God, your pregnancy brains are making you slow. Ian and I are moving back to NYC! I was just looking for the right time to tell you!"

"Can you please get over here and hug us so we don't have to get up?"

She laughed and came over to our side of the table.

"I'm so glad you're staying. I was just telling James how much I missed you."

"Me too, Penny. It's time to come home."

"So, what is Ian going to be doing when he comes back to New York?"

"Penny, you can't hire Ian back. It would be so weird now. He'd be working for family."

"I know, but I miss him," I said.

"And now you'll get to hang out with him all the time. Without him driving you around."

"I guess." I pretended to look sad.

"Stop it! You can't hire my fiancé as your driver."

"Wait, fiancé?" Daphne shrieked. She grabbed Jen's left hand.

"It took you bitches long enough to notice this rock."

"Congratulations!" Daphne and I said at the same time.

"Jennifer Hunter, you manipulation artist," Bee said as she walked up to us. "Jen called me a week ago with this crazy idea for a last minute baby shower. When she had zero interest in helping plan the last one. And she told me I had to coordinate everything because I'm on the right side of the country. Right before my wedding. When I've literally never been busier. And it was all because she wanted to tell everyone she was engaged. It was always all about you."

"Psh. That's not at all true," Jen said.

Bee shook her head. "Yes it is. But I am happy for you." She gave Jen a hug.

"Fine, you caught me, it is true. Not that I'm not excited about new nieces or nephews. But I'm engaged! And I'm moving back to New York!" She jumped up and down. "I am sorry for stealing the show, though." Jen put her hand on my shoulder.

She wasn't really sorry. But I was totally fine with that. I was just happy she was staying for good. Now we'd all be here. I smiled to myself.

Oh, shit. Except for Melissa. How did I forget about Melissa? "Hey guys, where is Melissa?" I asked.

"It was so last minute, she couldn't make it either."

"Oh, yeah. Of course." I had already asked about why my Mom wasn't there earlier. Bee said it was just a small thing thrown by friends. No grown-ups allowed. Which made me laugh because we were all grown-ups now, despite what we all thought. Besides, I knew what she really meant. Whenever anyone's mother was invited to something, Jen insisted that her mother be invited too.

Jen was quicker to forgive than the rest of us. Scarlett and Sophie hadn't met their grandmother on the Hunter side. I wasn't sure they ever would. I truly did believe in second chances. I drew the line at millions of chances, though. James, Rob, Daphne, and I were a unified front on this. Bee, Mason, and Matt were too. Maybe Jen had a bigger heart than us. No, James' mother hadn't been holding the gun. But she had helped enable a lunatic. She had taken Isabella's side over her son's side. I couldn't forgive any of that.

My son kicked me hard in the ribs. *Ow.* I wasn't sure if he was kicking me because I was unforgiving or because I hadn't once thought about Melissa. All of my friends were here. How had I completely missed the fact that she wasn't?

"Now, Bee, I think you'll forgive me for forcing you to plan this soiree. Because I have a huge surprise for you. The lame portion of the day has officially come to a close."

"Hey," Daphne said defensively, even though we had both been making fun of the party earlier.

I nudged her with my shoulder and we both laughed.

"And now it's time for your bachelorette party!" Jen screamed and threw her hands into the air.

"Um..." Bee looked at me and then back at Jen. "No, actually, it's not."

"We're doing a joint thing with the guys on Thursday," I said. "We already planned everything. Everyone already took off from work."

"I know," Jen said. "I heard all about your lame plan. But my girl wants something a little crazier. Am I right?" She pointed at Bee.

Bee looked confused. "Me? You never even asked me about it. I already signed off on Penny's idea."

"No," Jen pouted. "I missed out on Penny and Daphne's bachelorette parties because I was in stupid California. Now that I'm finally here for one we're not going on a day trip with the guys to a beach in the middle of nowhere. That's the stupidest thing I've ever heard."

"It's not the stupidest," I mumbled, slightly offended that she was shitting all over my idea.

"It's the beach that Penny and I both grew up going to," Bee said. "I'm actually really looking forward to it."

"Fine." Jen waved her hand through the air. "We can do that too. But we're also doing my thing. Because bachelorette parties aren't about nostalgia and playing stupid games in the sand. They're about making terrible choices that you regret for the rest of your life. Let's do shots!"

"I agree with Jen," Kendra said. Kendra was one of the first friends Bee made after moving to New York. To me, she embodied everything that the city had to offer. She was fun, classy, and usually up all night doing God knows what. Probably with a stranger she just met. "Besides, I remember Penny saying she was going to get us all back once we got married. After we tortured her at her bachelorette party."

I laughed. "I did actually say that." I shook my head, remembering that night. They had made me do this ridiculous list of activities which involved too many penis cookies.

Bee pleaded at me with her eyes.

"But I'm pregnant. And I don't exactly feel like walking all over the city torturing someone on a Sunday afternoon."

"Thank you," Bee mouthed silently.

"Afternoons turn to evenings pretty quickly in this city," Jen said. "And there's a bar right down the street."

"Damn it," Bee said under her breath.

"Everyone who wants to keep this party going, come with me," Jen said as she looped her arm through Bee's and practically dragged her out of the restaurant.

"So that was a weird baby shower," Daphne said.

"Actually I think I liked that one better than my first one."

Daphne laughed. "I'm glad Jen is moving back to the city. But you think she could have saved this crazy bachelorette party idea for her own bachelorette party."

"Well, that doesn't sound like Jen at all."

"Fair enough."

We both slowly stood up from our chairs.

"But what Jen doesn't know is that Rob and James are at that same bar they're heading to down the street," I said. "Which probably means Mason is with them. This little party will be broken up in no time. Bee and Mason already agreed that they didn't want traditional bachelor and bachelorette parties. And James and Rob are good at shutting down Jen's crazy ideas."

"And here I thought you were excited for a night on the town."

"God no. I'm exhausted."

"Me too," Daphne said with a laugh. "I'll probably join Sophie in her afternoon nap."

"Now that's something that sounds much more exciting than a night on the town."

We both waddled after our energetic friends who didn't know what it was like to carry a human inside of them.

CHAPTER 11

Sunday

"I feel like this is a bad idea," Hailey said as I caught up to her on the sidewalk. "It's all fun and games when everyone is single, but we're all married or soon to be. What is Jen's goal here? Does she want Mason and Bee to break up?"

I laughed. "No way. She loves Bee. Jen just likes having fun. And getting her way. Maybe I should have consulted with her on the original party planning process and she wouldn't have felt excluded."

"The Hunters are all so high maintenance."

She did realize that I was technically a Hunter too, right? "I don't really think that's true," I said.

"I was just joking, geez." She squeezed my shoulder. "You don't have to act all defensive. I'm going to go see if I can shut this thing down." She ran ahead of me on the sidewalk to catch up to Jen and Bee.

That was rather snarky. Usually Hailey was always so nice. Was she mad at me? I had a sinking feeling in my stomach. What if Tyler told her about my books? I bit the inside of my lip. That couldn't be it. She knew Tyler and I had a history. We were all friends now. And honestly, it didn't seem like anyone was ever going to read my books anyway. James had been bugging me to read it for ages, but when I finally gave him permission he hadn't even touched my manuscript. *Ow. Please stop kicking me, little dude.*

I had fallen way behind everyone walking to the bar. Part of me just wanted to hail down a taxi. The only thing that kept me going was that I knew James was at the bar. He could take me home. I wasn't going to partake in anything like what they had made me do for my bachelorette party. Thinking about that awful weekend made me want to start crying. I didn't want Hailey to be mad at me. I just wanted that nap that Daphne and I had discussed. Today had been exhausting. Bed rest was starting to sound more and more appealing.

To my dismay, my friends crossed the street up ahead. *Damn it.* Why were they crossing the street when there was a perfectly good bar just a little farther on this side of the street? I sighed as I crossed the street to follow them. I wasn't supposed to be walking around in this heat. James was going to be so mad at me. I slowly opened the door to the bar. The blast of cold air felt refreshing, but the smell of stale beer instantly made me feel nauseous. I placed my hand on my stomach. *Don't worry, I'm going to get you out of here.* I spotted my friends in the corner. As I made my way toward them, I pulled out my phone and sent a text to James asking him to come get me.

"I'm really sorry, but I have to get going in a second," I said as I joined them at the table.

"Time for shots!" Jen yelled and slid one down the table at Bee.

Bee grabbed my arm. "You can't leave me here with them. You're my matron of honor."

A month ago I would have stayed. A month ago it didn't feel like my heart physically hurt. "I'm sorry, Bee. I'm just really tired. I'm gonna call it a day."

She got a worried look on her face.

"Oh come on," Jen said. "What else would you be doing? You just sit around all day."

I swallowed hard. Why was everyone taking jabs at me today? *Fuck.* I put my hand on the center of my chest. *The pain is in my head. It's just in my head.*

"Jen," Bee said defensively.

"Well that's not true." Hailey reached out and grabbed the shot in front of Bee. "She's been writing. Right, Penny?" She downed the shot.

Yup, Hailey's definitely mad at me.

"Yes, her great romance," Bee's friend Marie said and lifted her shot glass. "I still can't wait to read it. I've been waiting to buy that for forever. When are you going to get it out into the world? I need my signed copy."

"I'm trying to get a deal with a publisher," I said, thankful that someone wasn't insulting me.

I glanced at Hailey. She was staring down at the table like she was in some sort of trance with the wood finish. Why did every bachelorette party I attended end up with arguments about Tyler? Unfortunately, I didn't have enough energy to discuss this with her right now. It would have to wait for another day. Maybe a few days to vent would be for the best.

It suddenly felt hard to breathe. The bar and it's blaring music was stifling. "Okay, I'm going to get going." I slid off my stool. Another sharp pain seemed to sear through my chest. *Fuck that hurts.*

"Actually, I'm going to head out with Penny," Daphne said. "Us pregnant girls need to stick together."

There were more protests, but Daphne had looped her arm through mine and was directing me toward the door. She was like my savior.

"Thank you," I said as we exited into the summer heat.

"Are you okay?"

"What?"

"Penny, you looked like you were going to throw up. And your face got really pale. And you kept putting your hand on your chest. Should I call your doctor? Is your chest hurting? You don't look well."

Why did everyone keep telling me how awful I looked? I grabbed my stomach as my son decided to kick me as hard as he could. Maybe I did feel a little nauseous. I tried to swallow down the lump in my throat.

"What's going on?" James' voice instantly calmed me down. He had materialized from out of nowhere. He looped his arm behind my back. "Baby, tell me what's hurting."

Yes his presence calmed me, but Daphne was right. "I don't feel good," I said as I melted into his side.

I heard him snap his fingers and the sound of rubber squeaking against the asphalt. "Call Dr. Nelson and tell him we're going to the ER," he said to someone. I wasn't even sure who he was talking to.

He lifted me into his arms and the smell of fresh leather soon washed away the scent of his strong cologne. I turned my head into his chest so that I could be engulfed in his familiar smell. The car door slammed and the tires squealed on the street.

"Baby, don't close your eyes." James gently tapped the side of my face.

I opened my eyes and looked up at James, a line of worry etched across his forehead. "I'm sorry," I said.

He lowered his eyebrows as he looked down at me. "You always have had a habit of apologizing when you've done nothing wrong."

I tried to smile but the pain made me wince. Hadn't I done something wrong? I wasn't supposed to be out. I should have been in bed today. "Is the baby going to be okay?" Tears were starting to well in my eyes. *He has to be okay.*

"The baby is fine," James said very matter-of-factly. He cupped my face in his hand and glanced at the front of the car. "Put your fucking foot on the gas, William!"

The car lurched forward.

The baby is fine. So that meant I wasn't fine, right? But if I wasn't okay, the baby wasn't either. I squeezed my eyes shut as it felt like someone was stabbing my heart.

"Penny, please open your eyes."

I looked back up at him. There was fear in his gaze. "It hurts." My voice came out as a whimper.

"What hurts, Penny?" He pushed my hair off my forehead.

"My heart." I knew what heartache felt like. I knew how painful that could be. But it wasn't like this. It felt as though my heart was literally breaking, cracking in two.

He clutched me a little tighter. "Okay, baby. We'll be there any second. Please just keep looking at me."

He didn't realize that it was hard to look at him like this. That looking at him made me feel like I was slipping away. Is that how I looked on our wedding day? When I watched his body collapse onto the ground? Was I dying too? The panic rising to my chest made the ache between my ribs increase.

"He's not kicking." The words that slipped out of my mouth terrified me. When was the last time I felt him kick?

"What?" James' hand slid down to my stomach.

"He always kicks me when I'm upset. Why isn't he kicking me?" *Please let my baby be okay.*

PART 2

CHAPTER 12

Sunday

I tightened my grip on James' hand.

The wand swept across my stomach once again. Dr. Nelson shifted in his seat and leaned closer to the monitor.

I looked up at James.

He gave me a tight smile. No fake optimism. No promise that everything was okay.

The silence was unnerving. Where were my son's heartbeats? Where was that tiny thudding noise that put a smile on my face? If I gripped James' hand any tighter my nails would surely have drawn blood. Would he notice? Would either of us notice a pain greater than this silence ever again?

I looked back at the monitor and counted my own heartbeats echoing in my ears. Could they beat for him? *Please, please, baby boy. Please be okay.*

Silence.

It felt like my whole world was slipping away. He was healthy. How could he just...stop? I felt the trickle of a tear run down my cheek. Now I was begging for his kicks. Begging for any sign that his tiny heart hadn't given out. *Please.*

"Oh, there we are," Dr. Nelson said.

I breathed out a sigh of relief and let my head flop down onto the pillow.

James placed a kiss on the back of my hand.

"A nice steady heartbeat. The baby is fine." He removed the wand from my stomach and handed me a towel to wipe off the jelly-like substance left behind.

"So he's okay?" I asked.

The doctor nodded. "You're both perfectly healthy."

"The nurse that came in said her heart rate and blood pressure were elevated. She mentioned that Penny might need medication for that."

"Well, that nurse was mistaken. Any medication we put her on would be dangerous for the baby. Everything is fine."

The word fine was starting to sound jarring to my ears.

"Dangerous for the baby, but how dangerous is this condition for my wife without treatment?"

Dr. Nelson looked down at his clipboard. "You're still taking those vitamins I gave you, right Penny?"

I nodded.

"I think that's enough. But let's double the dose every day just to be safe."

"You think?" James released my hand. "Can I please have a word with you in the hall?"

"Very well." The doctor took his clipboard and tucked it into his side. "I think maybe I issued bed rest prematurely. Go out and get your mind off everything, Penny. Sitting around thinking about it isn't helping anyone." He lightly patted my shin. His hand was so cold that it made me shiver. That was one of the things I disliked about Dr. Nelson. His hands were always freezing. And he always wore black scrubs instead of the pale pastel colors all the other hospital staff wore. I had been thinking about that Harry Potter movie that had scared Scarlett so much that Dr. Nelson was actually starting to resemble Professor Snape. And it wasn't just the black scrubs. It was the long gray hair that was always slightly messy looking. And the prominent nose. He really did look like an older version of the actor that played Professor Snape. I almost laughed out loud, envisioning him in a robe instead of scrubs. For some reason, it made me miss Dr. Jones. And his warm hands. And kind smile. And blue scrubs.

I shook the thought away. Dr. Nelson was great. I shouldn't have compared him to my last OB-GYN. Besides, I couldn't go back to Dr. Jones. He was retired. And James was thinking of suing him. God, I really hoped he didn't go through with that.

I watched the two of them walk out into the hall. As soon as the door closed, I could hear their heated exchange through the thin walls of the hospital room. I climbed out of the bed and started getting dressed, trying to ignore their words, but I couldn't.

"She said she had chest pains," James said.

"Which is ridiculous. You can't feel a heart murmur getting worse."

"Getting worse? Who said anything about it getting worse? Is the leak growing?"

"Mr. Hunter, it isn't getting worse. It would still be classified as moderate. I just meant that the condition can't be physically felt."

"Are you calling my wife a liar?"

"No, I didn't..."

"If she said her heart is hurting, then her fucking heart is hurting."

"And I just told you that such a thing is theoretically impossible."

"So you are calling her a liar."

"I'm just saying that bored housewives sometimes need attention!" Dr. Nelson snapped.

I bit the inside of my lip. *Bored housewife?* I smoothed my dress back into place. I actually had thought that the pain was in my head. It had only started after I was aware of my heart murmur. Was I really going crazy? I placed my hand on the center of my chest. So why did it hurt right now? I grabbed my purse off my chair. *Bored housewife.* Dr. Nelson's words echoed around in my head. I wasn't sure any combination of words had stung so badly. And it wasn't true. I was a wife and a mother and an author.

The taste of blood filled my mouth. I had bit the inside of my lip so hard that I had pierced the skin. *Bored housewife.* That's what people saw when they looked at me. It was basically what Jen had said to me just a few hours earlier today. What else was I going to do with my time if I didn't hang out with them? Well, I had things to do. I surely had new rejection letters to open. And agents turning me down via email. Fuck Dr. Nelson. And fuck everyone else too. *Bored housewife my ass.* I wasn't some young trophy wife like the tabloids claimed. Clearly. People who got rejected as much as me weren't trophies.

I pushed the door open and almost ran right into James. I could almost feel the heat radiating off of him from the way he was fuming.

Dr. Nelson plastered a smile on his face and turned to me. "Just keep taking the vitamins, Mrs. Hunter, and the rest of your pregnancy will go smoothly." He glanced at his watch. "Now, I have a tee time I need to get to. Good day to you both." He nodded curtly and walked away.

"Great. Everything is fine." I cringed at my use of the word fine.

"I'm going to make another appointment with the cardiologist," James said and reached for his cell phone in his pocket.

I grabbed his arm to stop him. "Really, James. It was just a false alarm. I'm sorry about ruining your afternoon."

"Ruining my afternoon?" He ran his hand through his hair. "You're not ruining anything. Your chest hurts. We're going to go see someone who will listen."

I felt the pain. I truly did. But that didn't mean that my mind wasn't somehow causing it to happen. If I thought about it enough, of course it would hurt. In the back of my head I knew that Dr. Nelson was right.

"Does it hurt right now?"

Yes. Maybe if I ignored it, the pain would go away. "James, the baby is okay. That's all that matters."

He lowered his eyebrows. "I didn't ask if the baby was okay. I'm asking about how you feel."

"I think Dr. Nelson is right. I'm thinking about it too much."

"God, don't listen to that prick." James lifted his cell to his ear and turned from me. "Yes I need to make an appointment for my wife."

"James." I put my hand on his bicep. "I don't think that's necessary." He shrugged away from my grip.

"She's been having chest pains," he said into the phone.

"James." He was being exasperating.

He put his hand over the receiver and turned toward me. "Penny, does your chest still hurt or not?"

I wasn't going to lie to him. "Yes, it hurts."

He gave me that stern look that always seemed to silence me and continued his conversation on the phone.

I tuned out his harsh words and leaned against the wall. I felt bad for the person on the other end of the line. The tone he was using could make someone feel like ice. I put my hands on my stomach and took a long, slow breath. *We're okay.*

When James was done on the phone, he turned back to me. "They couldn't fit you in for an appointment until Wednesday. I'll make a few calls and find someone a little more accommodating."

"Dr. Wells is the best cardiologist in the city. It's why we saw him in the first place. If he thinks this issue can wait until Wednesday, I'm sure it can."

"He told us that we should go to the ER in the meantime."

"And we did." I gestured to our surroundings. "Now we can wait until Wednesday."

"I don't..."

"Please, James. I'm tired. I just want to go home." I hated this hospital. Being here reminded me of when James was hurt. It reminded me of the feeling of almost losing him. The sterile smell in the air put a picture of Isabella in my mind. Her cold stare. Her taunting words.

The gun in her hand. I swallowed down the lump in my throat.

James pressed his lips together, like he had something to say but was holding himself back.

I looked up into his brown eyes. "Please."

Something in his eyes seemed to soften. He nodded and wrapped his arm behind my back. We slowly walked out of the hospital and into the sunshine.

For the first time this summer, I was happy for the heat. It was the only thing that could take the cold feeling of the hospital out of my bones.

CHAPTER 13

Tuesday

Sleep evaded me. My eyes traveled along the sharp line of James' jaw. I pressed my lips together as my gaze wandered over his parted lips. He was snoring lightly. He only did that when he was truly exhausted. Was he losing sleep over me? The past few days he had felt distant. Did he lay awake staring at me too? I wanted to reach out and run my fingers through his hair, but something held me back.

Five years ago, if I hadn't been able to sleep, I would have climbed on top of him and made him lose sleep too. There was something so pure about feeling his need for me with him barely being awake. His eyes opening, heavy with lust. I loved that. I loved him.

I swallowed hard. I wanted to climb on top of him right now. But I had a feeling he'd push me aside. He'd tell me I needed rest. He'd roll over so I couldn't even study his face while I was unable to sleep. When had we stopped making love in the middle of the night? When had we stopped letting passion overcome us?

I thought things might change once Scarlett was born. In a lot of ways they had. But James had still looked at me like he preferred me naked. Now he just looked at me like he preferred me in a wheelchair. He was worried about me. I understood that. It didn't mean I didn't miss that look, though. The one that made my knees weak. The one that could take my mind off all my worries. I needed that look right now. Couldn't he see how much I needed him?

But instead of reaching for him, I slowly climbed out of bed. His distance worried me. I looked down at the worn, stretched out t-shirt I was sleeping in. Maybe I needed to try a little harder. I pulled off the shirt and grabbed my silk robe from a hook on the door. I slid my arms into the sleeves and tied the sash tight. James stayed perfectly still in the bed. He used to swear he couldn't sleep without me by his side. Now he looked a little more comfortable with the extra room to spread out.

I turned away from our bed and headed into the hall. My feet stopped outside of Scarlett's bedroom. I leaned against the doorjamb as I watched her sleeping peacefully, her favorite stuffed animal held tight in her arms. No worries. No concerns. So peaceful. Whenever I saw her sleeping, I was always so tempted to lift her into my arms. I used to sing her to sleep every night. But now she preferred bedtime stories from James. My little girl was growing up. Hell, it already seemed like she was falling in love. Would time keep speeding up like this? Would I be looking at my son sleeping in a few years and wonder what happened to the time? I ran my hand across my stomach. I hoped I'd be so lucky.

I sighed and walked back into the hall. My feet tread lightly down the stairs. Writing always made me feel better. Maybe I could take another stab at the second book of my series. I grabbed my laptop off my desk and wandered into the kitchen. A late night snack couldn't hurt either. I switched on my computer, picked up a banana out of the basket on the counter, and sat down in one of the stools.

The light from the computer screen gave the kitchen an eerie glow. I stared at the first paragraph of my second book.

"My stomach was in knots. I couldn't eat. I couldn't sleep. I couldn't seem to focus in class. Every day that I saw Professor Hunter I had this pathetic hope that things would somehow be the way they were before. But it never happened. He wouldn't even look at me. It was like I didn't exist."

I took a bite of my banana and rested my chin in my hand. Every day James dressed in a pair of pants that hugged his ass perfectly and a shirt with the sleeves rolled up, revealing his strong forearms. He made his way to NYCU to teach. He had students that adored him. He was finally truly happy. And every day I wished he'd turn around and teach me a few things instead. Was I really jealous of his current students? It's not like I thought he was falling in love with some 19 year old in the back row of his class. Maybe I just missed that forbidden dynamic between us. I missed when his eyes begged me to call him Professor Hunter. When it turned him on just a little bit more. The only time I ever called him that now was when I was writing about it from the past.

"Is that how you feel?" James said from behind me.

I choked on the banana in my mouth and slammed my laptop shut. "What?" I turned around to face him.

Without the glow from the computer screen, the room was now dark. But the look in his eyes was unmistakable.

It was the one that I had been missing. My eyes wandered down his abs to the V of his waist. The rest of him was hidden underneath a pair of loose sweatpants. His impressive bulge, however, was quite visible through the fabric.

He crossed his arms and walked up to the kitchen island. "Like I don't look at you?" His voice was low and seductive. "Like you don't exist?" He put one elbow down on the counter and leaned against it.

My eyes gravitated back to his. "I wrote that about those weeks after you found out my age. When I thought I lost you." I tucked a loose strand of hair behind my ear. "It was a long time ago."

"That doesn't answer my question. Come here."

I swallowed hard. "It's not how I feel. But what Dr. Nelson said bothered me, yes. How could it not? And I'm not illiterate. I see what they say in the tabloids. It's...hurtful. Ever since I stopped working everyone questions what I'm doing with my time. For a while there, it felt like everyone was on our side. And now the whole city hates me. It's like they're waiting for you to move on to the next thing. Like they can't wait for you to cast me aside for someone more interesting."

"Come. Here."

The way he said it made me press my thighs together. My eyes met his again. He looked like he wanted to fuck the negative thoughts right out of me. Like he wanted to take away my pain. I didn't have any doubt that he could.

I probably moved faster than I had in weeks. The next thing I knew, his fingers were in my hair, pulling my head back so his lips could have easy access to mine. My back was pressed against the edge of the granite countertop.

And his other hand had slid beneath my silk robe and was squeezing my ass.

"Baby, I see you." His breath was hot against my skin as his lips traveled down my neck.

All I could do was moan.

He untied the string of my robe and separated the thin fabric.

My hand instinctively went to my stomach. "God, I'm huge. We don't have to do this right now. I know you can't really want me like this." I reached for the cord for my robe, but he grabbed my hand.

"You're beautiful when you're pregnant. If it was up to me, you'd be pregnant all the time."

I laughed as he easily lifted me onto the countertop. "Pregnant all the time?" I shook my head. "Remember when I didn't have any stretch marks? Remember when I could tie my own shoes?"

"I like your stretch marks." He kissed the side of my stomach. "They remind me of the gift you've given me." He kissed the other side of my stomach. "And I like tying your shoes." He dropped to his knees and kissed the inside of my ankle. He left a trail of kisses up the inside of my calf.

"James." My voice quivered. No, I didn't feel attractive. But the way he was kissing me made me feel so desired.

He gently parted my knees and continued his torturous ascent up the inside of my thigh. Suddenly I didn't care that I was seven months pregnant and felt like a whale. He took me back to when I was 19 and daring him to kiss me in his office.

"I always want you, Penny." His tongue thrust inside of me.

I fell back on my elbows. *God.* He made me feel so alive. I closed my eyes and let him pull me to the edge of the abyss. It was like he had awakened with a craving that only I could satisfy. That maybe he had been dreaming of having me just like this and then needed to make it a reality. This was so much fucking better than any dream.

His lips found my clit and he gently sucked.

In a matter of seconds, he had completely unwound me. I would have been embarrassed by how fast his tongue made me come. But we hadn't had sex in over a week. I was pretty sure he was minutes away from exploding himself.

"Fuck," he groaned and replaced this tongue with his fingers. "Another perk of being pregnant. You're crazy horny." He circled my clit with his thumb as he stood back up.

"That's just the effect you've always had on me."

He stood in silence, towering over me. He grabbed my hand, pulled me back to a seated position, and placed my hand on his erection. I wrapped my fingers around his length. He didn't have to say anything. This was proof that I still had the same effect on him too. I slowly ran my hand up and down through the fabric of his sweatpants. He placed his hands on either side of me, caging me in, making me feel like we were the only two people in the world.

He groaned as I tightened my fingers. "What do you want, baby? Because you're about five seconds away from being bent over this counter and fucked until you can't walk."

I gulped. *Yes, please.*

"Tell me exactly what you want. Tell me what will make you happy."

For a second I thought that question might have a bigger meaning. But the look in his eyes was solely one of desire. He wanted me screaming his name. God, I wanted that too.

"I want you to fuck me like I'm in your office at the University of New Castle. Like we could get caught at any second. I want to feel you lose control, Professor Hunter." Just calling him that made my heart race.

There was a twinkle in his eye as he raised his left eyebrow. "The threat of getting caught is real. I'm going to have you screaming so loudly that you'll probably wake Scarlett."

I laughed. "Well, don't..." My words caught in my throat as he pulled me off the counter. The look in his eyes was dead serious.

He put his hand on the side of my neck, a little tighter than a normal caress. I could feel my pulse against his palm. It was electrifying. I liked when he was rough with me. But he rarely ever was when I was pregnant.

"Turn around and place your hands on the counter, Miss Taylor."

He didn't have to tell me twice. I turned and pressed my hands against the cool granite.

He nudged my legs apart with his knee.

"Penny, you're dripping wet for me." He ran his fingers along the inside of my thigh and I could feel the moisture. "Have you been dreaming about this moment?"

"Every day." I arched my back, making my robe slip off my shoulders.

"Hmm." He gently bit the skin at the top of my shoulder blade.

"Have you?" I wasn't sure why I needed to hear him say it. Clearly he wanted this as much as I did.

His fingertips trailed up the back of my legs, pushing the silk up so he could cup my ass cheeks. "I dream of more than that, Miss Taylor. I want you to take my last name. I want to put my babies inside of you. I want to grow old with you. You want to relive a moment from our past. But you don't even know what was going through my head when I fucked you for the first time."

I wanted to laugh, but I was too turned on to think about anything but his hands on my ass. "You said it was a one time thing."

"Oh, baby." His fingertips dug into my hips. "It made you come back for more, didn't it?" He thrust himself inside of me with one movement.

Jesus. His fingers and tongue could never quite prepare me for his cock. But I loved the feeling of him stretching me wide. It was hard to think about his words. Had he really known? Had he known the whole time what he wanted from me?

We'd never really be able to go back to that moment. Yes, he was fucking me. But there was love in each stroke too. Love underlined everything we did.

His hands slid up my waist and grabbed my breasts. "Every fucking inch of you is perfect," he said as his thumbs and index fingers gently pinched my nipples.

"James," I moaned.

"Oh, no, Miss Taylor." He pinched my nipples even harder. "I don't believe we're on a first name basis yet. What are you going to scream when you come?"

"Professor Hunter," I panted.

"Scream it when you come, baby. Let everyone know how fucking wrong this is. How much you enjoy breaking the rules. How all you dream about is my cock deep inside of you."

"Professor Hunter!" I shattered around him as I felt his warmth spread up into me. I felt his naked chest against my back. His hands slid to my stomach. He placed a kiss on the top of my spine.

I shuddered once more and he groaned.

"Hearing you call me that still gets me so hard."

"Even when I'm as big as an elephant?" I didn't need to ask the question. He was still as hard as a rock and he had just cum.

He kissed the back of my neck. "I wasn't lying when I said I liked you pregnant. And guess what the best part is?"

I laughed and he groaned again.

"What?" I asked and peered at him over my shoulder.

"That there isn't a doubt in anyone's mind that you're mine. When they see this," he said as he ran his palm along my stomach again. "Everyone knows you're completely off limits."

"I have a ring for that."

"Hmm." He pulled out of me. "That's not quite the same."

I instantly felt an emptiness. It was like I never truly felt complete unless our bodies were intertwined.

"Now, my beautiful wife, let me show you how fucking right you and I actually are." He scooped me up into his arms.

I clasped my hands behind his neck. "What did you have in mind?"

"There's at least six hours before Scarlett wakes us up," he said as he carried me to the stairs.

"You have work in the morning."

"And you need my undivided attention for a few hours. But maybe not quite as much as I need yours." He smiled down at me. Any lingering sleepiness was gone from his face. That empty feeling was about to be extinguished. Maybe a couple more times.

CHAPTER 14

Wednesday

I closed the lid of my suitcase. James would be home any minute. I touched the center of my chest. All I needed to do was go to this appointment and get the all clear. Then I could focus on Bee's bachelorette party. We were leaving at the crack of dawn tomorrow morning. Separate cars so that we'd have a little girl time before meeting the guys at the beach. It was going to be so much fun. And I was beyond excited for their wedding on Saturday. I had been waiting for years for Bee and Mason to tie the knot.

My phone buzzed and I lifted it off the bed. There was a text from James. I clicked on it.

"We just pulled into the garage. We should probably get going if we're going to make the appointment on time."

I laughed and slid my phone into my purse. That was his nice way of saying, "get your ass down here or we're going to be late." I made my way down the stairs. The house was too quiet today. Scarlett had insisted on going to the park and Ellen had insisted that I wasn't allowed to accompany them. She usually tended to agree with James.

I stepped onto the elevator and watched the doors close. The day alone had given me time to read through my rough draft for my second book. And our heated night made it easy for the words to flow. I was pretty sure all the scenes with him were perfect. It was the moments with Tyler that were tripping me up. Picturing him in his Wesley costume on Halloween put this feeling of guilt in my stomach. And my son could feel it. It was as though he was trying to kick it out of me.

I needed to talk to Hails. That's what was bothering me. I'd be hanging out with her all day tomorrow. Certainly I could smooth things over. But maybe she wasn't even upset about that. We had never talked about my past with Tyler. She had always seemed cool about it. Was there something else bothering her? I tried to shake away the thought. The last thing I needed before going to the cardiologist was to get upset.

Breathe in. Breathe out. "Hi, William," I said as I walked up to the car. "How has your day been?"

"Very good, Mrs. Hunter." He bowed slightly as he opened up the door.

Had I just imagined him doing that? Our relationship or lack thereof was really starting to bother me. "You really can just call me Penny. Did James torture you all day?"

"Not at all, ma'am." He sounded slightly offended.

Ma'am? I wasn't seventy years old. If anything, I should have been the one that was offended. I stepped into the car and slid next to James in the back seat. The door closed behind me.

"Stop terrorizing him," James said with a smile.

"I'm trying to get to know him. How was class?"

"Good." He kissed my temple as he pulled me into his side. "Although, I was pretty tired all day."

"A sex marathon will do that to you."

He laughed and rested the back of his head against the seat.

"Are you okay?" He really did look exhausted.

"I've just been worried about this appointment all week."

"I'm sure the doctor will say there hasn't been any change." I rested my head on his shoulder. "How did the board meeting go this afternoon?" Rob had taken over as CEO of Hunter Tech. James still remained on the board, though. The company was still his baby, but he was happier teaching. Plus his blood pressure was back in the normal range now. His days of barking orders were over. And I was happier because of it too. He smiled more now. He was more relaxed grading papers and giving lectures. It helped that the university was crazy flexible with his hours. James was only teaching two classes this summer. He had even given a few lectures via video chat from bed. Those were my favorite mornings.

"The rollout is still on schedule. I think the board is still getting used to Rob's sense of humor, though."

"Why do you say that? Did Rob say something and hear crickets?"

"More like gasps. Today he said the launch was going to be as big as his dick."

I laughed. "Wait...you're not serious?"

"You've met my brother, right? He comes up to about here," he said and put his hand against his nose. "The one with no filter and the overtly sexual phrases?"

I shook my head and laughed again. "I'm still having trouble picturing him in a suit and tie all day. But I kind of just assumed he'd tone it down at work."

"I think the board secretly loves him. Besides, our client list is growing faster than ever. Everyone finds him super relatable, I guess."

"He's probably talking mostly to guys then."

"Or flirting with the ladies."

I lightly slapped James' arm. "Is that what you did? You grew your companies by schmoozing rich women?"

"A guy's gotta do what a guy's gotta do."

I rolled my eyes. "Fortunately for both of us, you're out of the game."

"Speaking of that, I may need to go to London for a few days. There's a deal that we really need to land. Rob's been flitting around with it for months. So I think it's best if I handle this one in person."

"When do you have to go?"

"Right after the wedding."

"Oh." I wasn't sure why, but I felt disappointed. Weddings were so romantic. I was hoping to spend a few days after the wedding with my head in the clouds. It was hard to do that when he was gone. I hated when he traveled. Scarlett did too. She always cried when he didn't tuck her into bed.

"It's just for a couple of days." He kissed my temple again.

The good I could draw from this was that James must not be too worried about my appointment today. If he was seriously concerned, he wouldn't be flying across the ocean in a few days. I took another slow, deep breath. That was good news.

The car pulled to a stop outside the high rise where my doctor's office was located. A minute later, William was helping me out of the car. *Stay calm.* This would all be over in about an hour.

***

"Okay, good news and bad news. What'll it be first?" Dr. Wells said as he scooted a chair over to me. His gray hair gave him a distinguished look. He had been doing this for over thirty years.

I bit the inside of my lip. I was going to believe whatever he was about to say. And I was terrified about what the bad news was.

James squeezed my hand.

"Let's just rip the Band-Aid off," I said.

"That's the spirit." Dr. Wells adjusted his glasses and looked down at his clipboard. "Your leak has progressed ever so slightly. Unnoticeable if it weren't for the echocardiogram. Despite your concerns, James, I truly believe that your OB-GYN wouldn't have been able to detect it with just a stethoscope."

"But shouldn't he have at least been a tiny bit alarmed?" James said. "Penny was having chest pains and he completely dismissed the possibility that something was actually wrong."

Dr. Wells nodded. "I understand. Us doctors all like to think we're right." He winked at me. "It is unusual to feel pain due to a murmur. It could have been a wide variety of things causing it. Your OB-GYN specializes in deliveries. I'm sure he's highly qualified in his profession."

I didn't care about Dr. Nelson right now and whether he was a good doctor. I wasn't even sure why we were discussing him. Dr. Wells had just said my leak had progressed and I really had no idea what that meant. "What do you mean that it progressed?"

Dr. Wells settled the notebook in his lap. "It's just a small amount, Penny. I'd probably classify the murmur as moderate to severe now. Somewhere in between the two classifications."

"That's bad, right?" Just talking about this made my chest hurt again.

"No, not necessarily. This baby is putting extra stress on your heart right now. I have every reason to believe the murmur will go back to being moderate after the birth."

"Before you said that it might go back to being mild after the delivery," James said.

Dr. Wells nodded and adjusted his glasses again. "This is something we're going to have to continue to monitor. But usually murmurs of this severity don't just disappear on their own. As long as you're not experiencing shortness of breath or any swelling in your legs and feet, your heart is working perfectly fine."

"When you say they don't disappear on their own, what do you mean by that?" James asked. "You mentioned before that if it got any worse she'd need surgical intervention."

"She'll live a long healthy life. Yes, a medical procedure may be in her future. But advancements in this area are astounding. By the time we need to surgically repair or replace the valve, we'll be looking at something a lot less invasive than open heart surgery."

For some reason my mind focused on the words, "open heart surgery." My mouth felt dry.

"The good news is, you're already on bed rest. So the odds of it progressing any further are very slim. I'd recommend staying off your feet as much as possible. We'll reevaluate your condition after your baby is born. Hopefully everything will go back to normal and you won't have to see my face anymore." He laughed at his own joke.

I didn't really know what to say. I placed my hand on my stomach. *It's okay little guy. We're going to be okay.*

"Should she be traveling at all?" James asked.

I glanced at him. He never let me fly when I was pregnant anyway. Did he suddenly have an urge to let me come to London with him?

"I'd recommend staying at home, Penny," Dr. Wells said. "The stress of travel isn't something I personally think is worth the risk."

James nodded his head. "And our incompetent OB-GYN said he may have prescribed bed rest too soon. Do you have names of any OB-GYN's that you'd recommend?"

"Why, certainly." He readjusted his glasses again. "My receptionist can give you a list of names. I've worked with all of them before. Top notch doctors."

"Thank you, Dr. Wells," James said.

"Did either of you have any other questions?"

"No, I think that about covers it." James stood up, put his hand out for me, and pulled me to my feet.

"Take it easy, Penny," Dr. Wells said. "And watch for any swelling or shortness of breath. You call me right away if you notice anything like that."

I nodded and let James escort me out of the doctor's office. His hand was gripping mine a little tighter than usual. And I couldn't help but think that it was because he thought I was slipping away.

CHAPTER 15

Wednesday

"But I don't want to stay with Grandpa. I want to come with you." Scarlett pulled on the hem of my dress to get my attention.

I looked down at her cute little scowl. "I know, Scar. But Grandpa has all sorts of fun activities planned. You're going to have so much fun. Rumor has it he's taking you to the zoo." I reached down and picked up the sandals I had been searching everywhere for. Of course they were exactly where they should be in the closet. I had almost forgotten to pack them.

"Hmph." Scarlett crossed her arms. "I don't want to go to the zoo. I want to come with you, Mommy." She plopped down in the middle of the closet in protest.

"Scar, get up off the floor and we'll get your stuff ready to go to Grandpa's."

"Mommy, please let me come with you!" She flopped backwards and spread her arms and legs out like she was about to make snow angels. But she stayed perfectly still like the thought of not coming with us had killed her.

"What are you two doing?" James said. He was staring down at our daughter sprawled out on the floor.

Scarlett immediately got up. "I'm helping Mommy pack. She said if I was good I could come with you."

"Scarlett Hunter." I couldn't believe what I was hearing. "What have we told you about lying?"

She gave me the most innocent look. "I don't remember. Daddy, please let me come!" She ran over to James and wrapped her arms around his leg.

"Pumpkin, why don't you go downstairs and help Ellen with dinner." He ruffled her hair.

"If I do will you let me come?"

"I'm going to give you to the count of ten to do as I asked," said James.

"You're a mean daddy!" She ran out the door and her little feet could be heard sprinting down the stairs.

James frowned and turned his attention back to me. At first I thought he was upset by what Scarlett had said. But he looked upset with me.

"What's wrong? I had already told her no. We really need to talk to her about lying again." I walked past him and back into our bedroom. I tossed my sandals on my suitcase.

"Penny, we discussed traveling with the doctor. I thought this was already settled. You're not going anywhere."

I turned back toward him. "What?"

"We're not going."

"James." I laughed, because he must have been kidding. "I thought you were talking about London. Driving a few hours to the beach is hardly traveling."

"We're. Not. Going."

I swallowed hard. The way he said it was as condescending as it was sexy. But I was way more focused on the condescending aspect of his statement. "Yes we are. I'll be sitting down in the car. And sitting on the beach. It's practically bed rest."

"I already called them and told them we couldn't come. This discussion is over."

Like hell it is. "You canceled without asking me?"

"The doctor said..."

"James, I'm Bee's matron of honor! I have to be there." Why was he acting like this?

"And you're my wife. What's more important to you?"

How could he even ask me that? I swallowed down the lump in my throat. "So that's it? You want me to sit around for two months while you fly off to God knows where and abandon me?"

He shook his head. "Jesus, Penny. I'll be gone for two days. Three tops. Why do you insist on pushing yourself? Why can't you just stay still for once?"

Suddenly it felt like the weight of the world had fallen on my shoulders. Honestly, I wasn't upset about his tone. I knew he was doing it because he cared. I wasn't even upset that he had made the decision not to go without asking me. It was so much deeper than that. I blinked away my tears. "Because what if this is it, James?" My voice cracked. "What if I go into labor and the stress on my heart is too much and I die on that table?" I voiced my fears and hearing them out loud was so much worse than thinking about them in my head.

He took a step toward me, but I held up my hand.

"What if these are my last two months? Time doesn't stand still just because I have to."

"Baby."

"And I'm so scared about what'll happen once I'm gone. Everyone will forget about me. Scarlett won't even remember me, she's too young. All I have is a stupid book that no one wants to fucking read. That's my legacy."

"Nothing is going to happen to you."

"But what if it does?" I wiped my tears away with my hands. "You have to promise me you'll keep living. Promise me you'll keep your heart open."

"No." He said it so matter-of-factly, I could have thought he was responding to a simple question about if he wanted Chinese food for dinner.

"James." God, he was so exasperating. "Just promise me."

He ignored my outstretched hand and pulled me into his arms. "No. I will never fall for someone new. You're it for me, Penny. You're everything. My heart will stop beating the second that yours does."

"That's very romantic, but what about Scarlett? What about this baby? They'll be relying on you. You have a family that needs you."

He shook his head.

"Promise me, James."

"I'm not going to make you a promise that I can't keep. I don't know how to live without you. So you're just going to have to keep living, baby. And that means no trip to the beach. It's not worth risking your health."

"Fine. I'll agree to no bachelorette party. But you have to agree to my request too. Your heart will in fact keep beating once mine stops." I put my hand on the center of his chest. "And I'm asking you to please be willing to keep it open to love. Our kids will need you to smile and laugh and maybe, just maybe, find someone to share all that joy with."

"No."

"James!" For some reason his stubbornness made me start laughing. "Do you think I want to imagine you with another woman? The thought makes me feel sick to my stomach."

"Good, me too."

"You have to promise me." Now that I was smiling, I wasn't sure he was talking me seriously at all.

"Absolutely not." He was smiling now too.

"God, what am I going to do with you?" I ran my fingers down the collar of his dress shirt.

He tilted his head down and ran the tip of his nose down the length of mine. "Does that mean we can stay here tomorrow?"

Now he's asking. "You didn't agree to my demands."

"Demands?" He cupped the side of my face in his hand. "Surely you can think of better demands than that."

I laughed.

"That one sound." He closed his eyes. "How can a sound be my favorite thing in the world?"

"I love you, James."

He opened his eyes again. "You're unforgettable, Penny. To me. To our daughter. To our family and friends. Nothing is going to happen to you. But don't you ever think that if it did, we'd forget you."

I stood on my tiptoes and kissed him. I understood why he couldn't promise me he'd move on. I could still remember the feeling in my soul when I thought I was going to lose him. That was it. My heart would have stopped beating when his did. I truly believed that it was possible to meet someone so perfect for you that you could no longer exist without them. James was my heart. My soul. My everything.

CHAPTER 16

Thursday

A light knocking on our bedroom door made me yawn. "James," I said and nudged him. "Who's at the door?"

"What?" he grumbled.

"James," Ellen said and knocked on the door again. "I hate to disturb you, but your brother is downstairs asking for you."

James groaned and looked at the clock on his nightstand. "It's 5 o'clock in the morning. Why is Rob here so early?"

"Do you think something is wrong?" I was about to sit up when James put his hand on top of my massive stomach.

"I got it. He probably just wants to say goodbye before they head down to the beach. I'll go tell him to go away."

I laughed and rolled onto my side in search of a cool spot on my pillow. I was just drifting back to sleep when I heard James clear his throat.

"So, bad news," he said. "My dad came down with some kind of bug. And..."

"Aunt Penny!" Sophie yelled and pulled on my hand that was hanging off of the bed.

I opened up my eyes. "Hi, sweetie. What are you doing here?" I tapped the tip of her nose with my index finger.

"My daddy said I get to spend all day and night here."

"And we're going to go spend that time downstairs," James said and swooped Sophie up into his arms. "And we're going to be quiet so we don't wake anyone who's sleeping. Right, Soph?"

Sophie giggled. It didn't look like she had any interest in listening to what he said.

"Is your dad okay?" I asked as I pushed myself into a seated position. I yawned again. It had been awhile since I had woken up this early.

"He'll be fine. Keep sleeping, baby, I've got this."

I watched him walk out of the room with Sophie. I was still tired. Plus, Ellen was already here to help. I lay back down and closed my eyes.

***

When I finally wandered downstairs, I followed all the noise into the family room. I smiled at the scene in front of me. Axel was standing on the couch repeatedly hitting James in the back of the head with a pillow, while James played the board game Pretty Pretty Princess with Scarlett and Sophie on the floor. James was decked out in a pink necklace, ring, and bracelet. Why he got stuck with the color pink was beyond me. It looked like Axel had played long enough just to snag the crown.

I used to love that game when I was little. But I certainly couldn't remember my dad playing with me. "Are you the winning princess?" I asked Axel as I walked into the room.

Axel scowled. "No. I'm the prince. They're the princesses."

Scarlett was clipping on a pair of earrings. I was almost positive that it wasn't even her turn.

"Axel won't play," she said. "He thinks it's a game just for girls. But Daddy's playing, so Axel is wrong."

"I am not," Axel said, and whacked James on the back of the head again.

"Okay, enough of that," James said. He turned and lifted Axel off the couch. "You get to choose what we play next, but right now we need to finish Pretty Pretty Princess. And it's your turn."

He stuck his tongue out at Scarlett and then sat down next to her.

"Here you go, Axel," Scarlett said and put a necklace over his head. "Now you're a beautiful princess."

"I'm not a princess! I'm a boy!"

"But my Daddy is playing and he's a boy."

"That's different. He's a dad, not a boy."

James and I both laughed. James looked up at me and smiled. He looked completely ridiculous decked out in his garish jewelry. But I wasn't sure I had ever seen him more handsome, jewels and all. Being a dad definitely didn't take the man out of James. It certainly took a level of confidence to willingly dress like a princess, and to me that exuded a level of sexiness that was hard to put into words.

When no one was looking, Sophie grabbed a ring, the last piece of jewelry she was missing. "I win!" she shouted.

"But it wasn't your turn," Scarlett said.

"I'm the prettiest princess!" Sophie stood up and started to twirl around in circles.

Scarlett folded her arms across her chest. It looked like she was about to cry.

But then Axel leaned over and whispered something in her ear. Her frown was replaced by the biggest smile. She turned to Axel and kissed him on the cheek.

"Ew!" Axel shouted. He rubbed his cheek where her lips had been, then got up and jumped back onto the couch, retrieving the pillow he had dropped earlier. He tossed it at Scarlett and then picked up another and slammed it against the back of James' head.

"Okay, that's it. Princesses, attack the prince!" James said.

Axel jumped off the back of the couch as everyone else grabbed pillows and chased after him.

I ran my hand across my stomach and turned back toward the kitchen. *We can join them as soon as you're out, baby boy.* In the meantime, I was starving. I opened up the fridge and looked at the scarce remains. The kids must have ransacked it for breakfast. That was probably why Ellen was nowhere in sight. She handled our grocery shopping and there wasn't much she could make with the current contents of the fridge. I grabbed the bottle of orange juice and closed the fridge. I opened up the cupboard to grab a glass but my eyes landed on a banana instead. And a small note with James' handwriting on it:

Saved this for you. Don't let Soph see you eating it. She was very upset that she couldn't have one. I had to pretend that this one was rotten.

I smiled and picked up the banana and a glass. *The perfect breakfast.* Well, maybe not on a normal basis. But recently all I was craving was fruit. I quickly ate so I could join in on the fun. I was just like Scarlett in that way. The thought of missing out on a second of family time made me sad. Plus, I didn't want Sophie seeing me eat the banana. Saying no to Scarlett was hard. Saying no to Sophie was almost impossible. She could cry at the drop of a hat. I was pretty sure she was going to be an actress when she grew up. She'd probably win an Oscar.

When I walked out of the kitchen, I couldn't help but laugh. James was lying in the middle of the foyer surrounding by all the kids who were repeatedly smacking their pillows against his back.

"We killed the beast!" Axel yelled.

I wasn't sure how it had morphed into killing a beast instead of attacking a prince.

James opened one eye to look at me laughing.

"Kids, I think he's still alive!" I pointed to his opened eye.

"Get 'em!" Scarlett jumped onto his back.

James cringed when she landed right on his spine.

Crap. Every now and then James' back would give out. Based on the expression on his face, I was pretty sure Scarlett's landing hadn't magically fixed it. And I couldn't imagine taking care of these kids all day without his help. "Okay," I said and lifted Scarlett off his back. "How about you guys go clean up the board game and pick out a new one to play?"

The three of them ran off toward the family room.

"Are you alright?" I asked.

"Ow," he mumbled and turned his face away from me. He hated when I saw him in pain. The years together hadn't changed that.

I knelt down next to him on the floor and gently touched his lower back. He didn't seem to have any reaction to that, which was good. I pushed up the bottom of his t-shirt and applied the smallest amount of pressure on his skin. "Does that hurt?"

Suddenly, he rolled onto his back, pulled me on top of him, and started tickling my sides.

"James!" I said in the small amount of breath I could take between fits of giggles. "You liar! You're not hurt at all."

He continued tickling me.

"Stop!" I laughed. "I can't breathe."

His hands settled on my waist. "How many times do you think we've had sex right here?"

I put my index finger against his lips. "James, lower your voice. The kids are in the other room."

He tickled my side again so my hand slipped from his mouth. "God you're beautiful."

I smiled down at him. "You can't flatter me out of this one. I think Scarlett picked up this lying fix from you."

He shook his head. "A trick is different than a lie."

"I thought you were really hurt."

"No. I just wanted you on top of me." He reached up and tucked a loose strand of hair behind my ear. "But really. We used to come back from events and have sex right when we stepped into our apartment. Do you remember that?"

I bit the inside of my lip. How could I possibly forget? "I might need a reminder."

He ran his thumb along my lip so that I'd stop biting it. "Kiss me, Penny."

I leaned down and placed my lips against his.

He grabbed the back of my head to deepen the kiss. And he wasn't kissing me like our house was filled with company. He was kissing me like we had just gotten back from a gala where we both had too much to drink.

"I remember," I whispered.

I could feel his smile in the kiss. I could feel every emotion when our bodies were intertwined like this.

"What on earth are you two doing on the floor?" Ellen said as she came into the apartment. "James, you're going to throw out your back again."

"We were just getting up," he said and slapped my ass.

"Ellie!" Scarlett yelled as she ran into the foyer. "The ice cream is here!"

"Ice cream!" Axel and Sophie yelled in unison.

"Do you really think that's a good idea?" I asked James as I got up off the floor. "They're going to be wired up all day."

"You try telling them no. It was three against two down here for a couple of hours. But now that you're up at least we won't be outnumbered."

I watched the kids run into the kitchen after Ellen. "Thanks for saving me a banana."

"Mhm." He placed a soft kiss against my lips as he pulled me back into his arms. "Ellen said she'd grab some more at the store too."

"Did you know you were still wearing this?" I asked and touched the silly pink necklace.

James laughed. "No. Do you like it?"

"I've never seen it worn better. So they're still refusing to learn the actual rules of Pretty Pretty Princess? It's just a free-for-all with jewelry?"

"They have no idea how to play, but Scarlett and Soph insist that it's their favorite game. I think they just like torturing Axel."

"Speaking of Axel. What did he whisper to Scarlett to calm her down? She's an extremely sore loser and I know she was about to throw a fit."

James laughed. "That kid's a bad whisperer. He said that she was the prettiest princess he ever saw."

"No way. Did he really?"

"That's a direct quote."

"Aw," I said. "That's the most adorable thing I've ever heard."

"Tyler can joke around all he wants about Scarlett being in love with his son. But that boy is just as smitten with her."

I laughed. "I think they make a cute couple."

"They're only three and a half."

"Exactly. And they're already perfect for each other."

James shook his head. "They're practically cousins. Axel calls us Uncle James and Aunt Penny. And Scarlett does the same with Tyler and Hailey."

"Oh, the forbidden nature of it all. Like that hasn't ever intrigued a girl?"

"They're three and a half," he said again. "I don't think they even know what forbidden means. Besides, Scarlett isn't allowed to date until she's 30."

I laughed. "If she was more like me you wouldn't have to worry so much. I didn't even have my first kiss until college."

"But then you started sleeping with your professor. You're a terrible influence."

"Me? I'm the one saying I'd be happy if she ended up with a boy we already know and love."

"Now that I know what it's like to have a daughter, I'm lucky your father didn't kill me. I'm going to want to murder anyone who even kisses Scarlett." He pulled away from me and reached up to unhook his necklace. "I'll be right back. I need to de-princess myself." He winked at me and disappeared back into the family room.

CHAPTER 17

Thursday

I picked up the last slice of pizza and took a huge bite. "Today was way better than the beach. And honestly, I was craving this pizza, not Grottos."

"Really? Did you finally just admit that Grottos is second best to Totonno's Pizzeria?"

"I was just in the mood for it."

"You, Mrs. Hunter, are officially a New Yorker."

"I am not. I'm a Delawarean." But I smiled at the thought of truly being a New Yorker.

James laughed. "Do you ever want to go back?"

I set my slice of pizza down. "You know, I thought I would. Especially once we had kids. But our whole life is here." I looked into the other room where the kids were bouncing around the room giggling. They were addicted to this game where an elephant shot butterflies out of its nose. They had to run around catching the butterflies in their nets before they hit the ground. It was one of the only things that could entertain all of them for at least an hour, so it was one of my favorite games too. "Suburbia wouldn't really feel like home anymore," I said and turned back to James. "I do wish my parents visited more, though."

"Your mom has been threatening to stay with us for a few weeks after the baby is born. So we'll be seeing plenty of them soon enough."

"Why does the thought of my mother staying here bother you so much? You really don't have to put them up in a hotel every time they visit. We have plenty of room."

He leaned forward slightly. "The thought of your parents hearing us make love doesn't exactly get me going."

I laughed. "We're not going to be having sex after the baby is born. For awhile anyway."

"Don't remind me." He put his chin in his hand and stared at me.

I lifted up my slice of pizza again.

"You know, I wouldn't mind if it was a boy."

I stopped chewing mid-bite. That was the first time James had ever said that. The whole time I was pregnant with Scarlett he insisted it was going to be a girl. And he had been doing the same this time. "Really?"

"I don't know. It might be fun to have another guy in the house. And I could teach him how to throw a football. And hit a baseball." He grabbed the piece of pizza out of my hand and took a bite. "It wouldn't be all bad is what I'm saying."

I couldn't even believe my ears. "You want a boy."

He laughed. "I didn't say that. I said I wouldn't mind if it was a boy."

"No, you totally want a little boy. If it was a boy, what would you want to name him?"

"I don't know."

We hadn't really discussed boy names at all, but I had a list in my head. "What about Rowan?"

James scrunched up his nose.

"Lucas." When he didn't have a reaction, I decided to just start giving him more options. "Noah. Oliver. Elijah. Ryan."

He just stared blankly at me.

"James Junior?"

He laughed. "Absolutely not. Rob Junior is going to be enough juniors."

"Jace?"

"Two J names in the house would be bad. You'd probably yell Jace when you meant to yell James."

I laughed. "I don't make a habit of yelling at you."

"But if you did, it would be a problem."

"How about Liam Hunter?" I held my breath as I waited for his response. Liam was at the very top of my mental list.

"Yeah. Maybe. But it's probably going to be a girl." He leaned forward and put his hand on my stomach. "Isn't that right, Arya?"

I laughed. "We are not naming her after a Game of Thrones character. I've already vetoed that one."

"But you like Game of Thrones too. I don't understand what the big deal is."

"Everyone is going to be naming their little girls Arya. And it doesn't even sound good with Hunter."

"Arya Hunter," he said slowly. "It slides right off the tongue."

"Fine, it sounds okay. I just feel like I picture the character from the show when you say it. I don't want our daughter having an identity crisis."

"That character from the Big Bang Theory has the name Penny. Does seeing that show give you an identity crisis?" He let his hand drop from my stomach.

"No. But I look nothing like her."

James laughed. "So if our daughter comes out with red hair, which she probably will given our last one, we can name her Arya since she'll look different from the character?"

"That's not what I said."

"But we couldn't name her Sansa because they'd both have red hair and it would be super confusing for her growing up."

"I don't know. No one had my name growing up. The Big Bang Theory didn't come out until I was in high school."

"Well, plenty of kids had the name James and I turned out fine. By the way, Liam is on the top of the list for boy's names this year, so doesn't that kind of count that name out?"

"You've been looking at the list of most popular boy's names?"

"I mean...I may have glanced at it."

I smiled and grabbed his hand, pulling it back to my stomach. "I swear to you, this is a little boy."

His eyes twinkled as he spread his fingers out. "You said that last time."

"Everyone likes to rub that in my face. But now I have experience. And I'm telling you James, I feel it. He's stronger and more energetic and he's just...he's a he."

"I'm kind of used to coming home and asking how my girls are doing." He stared at my stomach. "What if it is a boy? What if I mess him up?"

His words hurt me because I knew what he was referring to. But how could he think that? He was so good with Scarlett. He'd be good with a son too. "You're not your parents, James."

He continued to stare at my stomach.

"And you're the best father I know. You know, my dad never played Pretty Pretty Princess with me."

James laughed. "God, I really want it to be another girl." He leaned down and placed a kiss against my stomach. "But I guess the name Liam isn't so bad if it's not."

I touched the bottom of his chin so that he'd look up at me. "You're a great father. The sex of the baby doesn't matter. It's the love that you have that makes you so wonderful."

A pounding on the front door made me jump.

"Who could that be?" James said as he stood up. "If it's Rob dropping more children off, I'm not letting them in this time."

I laughed and followed James to the door. I did not expect to see Scarlett being held out to us when the door opened.

"I believe this little girl belongs to you." Porter, the head of our security detail, set Scarlett down in the foyer. He patted her head affectionately.

"Scarlett, how did you get out of the apartment?" James said sternly.

"The door." She pointed to the very obvious answer behind her.

"You know you're not supposed to leave without an adult," I said. Or at all. Seriously, how was she getting through the child locks?

"Mr. Porter said I wasn't in trouble." She blinked innocently up at us.

"Did he?" James said and knelt down in front of her. "Pumpkin, why did you leave without telling us?"

"I saw a real butterfly outside. And I wanted to catch it. I was supposed to get to play with the animals today."

"You should have asked us to come with you."

"But you would have said no! Mommy can never do anything because the storks haven't come yet. It's not fair!"

"I'm just going to..." Porter's voice trailed off as he walked back into the hall and closed the door behind him.

"Pumpkin, Mommy will do whatever you want as long as we stay inside, okay?" James said. "It's just too hot out today."

"It's not fair!" Scarlett screamed again. "Grandpa was going to take us to the zoo today. You promised! I want the zoo!"

"Scar," I said as soothingly as I knew how. "I'm sorry about the zoo. But we can go a different day, okay?"

My words didn't help at all. She just looked at me and shrieked at the top of her lungs. Tears immediately started falling from her eyes.

"Scarlett," James said sternly. "That is enough. Plans change. We'll go a different day."

She screamed even louder. It was like a chain effect and in a second I heard Sophie crying from the other room.

Damn it. One crying kid was bad enough. "Please look at Mommy," I said as I knelt down next to James. "I promise you we'll go a different day. We can even take Sophie and Axel with us."

"You're a liar! You're a mean mommy!"

Ouch.

"Scarlett Hunter, go to our room right now," James said. His tone probably would have made me go to my room.

"I hate the baby! I hope the storks cook her too long in the oven!"

"Now," James said.

"Fine! But you're a mean daddy too!" She screamed at the top of her lungs again and ran past us.

I sat backwards onto the floor. "What the hell was that? Her scream could rupture someone's eardrums."

"I have no idea." James ran his fingers through his hair as he stood up. "I hate when she calls me a mean daddy. How can she use such a cute phrase to break my heart in two?"

"She doesn't mean it," I said as he helped me to my feet. "We should go calm Sophie down."

A door slamming upstairs made me wince.

"I'll handle Soph," James said. "You can go talk to that little monster upstairs that I don't recognize at all."

I sighed and followed the path of the little girl I didn't recognize either. Scarlett rarely ever screamed. She'd cry when she was upset, but what I just witnessed was more of a wild banshee. What had gotten into her? I ran my hand across my stomach. *She didn't mean it, baby boy. She's going to love you.*

I made my way upstairs and knocked on her door.

"Go away!"

"Scar, can I please come in?"

"No!"

I opened up the door anyway. Scarlett was lying in the middle of her floor with her face buried in the carpet.

"Hey," I said and slowly sat down cross-legged beside her. "Can you please look at me?" I gently ran my fingers through her curly hair.

"No," she mumbled into the floor.

"Okay." I lay down beside her and just stared at her in silence for a few minutes until she finally turned her head toward me.

"Mommy, it's not fair. The stork is going to take the baby. And then the snake is going to take you. And I'll only have Daddy. And Daddy will be too sad to be a good daddy when you're gone."

For just a second, I was too stunned to say anything. "Scar, what are you talking about? There are no evil snakes, it was just a movie. I'm not going anywhere."

She scrunched her eyes closed. "We need you, Mommy. It's not fair."

"Baby girl, I'm not going anywhere. That movie wasn't real. It's just made up. There are no evil snakes."

"No, Mommy." She scooted forward and wrapped her arms around me. "He was already here."

Her words sent a chill down my spine. What was she talking about? "Scarlett, who's here?"

"The snake! Mommy, I don't even want a baby sister. No one asked me. I never wanted one. I just wanted you."

She was crying again. I could feel her tears soaking through my shirt.

"You have me," I said and ran my fingers through her hair again. "I promise I'm not going anywhere." I held her tight as she cried. We really shouldn't have let her watch Harry Potter and the Chamber of Secrets. First the stork story and then the movie that was giving her nightmares. Were we awful parents?

She lifted her tear stained face to mine. "You promise?"

I swallowed hard. "I promise I'm not going anywhere." I didn't want to lie to her. But she believed in Santa Claus. She believed in the Easter Bunny. What would another white lie hurt? The logic was sound, but for some reason I felt an ache in my chest. She might lose me before she finds out that Santa isn't real. That there is no Easter Bunny. Would she resent me forever if I broke that promise? "I promise," I said again. God, I was an awful parent.

She sniffled through her nose. "Am I in trouble?"

"No." I kissed her forehead. "But you need to promise me you won't leave the house without a grown-up. And when you don't get what you want, you need to talk to us instead of screaming at the top of your lungs." I tried to give her a stern look, but it just made her smile.

"I promise."

I found a little solace in the fact that she would most likely not keep either of those promises either. Maybe she did get the lying thing from me. "Now, we're going to go finish catching fake butterflies and then have another slumber party. But this time you'll be having one with Soph and Axel." I sat up and pulled her into my lap.

She scrunched her mouth to the side, like she was thinking. "With my best friends?"

"That's right."

"Axel isn't one of my best friends. My best friends are you, Daddy, and Sophie."

"Scar." I frowned. Where had all this sass come from? "Why would you say that? You and Axel get along so well. Did something happen?"

"No, Mommy, he's my boyfriend. That's different. You can't be best friends with your boyfriend."

Oh my God. I couldn't help but smile. "Actually, you can be. Daddy's my best friend too."

"Really?"

"Mhm."

"What about Aunt Melissa? And Aunt Bee? And Aunt..."

"You can have more than one best friend. You just named a few yourself."

"Okay. Then Axel is my best friend and my boy-friend." She nodded her head like she was completely convinced of Axel's new title.

As we wandered out of her room, her little hand in mine, I really hoped that we could both keep our promises. I wanted her to stay safe. And I wanted to be there to witness it.

CHAPTER 18

Thursday

"James, what are you doing?" I put my hand out to block the lens of the video camera he was holding. I had just collapsed onto the couch after getting the least amount of butterflies in my net. And I was sweaty and gross from the exertion.

James continued filming me.

"Really, James." I held up my other hand, hoping it was enough.

"Scarlett, go tickle Mommy," he said.

I started laughing as soon as Scarlett jumped onto my lap. I laughed even harder when Axel hit me in the back of the head with a pillow and Sophie joined in on the tickling session. "Cut it out, you guys!" I said through fits of giggles. It took me several minutes to get all three kids back on the ground.

James stepped closer to me with the camera. What was he doing? I picked up one of the throw pillows and tossed it at him.

He laughed and caught it in his free hand before joining me on the couch. I grabbed the camera out of his hands and pointed the lens at him. "You thought it would be fun to film me not being able to breathe?" I was staring into the little monitor on the camera. I slowly zoomed up on his face.

"No," he said.

Something about the way he said no made me look back up at him instead of at the screen.

"I just wanted to capture your laughter on film."

The same chill that Scar had given me when she was talking about snakes ran back down my spine. Did everyone think I was doomed? I looked back down at the screen on the video camera. "Why?" I asked. For some reason not staring directly at him made my question easier. I watched his eyebrows lower on the screen. I watched a dark expression cross over his face, one that I had never seen before. Again I felt a chill down my spine.

"Because I wanted to capture my favorite sound. It's the only thing that truly makes me happy," he said slowly.

I looked back up at him. He wanted to capture my laughter on film. So that when I died, he could listen to it? I swallowed hard. I wasn't going to die. I was going to live long enough to see my daughter lie again. And to keep seeing him laugh. I looked down at the camera. "I don't think that's true, James," I said as I slowly got up off the couch. "Get 'em kids!"

The three kids launched themselves on James and started tickling him. His laughter rippled through the awkward silence his words had left. I looked down at the camera and smiled. That sound made me happy too. But so did Scarlett's laughter. And Soph's. And Axel's. Before I gave birth to my son, I'd need James to promise me what he currently refused to promise. I refused to go into labor before he promised me that he would keep living if I stopped. That he would keep laughing. That he would keep our children smiling.

I switched off the camera and joined in on the tickle fight.

**

My chest hurt again. The pain was keeping me up. Or maybe it was something else. I just had this eerie feeling ever since Scarlett had mentioned that a snake was going to take me away. I had read that book probably a dozen times and seen the movie half as many. The snake talked to Harry. Was Scar hearing voices?

James turned away from me in his sleep. I propped myself up on my elbow and stared at him. He was always so happy around Scar. Why did she fear that he wouldn't be a good father if I was gone? It didn't make any sense. I reached out and traced James' tattoo with my finger. The pulse. The reminder that his heart beat for me. But our family was three now, instead of two. And it was about to grow to four. He should have Scarlett's birth date under the date he met me. His heart beat for all of us. I let my fingers fall from his skin.

"Penny," he breathed out, like he felt the absence of my touch.

"Promise me." The words tumbled out of my mouth before I could stop them. But I had spoken them in a whisper. At first, I thought he may not have even heard me. Or maybe he just didn't remember what I was asking of him.

He rolled over so that he was facing me. "No." He looked completely alert, like he hadn't been sleeping at all. His mind must have been tossing and turning as much as mine.

"But Scarlett..."

"She looks just like you," he said, cutting me off. As if that was a reasonable response.

"She has your eyes." I reached out and gently touched the side of his face. "I don't understand your point."

He smiled and turned his head to kiss my palm. "I'm worried that if something happens to you, I won't be able to look at her."

"Don't say that." I turned his face back to mine.

He pressed his lips together. "I don't want to talk about this anymore."

Didn't we need to? "Today Scarlett said she thought a snake was going to take me away. It was like she could feel our fear. We're scaring her, and I don't think it's just the movie choices she's making."

"She's just a kid. Kid's say weird things. She doesn't understand what's going on."

"She has your eyes. And she also has your intelligence, James. I'm almost positive I wasn't as smart as she is when I was three and a half. She gets that from you. And she can tell something is off."

He lowered his eyebrows slightly but didn't say a word.

I was tempted to tell him what Scarlett had said about him. But I stayed silent too. It just reinforced the fact that he might not be the best father if something happened to me. I didn't want fear in Scarlett's heart and I didn't want it in James' either. "Do you think maybe there's a snake in her bedroom?"

James' smile returned. "The way Ellen cleans, she would have found it by now."

"That's true." My eyes drifted down to his smile. "I need you to stop doing things like recording my laughter on camera. You're putting bad vibes out into the world, and I don't want any part in it."

He laughed. "Bad vibes?"

"Remember, I'm a believer in fate. I'm a believer in vibes too. You knew what you were getting into when you married me." I lightly tapped on his chest.

"Yes. I certainly did." He leaned forward and placed a kiss against my lips. His hand slowly wandered down my back. "Why did you stop sleeping in my old t-shirts?" He kissed the side of my jaw.

I was wearing one of my silk nightgowns that matched my robe. "We stopped having sex in the middle of the night. I was worried it was because you thought I wasn't trying anymore."

He kissed the top of my shoulder. "We stopped having sex in the middle of the night because that little monster you created downstairs wears us out."

"That I created?" I laughed. "She's all you."

"I beg to differ. And, baby, I've always thought you looked better in my clothes than I did." He kissed between my breasts.

"Yeah, when I wasn't the size of a whale."

"I've said it before and I'll say it again. I think you're beautiful when you're pregnant." He kissed my stomach. "If it was up to me, you'd be pregnant all the time."

"You want me to have a huge stomach all the time?"

"It's just more of you to kiss."

I couldn't repress my smile. God, he was the sweetest man I had ever met. The feeling of his hands pushing the silk up my thighs made my smile grow.

"Being pregnant also makes you so fucking horny."

He was the sweetest, but he was also the sexiest and had the dirtiest mouth.

Oh God. And his mouth was currently devouring me. The feeling of his tongue inside of me made my back arch. His fingers against my clit made me stifle a moan. I closed my eyes as I let the sensation of his love start to overtake me. But suddenly his lips were gone.

"See," he whispered, his hot breath still close enough to make me even wetter. "So fucking horny," he said.

"Yes, okay? I'm horny." Damn it, why was he torturing me? "So how about you stop teasing me and give me your cock."

He raised his left eyebrow. "I do like when you tell me what you want. However, the answer is...no." He climbed off the bed.

What was he doing? *He isn't seriously going to leave me like this?* "Why do you always say no to me recently?"

"By saying no to you right now," he cupped his hands beneath my thighs and pulled me to the edge of the bed, "I'm going to have you screaming a whole lot of yes."

He knelt down in front of me. I closed my eyes, waiting to feel him once again, but instead I heard a soft knock on our bedroom door.

"You've got to be kidding me," James groaned.

I slid away from his hands, pulling my nightgown back in place. "I'll take care of it. Just, hold that thought, okay?" I quickly climbed out of bed. "And get under the covers to hide...that." I pointed to his erection that was extremely evident through his boxers.

James sighed and climbed back into bed.

I opened up the door. Axel was standing there with a worn puppy dog stuffed animal in his hand. He looked up at me with his big blue eyes.

"Aunt Penny?" He looked so sad. But at least he wasn't crying.

"Axel, sweetie, what's wrong?" I crouched down in front of him.

"I miss my mommy."

"I know. But you'll see her tomorrow morning right after you wake up." I pushed his hair away from his forehead. "How about we go back downstairs and I'll tuck you in again?"

"I want to say goodnight to my mommy."

"Sweetie, it's..." I looked over my shoulder at the alarm clock. "It's past 3 o'clock in the morning. Your parents are asleep."

His lip started to quiver and he began blinking faster. A single tear ran down his cheek.

"You know what?" I tapped the tip of his nose. "We can try to call them. How about that?"

He nodded furiously.

"I'll be right back, James," I said. I ignored his groan. He could wait five minutes. He hadn't seen Axel's face. If he had, he'd be doing the same thing as me. I stood up, grabbed Axel's hand that wasn't carrying his stuffed animal, and led him back out into the hall. When we reached the stairs he stopped and tugged on the bottom of my nightgown.

I looked down at him. He made the same grabbing motion Scarlett did when she wanted to be picked up. I wondered if he had learned it from her. "Okay, sweetie." I lifted him up and balanced him on my hip as I walked down the stairs. He was significantly heavier than Scarlett. He wasn't that much taller than her, but the kid was pretty solid. I grabbed my phone out of my purse and walked through the living room. Scarlett and Sophie were still sleeping peacefully. I made my way down the hall and opened up the door to my office.

"Here we go," I said and tried to set him on the floor.

"No," he said and wrapped his arms around my neck.

"Okay, I've got you." I kicked the door closed with my foot and made my way over to my desk chair so I could at least distribute some of his weight. I sat down with a sigh and clicked on Hailey's name in my phone. I didn't think anyone would answer. And now I was worried it was the wrong move. What if them not answering freaked Axel out. I pushed his blonde hair off his forehead again, the way Hailey always did for him. Hopefully the action would be soothing.

"Penny!" Tyler said. There was music blaring in the background. "What's up?"

"Tyler, hey. I thought you guys would be asleep."

"Nope. I had no idea how much Mason liked to party. I'm not sure we're going to get any sleep tonight."

"Is that Penny?" I heard Rob say in the background. "What is the beautiful goddess doing up in the middle of the night? Is James not pleasing you?"

God. I pressed Axel's head to my chest and put my hand over his other ear. It didn't even sound like Rob was near the phone. Which meant he was screaming those words in whatever club he was in. "Tyler, can I talk to Hailey? Axel's having trouble sleeping. He needs to hear her voice."

"Put him on. I'll talk to him."

I took my hand off Axel's ear and put the phone on speaker. "Here's your daddy."

Axel looked down at the phone. "Daddy?"

"Hey, Axel. Having trouble sleeping? Do you have Bert with you? You know that whenever you have Bert with you you're not alone."

Axel hugged his stuffed animal to his chest and leaned toward the phone. "Daddy, I want Mommy," Axel said into the receiver.

Tyler laughed. "Okay. Give me one second to get her." Loud music blared through the phone as Tyler went to find her. "Hails, Penny's on the phone..."

"Why is she calling you in the middle of the night?" I heard Hailey say on the other end, cutting off Tyler's words.

"She's calling you. You gave me your phone because you didn't want to bring a purse. Axel needs you."

"Oh."

I heard the phone exchanging hands.

"Axel, what are you doing up so late?" Hailey asked. "You should be in bed."

"Mommy!" Axel grabbed the phone out of my hand. "Mommy, can you come home? I need you."

"Axel, Mommy can't come home right now. You need to go back to sleep and I'll see you in the morning."

"But...but I need the song."

There was a pause on the other end and suddenly the music died away. "Hey, Penny, can you hear me?" Hailey asked.

"Yeah," I said.

"Can you turn it off of speaker?"

"Of course." I grabbed the phone and turned it off of speaker mode and then gave it back to Axel.

"Mommy?" He pressed the phone to his ear and moved so that he was sitting on my lap. In a second a huge smile crossed his face.

I watched him as his eyes slowly drooped. He shifted so that his head could rest against the desk. And in one minute flat he was fast asleep.

I removed the phone from Axel's hand, being careful not to wake him, and put it to my ear. I was just about to say hi to Hailey when I heard her singing. Her voice was beautiful. I had never heard her sing before.

"We ain't ever getting older," Hailey sang. "You look as good as the day I met you. I forget just why I left you, I was insane." The lyrics from Closer sounded just as good as when The Chainsmokers sang it.

"Hails," I said, cutting off the song, knowing perfectly well she didn't want me to hear it.

She immediately stopped singing. "Hey." She cleared her throat. "Did he fall asleep?"

"Yeah." I smiled at Axel who was now snoring softly. "Whatever you did was exactly what he needed."

"Good. I should probably get back. Thanks for watching him, Penny."

I looked down at my laptop that was right by Axel's head. "I'm not going to publish the book." I pushed his hair off his forehead again. He really did look just like his father.

There was silence on her end.

"You're one of my best friends, Hails. So is Tyler. And I'm not going to publish it. I'm so sorry that I even wrote it in the first place. Can we please just go back to the way things were?"

"Do you know why we named our son Axel?"

It took me a second to register the weird segue. "No."

"It's because I'm 99 percent sure that he was conceived on the side of the road in Texas. When I crashed Tyler's car and almost killed both of us. I bent the axle of his car."

I smiled. How had I never heard this story?

"Penny, I love my husband," the emotion in her voice made tears come to my eyes. "Of course it bothers me that you've slept with him."

"That's why I'm not going to write it. I'm sorry..."

"You didn't let me finish. It's not about that. I know you two are friends. We're all friends. That part of your relationship with him was so long ago. I've never resented you for that. I'm upset because you're going to write a book that involves him, but it's not going to be the whole truth. It's just...you have to get the story right. He wasn't in a good place when he met you. And I'm just worried that you're going to portray him wrong. What if Axel reads that one day? What if he reads it and doesn't get the whole truth?"

"I would never write something bad about Tyler. I love him. I love you. And I love your son. You're my family. I changed everyone's names and I'm using a pen name myself. No one will ever even know I wrote it."

"They will when it takes off."

I laughed. "I've been denied by 15 publishers. It's never going to take off."

There was another pause on her end. "One day I'm going to tell you the whole story from my perspective. How I met Tyler. How we were both lost without each other."

"I'd love to hear it."

"Good. I heard you promised him a redemption story after you're done writing about you and James. I just want to make sure you get all the details right. That you paint him honestly. I'm going to help you make it perfect."

"That sounds like a good plan." I breathed a sigh of relief. She wasn't upset with me. She was just worried that I was going to portray her husband wrong. But that was never going to happen. I knew what Tyler had been through. I knew the pain I had caused him. The pain he had suffered after losing his father and grandfather. I knew it. He wasn't just some frat boy I hooked up with once. He was one of my best friends. I respected him and I cared about him. He just wasn't the hero of my story. He was the hero of Hailey's.

"In the meantime, go tuck my son in."

I laughed. "Thanks, Hails. I love you, you know."

"Goodnight, Penny. I love you too."

"Goodnight." I looked down at Axel sleeping. "Good vibes," I said softly. "Everything is working out okay. Now let's tuck you back in." I lifted him up into my arms as I stood. We slowly made our way back out to the family room.

When I set him down on his sleeping bag he immediately opened his eyes and reached his hands back up to me.

"Axel, you need to go back to sleep."

"Can't I sleep with you? It's scary down here."

I looked at Scarlett and Soph sleeping soundlessly. There was nothing scary about this room. Unless Scarlett had a pet snake I wasn't aware of.

"Please, Aunt Penny." He gave me that same sad look he had when I opened up the bedroom door to find him.

"Okay, sweetie." I lifted him back into my arms and carried him upstairs. He was asleep before I even reached my bedroom door. It was tempting to turn back around and try to tuck him in again. But James had probably already fallen asleep. Besides, Axel looked so cute when he was sleeping. I didn't want to break my word to that innocent little face of his. I couldn't seem to say no to him.

"Finally..." James' voice died away as I walked back into the room with Axel in my arms. "What are you doing?" he whispered.

"He wants to sleep up here with us."

"Are you serious? Why? Go put him back downstairs."

"He's scared downstairs, James. He's just going to wake us up again in a few minutes if I do. It's fine." I set him down in the bed and crawled in next to him.

"Fucking Stevenses, always getting in the way."

"Language, James."

"He's asleep." He gestured to Axel, who was snoring peacefully.

"Still."

James sighed and rested his head back on the pillow. "So you want this scaredy pants to marry our daughter, huh?"

"He's three and a half."

"That's exactly what I've been saying."

I laughed. "No, I mean, he's scared because he's three and a half. He won't be scared when he's our age."

"Maybe."

"Scarlett referred to him as her boyfriend today."

James lowered his eyebrows.

"Don't look so serious. It's innocent and cute."

"Now. It won't be so innocent and cute when they're older. I like him now but in a few years I have a feeling I'm going to hate this kid."

I laughed. "You're impossible."

James pulled the covers up slightly to tuck them under Axel's chin. "When he's older I'm going to do my very best to do to him what he just did to me. It's my new mission."

"What are you talking about?"

"I'm going to be a total cock block."

"Language, James." But I couldn't help but laugh. I reached over and playfully shoved his arm.

He smiled.

"Fortunately we have a long time before that happens."

"Yeah." James pushed Axel's hair off his forehead like I had been doing. "And fortunately for him, he is a cute kid."

"You totally want a boy."

"It wouldn't be the worst thing that ever happened if it was a boy. That's as far as I'll go."

But all I heard was that he desperately wanted a baby boy. And I was positive that in two months time, I'd be giving him what he really wanted. A son.

CHAPTER 19

Friday

"You guys look terrible," I said as I put the tea kettle on the stove. Everyone else had picked up their kids and left. Bee and Mason, however, didn't look like they could move.

"It's his fault," Bee said and pointed at Mason. "For some reason he decided his last night as a single man meant no sleep."

Mason laughed. "You had fun."

"I didn't say it wasn't fun. But I have a hangover and in a few hours we need to go to our rehearsal. Penny, what are you doing?"

"Making tea."

"Why?"

I shrugged. "Because tea fixes everything."

"Is that what's going to happen to me once I get married? Will I automatically turn into an old lady?"

"Hey." I frowned.

"Sorry. Hangover." She pointed to her forehead.

"Penny's right," James said. "Tea really does fix everything."

I smiled at him. A couple years ago we had both decided to give up coffee in favor of tea. I had read some article about the soothing properties of herbal tea. And

James was always really supportive with my weird ideas. I did feel healthier though. Although, when I drank coffee I didn't have a heart murmur. I shook away the thought.

Bee and Mason just stared at us.

"Yeah, we're going to become old people when we get married," Mason said. "I knew this was a bad idea. Is there still time to back out?"

"Approximately 30 hours," Bee said. "But then there's the issue of me really loving you. Decisions, decisions."

Mason laughed. "Don't you dare get cold feet, babe. I was only kidding. And really we should be mad at Penny. This beach trip was her idea. It's her fault that we have hangovers."

I placed a cup of tea down in front of each of them. "You're both ridiculous. How was it my fault that you drank too much? I wasn't even there."

"Exactly," Bee said. "My matron of honor ditched me. I had to drink away my sorrows."

"You know I would have loved to have been there."

"I know." Bee reached out and squeezed my hand before taking a sip of the tea. "Damn, it's actually really good."

I smiled. "See."

Mason took a sip. "Eh," he said and set it aside. "How are you feeling anyway?"

James wrapped his arm around my back.

"I'm good. The doctor said no travel, so we decided to listen to him for once. I really am sorry that we couldn't come."

"James, the beaches down in Delaware are awesome," he said. "You were holding out on me all these years. We'll have to make a trip some other time after your kid pops out."

"Sounds like a plan," James said. "A nice family beach trip is definitely in order."

"Ugh, no. I meant without the kids."

James laughed.

"Uncle Mason!" Scarlett squealed as she ran into the kitchen. "Aunt Bee!"

Mason put his hand on his forehead, wincing from her voice due to his hangover. But he still managed to smile at her.

Scarlett stopped at the stool he was sitting on and pulled on his pant leg.

"Hey, kiddo." He lifted Scarlett up onto his lap. "What do you have there?"

For not liking kids, he really seemed to adore Scarlett.

"I drew a picture of your wedding." She put the piece of paper she was holding down on the countertop. "This is you," she said to Mason and pointed to a stick figure with brown hair and a black outfit. "And this is Aunt Bee." She pointed to the figure with long blonde hair and a white outfit. I smiled as I recognized myself standing next to Bee. And there was James, depicted holding Scarlett in his arms. Tyler and Hailey were standing with Axel. Rob and Daphne had their arms wrapped around Sophie . Matt looked just like Mason but he was standing next to Jen and Ian. Bee's friends Marie and Kendra were standing to one side with glasses in their hands, which I found particularly funny, because Scarlett only knew them from a few girls' nights I had thrown here. Marie's husband, Carter, was even in the picture. I smiled down at the image. It was the most beautiful stick figure drawing I had ever seen.

"Can we keep this, Scarlett?" Bee said. "I think it's going to be better than any pictures we get taken tomorrow."

"Mhm. It's your wedding pres... presen ... pre..." her voice trailed off and she frowned, unable to remember the word.

"Present?" Bee offered.

"Yes! Wedding present." She slid it toward Bee. "Mommy, can I put on my dress *now*?"

She had been asking me every half hour all morning.

"Not yet. The wedding isn't until tomorrow."

"But I don't mind sleeping in it. Pleeeeease?"

Bee laughed. "If you sleep in it, it will get all wrinkled. And you don't want that, do you?"

Scarlett scrunched her mouth to one side as she thought it over. "No. A flower girl shouldn't have a wrinkled dress. I'll go put it back."

"Put it back? Where did you put it?" I asked.

But Scarlett had already crawled down from Mason's lap and was running back up to her room.

"I promise I'm going to follow up on that," I said and sat down in one of the empty stools.

Bee laughed. "It's fine. The kids are going to be so cute tomorrow even if their outfits are wrinkled."

"Hopefully they'll be well behaved," James said.

"They'll be great, I know it."

I hoped that Bee was right. But I could just imagine Scarlett and Sophie throwing flower petals at each other instead of on the aisle. And after last night, Axel might just run off and try to find his mother instead of safely delivering the rings to the altar. It was good that the kids were coming to the rehearsal tonight. They needed all the practice they could get.

Bee set her empty mug down. "We really should get going. I'm in desperate need of a nap. Thank you for the tea, it actually made me feel a lot better."

"Of course. We'll see you tonight." I gave them each a hug goodbye and continued to sip my tea as James showed them out.

"Do you mind if I grade a few papers before we have to get ready for the rehearsal? I'm a little behind, especially since I'll be jet lagged after my flight tomorrow night."

"Yeah, that's fine. I need to get some work done anyway. What time is your flight?"

"I'm taking the red-eye. That way I won't have to cut out from the wedding early."

"Smart thinking."

He kissed my cheek. "Let me know when you're going to start hogging the bathroom so I can shower real quick beforehand."

I laughed. "You could just shower with me."

"I thought you'd never ask." He winked at me and grabbed a cup of tea before heading toward his study.

Now I definitely had something to look forward to. Just a few hours of work and I could get my favorite reward. I carried my tea to the library, sat down at my desk, and opened up my computer. Now that I had cleared the air with Hails, typing came easily to me. I poured my heart and soul out on the paper. I wiped away tears. I laughed. I immersed myself to the point where someone watching me probably would have thought I was suffering through emotional distress. I swallowed hard as I read the words that had once appeared in a note from James that I had typed up before I started writing the second book of my series. His notes were one of the reasons why fiction blurred with the truth. Because I couldn't change the words in his notes. They were perfect just the way they were.

"Only with you am I strong. Only with you am I good. Only with you am I whole."

I wiped away the tears on my cheeks. *That's not true.* He was strong. And good. And whole. He was all of those things without me. For some reason I couldn't move past those words. My two hours of productive writing had come to a grinding halt.

I put my hand on my chest. What if something did happen to me? How could I leave like this? With him thinking that was true. I pulled up a blank Word document and stared at the blinking cursor. James had a will. It was irresponsible for me not to. I'd feel better if I had one too. Not necessarily for leaving monetary things to people. I just needed James to remember my words. I needed to leave him with something. My eyes continued to focus on the blinking cursor. Scarlett's weird snake fears had gotten into my head. James' capturing my laughter had too. I needed to do this.

But for some reason my mind only got as far as writing "James" before shutting down. I said I didn't want any bad vibes. Making a will was the worst possible vibe. I closed my laptop and slowly stood up. *We don't need a will, do we baby boy?* I thought to myself as I wandered out of the library. Besides, what was the point of focusing on something terrible happening when my husband was waiting for me naked in the shower?

CHAPTER 20

Friday

"I don't remember it being this hot when I was getting married," I said and sat down next to Matt. Apparently the matron of honor and best man had everything perfect and were allowed to take a break. I knew that was code for Bee being scared I was going to die the night before their wedding.

"June isn't quite as bad as August," Matt said. "And you weren't this high up. Maybe that has something to do with it."

"That could be." I looked out at the expansive view of New York City. The ceremony was taking place at the top of a high rise. And not just any high rise. Mason and Bee owned the building and their successful Marketing firm, Bee Inspired Media Group, was located on the top floor. The ceremony was going to be beautiful. Just the view made it breathtaking and they hadn't even started decorating yet. The rehearsal dinner was being held in their office, which I totally understood. After all, Mason had named his firm after Bee in a grand gesture to win her back. It was so romantic.

"I almost made a point of saying you weren't pregnant during your wedding, but technically you were," Matt said, drawing me back to the present.

I laughed.

"But not nearly as pregnant. You couldn't tell or anything. Not that you can really tell now. I didn't mean..."

"It's fine," I said. "I know I'm huge." I put my hand on my stomach. "And uncomfortable. God, I swear I was this big at nine months for Scarlett."

"No, you were definitely bigger."

I laughed again. "Bigger? It's not possible."

"You still look good, though. You're always beautiful. And you make adorable babies." He nodded at Scarlett who had just decided to sit down in the middle of the aisle.

"Thanks, Matt." I watched as everyone else practiced standing there, waiting for Bee. "When do you think you'll settle down?"

"Me?" He whistled and put his arm on the back of the empty chair beside him. "I'm too young to get married. My big brother is only just tying the knot now. Give me some time, woman."

I shook my head. "I just think you're going to make a really good father."

"Just because I'm good at hanging out with your kid on occasion doesn't mean I'll be a good dad. But I do have the uncle thing down pretty well, don't I?" He flashed me a smile.

"Absolutely."

"Did you want me to go tell her to finish walking down the aisle?"

"You can certainly try."

He laughed and got up to join Scarlett. He leaned down and whispered something in her ear. Whatever he said to her seemed to work. She put her hand in his and let him walk her down the aisle. I looked at James standing on the right side of the altar. He was staring at our daughter with a smile on his face. That small action calmed me. *See, he's whole because of Scarlett too.* I looked down at my stomach. I wasn't really saying it to the baby. Maybe I was insane. Talking to oneself counted as insanity, right? *Damn it, stop talking to yourself!*

I took a deep breath and looked back up at James. All that mattered was that I wasn't going anywhere. I refused to. But I loved seeing him smile because of someone besides just me. He had so much love to give. So much more than he even realized.

Justin clapped his hands. Bee and Mason had opted to use the same wedding planner that we had. I'm pretty sure Justin was happy to be working with James again. I swear if Justin had his way, he would try to steal my husband.

"The sexy couple needs to get their rehearsal dinner on! And I'm starving! Chop chop!" Justin unceremoniously slapped Mason on the ass.

I tried to stifle my laugh at Mason's reaction. It looked like he wanted to punch Justin in the face. Maybe I didn't have to worry about Justin hitting on James after all. He seemed to be ogling Mason more now. Justin would probably try to steal Mason away before tomorrow. I smiled as I got to my feet. All preposterous thoughts. Mason and James were both certainly straight. No, I couldn't verify it for Mason first hand. But I had heard so many stories. I shook away the thought. His promiscuous past had nothing to do with the current events. I watched him and Bee exit the pavilion hand in hand, any trace of their hangovers completely gone. They were all smiles.

"How'd we look?" James asked as he put his hand out for me. Scarlett was balanced on his hip with a huge smile on her face.

"Did I do it right, Mommy?"

"You were both perfect. Just make sure to keep walking tomorrow, Scar." *Please don't ruin their wedding.* I grabbed James' hand and the three of us walked toward the elevators to head down to Mason and Bee's offices. My jaw probably dropped when I stepped off the elevator. I had visited them at work countless times. But they had completely transformed the floor. There were royal blue decorations everywhere. Even the wait staff and bartenders were wearing blue vests. It was worthy of the reception itself. Although, I was excited to see what they had planned for that if this was the rehearsal dinner. The reception tomorrow was being held at The Plaza. The ballroom was otherworldly. I had been there a few times for different functions with James. I smiled to myself. Actually, I was pretty sure the first time Bee and I had met was a gala at The Plaza. I still remembered how surprised I was to find out that Mason was dating someone. Times really did change.

Scarlett squirmed out of James' grip and ran off toward Axel.

"We really do make adorable babies," I said and smiled up at James.

"It must be the curly red hair."

I laughed. "Or the intense brown eyes. Or the perfect skin. Or that genius brain of yours." I tilted my face up toward his and he responded with the kiss I desired.

He pressed his forehead against mine. "I can't believe Mason is making me hang out with him all night. I hate spending the nights away from you. And with the trip tomorrow night..."

"It's okay. We made our bridal parties hang out with us all night, remember? The wedding is going to be so much fun. And when you get back from London I'll catch you up on whatever boring things you missed in between."

He smiled. "Not a day with you is boring."

"Trust me, sitting around all day is going to get terribly boring. I'm officially going on bed rest after the wedding."

"Finally. I'm going to go grab a drink. Do you want me to find you some fruit?"

"Do you even have to ask?"

He kissed my temple and wandered off toward the bar set up in the corner.

"Okay, that's enough standing," Daphne said and looped her arm through mine. "I've scoped out two seats over there with our names on them."

I laughed. It was like she had materialized behind me. "Not you too? Bee's already worried enough about me. And I'm fine. I don't know how many times I need to keep saying that. Besides, you're pregnant too."

"Just a normal boring pregnancy for me." Daphne pointed to the chair she had escorted me to. "Now sit. And yes, since I am pregnant, I'm sitting too." She plopped down in the chair beside me. "God, these shoes are killing me."

I looked down at the high heels she was wearing. "No one forced you to wear heels." I held up my leg to show off my flat sandals.

"But Rob loves when I wear heels."

I laughed.

"Don't you even start with me, Penny. You cater to James just as much as I cater to Rob. And they're both spoiled rotten."

"You know, I never really thought about it before, but you're right. They are spoiled, aren't they?"

"Extremely." Daphne took a sip of her water. "But they're also loving, caring, kind, thoughtful, romantic..." her voice trailed off. "We're so lucky."

I smiled as I spotted James in the crowd. He was holding a bowl of fruit in one hand and his drink in the other. Scarlett was pulling on his pant leg and he was in the middle of a conversation with Mason's father. James didn't look at all perturbed. He was still in his element despite the balancing act.

"We're the luckiest," I said.

Mr. Caldwell picked up Scarlett and all three of them started walking toward us. "How are the Hunter women doing tonight?" he asked.

"Good," Scarlett said.

He laughed and set her down beside me. "Beautiful as always, my dear," he said as he leaned down and kissed my cheek. "As lovely as ever," he said to Daphne and kissed her cheek too.

"Your fruit, madam," James said with a smile and a bow as he handed me the bowl he was carrying. "Can I get you something, Daphne?" He ran his hand through his hair.

"I'm okay, Rob is in search of pickles."

Mr. Caldwell laughed. "Oh, I remember the pickle phase. My wife couldn't get enough of them when she was seven months along either. I saw some back there. Let me go get you a plate."

"Oh, I'm sure Rob will find them," Daphne said.

"It's no problem at all. I'll be back." He smiled at us and then turned to James. He patted him on the back and gave him a much more tight-lipped smile and a nod.

That was odd. I was about to say something but James broke the awkward silence by kneeling down to talk to Scarlett.

"Say goodnight to Mommy. And we'll go meet Ellen, okay?"

Scarlett made the grabbing motion for me to pick her up. I lifted her into my arms.

"Goodnight, Mommy!" Scarlett said.

"Goodnight, Scar." I placed a kiss on her forehead. "Be good for Ellen, okay?" I gave her a tight hug.

"I will, Mommy," she said as she hugged me back. And then in my ear she whispered, "Be careful of the snake."

The now familiar chills ran down my spine. Why did she keep talking about snakes? "Scar, we talked about this. There is no snake. It was just a movie."

"Just because you can't see it doesn't mean it's not there, Mommy." She squeezed me once more and then jumped off my lap. "I'm ready to go!"

"Okay, pumpkin." James lifted her up. "I'll be right back."

"I should probably go find Sophie so I can say goodnight," Daphne said. "And I need to thank Ellen again for watching her tonight. That was so sweet of her to offer. Save my seat?"

"Mhm." But I wasn't focused on her words at all. Scarlett's warning was going round and round in my head. She was starting to scare me. I needed to search our house for snakes. Or at least tell Ellen to be on the lookout when she cleaned. I ran my hand across my stomach. *When you can talk, don't say creepy things like that to me, baby boy.*

I plopped a strawberry in my mouth. Screw bananas. Strawberries were now my favorite thing. I closed my eyes to relish the taste on my tongue.

***

"Baby," James whispered. "It's time to get going."

His scent was the only thing my mind seemed to register. I slowly opened my eyes and saw his smiling face. "But we only just got here."

He leaned forward and tucked a loose strand of hair behind my ear. "You fell asleep."

"No I didn't. I just closed my eyes for a second..." my voice trailed off as I looked around the almost empty room. "Oh, I missed everything. The toasts. I was going to take pictures. How could you let me sleep through the whole thing?" The real question was how could I have slept through the whole thing. What was I, eighty years old?

"The photographer handled the pictures. And you've heard plenty of Mr. Caldwell's toasts. The real fun is tomorrow night anyway."

I sighed. "I guess. God, I can't believe you let me miss it though." I swatted his arm.

"I think you needed your rest. Especially since you're going to be staying up all night."

"Isn't that the truth," Jen said, butting into our conversation. She practically pushed James out of her way. "Time to go, sis."

"Give us a minute, Jen," James said without looking at her.

"You have exactly one minute. We're all waiting by the door, Penny."

"I'll be right there," I said.

James put his arm behind me on the chair. "I'm sure I can get us out of the shenanigans tonight if you want."

"I already missed the bachelorette party. And the rehearsal dinner. I can't miss tonight."

He frowned. "Until tomorrow then."

"Don't look so glum." I ran my fingers along the side of his jaw. "It'll just make our reunion that much better."

"I know, I'm just going to miss my girls." He put his hand on my stomach and leaned in to kiss me.

I didn't even care that he was back to his old ways of wishing for a girl. I was much too focused on his lips. And the fact that I really wanted to give in to spending the night with him instead.

He groaned into my mouth. "Don't kiss me like that when you have no intention of sealing the deal."

I laughed. "I love you."

"I love you too, Penny. Call me if you need anything tonight."

CHAPTER 21

Friday

"On a scale of one to ten, how terrified are you of tomorrow?" Jen asked.

"An eleven," Bee said and laughed.

"What? Why? It's not like Mason is going to not show up."

"Don't even joke about that." Bee sighed and leaned her head against the back of the couch.

"I've known him since he was born. If there was ever someone set in his decisions, it's Mason. He's showing up."

"I always forget that you knew the Caldwells growing up," I said. "You must have so many stories." I took a sip of my tea as Jen downed another shot.

"Not really," she said. "But Matt is great in bed."

"Wait, you've slept with Matt?"

"Hasn't everyone?"

"Umm...obviously not," Hailey said. "We were all dating someone when we met him."

"Seriously. None of you have slept with Matt? I kind of just assumed you all had."

Bee laughed. "Of course I haven't slept with him. I'm marrying his brother."

"And I'm married to your brother," I said.

"Ditto." Daphne tapped her teacup against mine.

"But it's Matt," Jen protested. "How could you guys not sleep with Matt before you got married? It's like a rite of passage."

"Because Rob's a perfect ten in bed," Daphne said.

"And so is James," I added.

"Stop." Jen put her hands over her ears. "Those are my brothers that you're talking about."

Daphne and I both laughed.

"Can we go back to talking about you sleeping with Matt, though?" I asked. "When did you do it? Was it just once?"

"No, a bunch of times." Jen waved her hand dismissively.

"Isn't there like a seven year age difference there?" Daphne asked.

"Age is just a number," I said.

"Mhm, Penny." Jen rolled her eyes. "We all know that you're much too young for my brother. We get it."

I shrugged. "Sorry I brought it up. Tell us the story about you and Matt. Spit it out."

Jen laughed. "There's nothing to tell. When I came home from college for summer break one year, our pool was being cleaned or something. So I went over to the Caldwell's instead. And it was just Matt and me hanging out. My boyfriend had just dumped me and I was terribly upset. Matt made me feel a whole lot better. Over and over and over again. It was probably the thrill of doing it right there in the open. His parents or Mason could have come home at any moment. It was so fun being young."

"Wait," Bee said. "So it was just like a one day thing with tons of sex?"

"Oh, no, it was the whole summer. I'm pretty sure we banged on every surface in their house. God, it was so much fun."

"So what happened?" I asked. "Why wasn't it more than just sex?"

"The guy is a brick wall. He fucks. He has no emotion. He uses your body for pleasure. It's kind of exhilarating."

"Says the woman betrothed to someone else."

"Well, yeah. I wanted love. Ian's my other half. Matt was just like...a sex slave. Besides, our parents would have been thrilled if we ended up together. Despite the age difference. And just that fact alone was a total boner killer. I mean, not literally. I'm pretty sure Matt is at attention 24/7."

I laughed. "A summer fling with you and Matt? I just can't imagine it. Wait, hold on a second. I could have sworn that when we tried to set him up with Melissa that you said he wasn't a..." I bit the inside of my lip, trying to think of the proper phrase.

"A mindless sex robot," Bee said with a laugh.

"Yes! Jen, you said he wasn't a mindless sex robot!" I emphasized the word wasn't.

Jen shrugged her shoulders. "Well, I lied. I thought they'd be cute together."

"Jen!"

"What? I did her a favor. She'd never be mad at me for helping her experience the perfect specimen in bed."

"A favor? You called him an unemotional brick wall that uses your body for pleasure."

"Are we talking about Matt?" Kendra asked as her and Marie walked into the suite. "God, he's a fucking stallion in bed."

"Finally!" Jen said. "I knew I couldn't be the only one who slept with him. He's amazing, right?"

"I get goose bumps just thinking about it. We got more tequila!" She and Marie lifted the bottles they were carrying.

"Tequila!" Bee shouted. "Time for shots."

"I really don't get it," I said. "Matt has always been so sweet to me. And to Scarlett. He's not an unemotional brick wall at all."

"Yeah, around you," Bee said and sat back down with a shot glass in her hand.

"What is that supposed to mean?"

"You're the girl that everyone falls for before they find the one."

"What? That is so not true."

Bee looked around for help, but no one seemed eager to assist her. "Hear me out," she said. "Take Mason for instance."

"Mason never, ever, ever had a crush on me. We were always just friends. Through James. My husband. You know that."

Bee laughed. "Maybe he didn't have a crush on you per se. But it was because of your relationship with James that he realized he was ready to settle down with me. He loved the idea of you."

"That's very different."

"No, Bee has a point," Daphne said. "Rob was the same way. Joke around about it as much as you want, but I really think he used to have a thing for you. And he looks up to James. Maybe it was the idea of you thing like Bee said."

"That's completely ridiculous," I said. "Rob and I just have a joking relationship. He was never in love with me. We're always kidding around."

"That's another point," Jen said. "You are kind of one of the guys. You drink beer with them and play video games. Watch football games. Way more than the rest of us do."

"But I..."

"And Tyler actually was in love with you," Hails said with a laugh. "I mean, you were all there for that. I caught the end of the show, but he was pretty torn up after you married James. He had it the worst of anyone."

"That's true," Bee said. "I had to witness that fatal love story for years. But then he met Hails. And Rob met Daphne. And Mason met me."

"Ugh. You're all ridiculous" I took a sip of my tea. "God, I wish this was stronger. Just because you guys have a few examples..."

"Honey child, three examples is pretty solid evidence if you ask me," Kendra said. "All of their spouses have basically mind fucked you."

"Don't be gross," Marie said and swatted her friend's arm.

I shook my head. "So you all seriously think Matt is in love with me?" I laughed. "So not true. You're all crazy."

"He's at least in love with the idea of you," Bee said.

"Haven't you noticed the way he looks at you?" Jen asked. "He used to look at me like that before he fucked me in his parents' pool."

"Okay. Enough talk about this," I said. "He's sweet and kind and his mind is not at all in the gutter. Plus I'm a whale." I gestured to my stomach. "And now you guys freaked me out. The next time he asks to touch my stomach I'm going to think he's hitting on me."

"He probably is," Jen said. "We already verified that he's super kinky."

"Gross. I'll reiterate the fact that I'm happily married...to your brother! And seven months pregnant. And you know what? James fell in love with me. So by default I couldn't possibly be the girl that everyone falls for before they find the one."

Jen shrugged. "Fine. But I do agree with everyone else. Don't sweat it though. Matt will find his person soon enough and stop hitting on you."

"He hasn't been hitting on me."

"Mhm."

The conversation made me realize that my friends were all insane. Matt in love with me? Utter nonsense. But I couldn't really be upset with them. It all meant that James and I had a relationship worth emulating. That's basically what they meant. I bit the inside of my lip. But Mason did go from a man-whore to a loving boyfriend within a few years of meeting me. And so did Rob. Tyler had actually told me that he loved me several times, including right before leaving on his road trip where he fell in love with Hailey. Did they have a point?

I shook away the thought. At least James hadn't found someone better after me. I didn't even want to think about that happening. I swallowed hard. So why was I trying to get him to promise me he'd do just that if I died? *God, I'm making my crazy friends right!* "Excuse me for one sec," I said.

"You okay, big momma?" Bee asked.

I laughed. "I'm fine. I just need to use the restroom." I quickly retreated to the hotel bathroom and locked the door. Panic had settled into my stomach. It almost felt like I was going to puke. I pulled out my phone and clicked on James' name. Maybe I'd calm down once I heard his voice.

"Hey, baby," James said. There was laughter in the background on his end.

"James?" My voice sounded desperate. Any hope I had of calming down was gone. Hearing his voice just got me more upset. *I was his one, wasn't I?*

"Penny, what's wrong? Are your ankles swelling?"

"No. I just...I don't want you to make that promise."

"What promise?"

"The promise to move on from me. The promise that I've been nagging you about."

"I already told you no, baby."

A stifled laugh escaped my throat. "James, am I the girl that everyone falls for before they find the one? If that's true then your one is still out there. And it's not me. And Scarlett's right and a snake is going to kill me. And then you're going to find your soul mate and replace me."

There was silence on the other end.

"James?" I croaked into the phone. *Oh God, it was all true.* "James?" I placed my forehead in my hand.

"Penny?" Jen said and knocked on the door. "Is it true that your pregnancy hormones have taken over your mind and you're crying in there?"

I sniffled. "Maybe."

"Okay, you can let him in!" Jen shouted.

"What are you talking about?" I asked and grabbed a tissue.

A few seconds later there was another knock on the door. "Penny, can you let me in?" James said from the other side.

I quickly unlocked the door. My knight in shining armor was standing there with a worried expression on his face. His chest was rising and falling like he had run through the hotel to find me. He shoved his phone into his pocket, joined me in the bathroom, and locked the door.

"Baby, what's wrong?" He put his hands on either side of my face and brushed away my tears with his thumbs.

"Jen was right, it's just my hormones."

He gripped my face a little harder. "Talk to me."

"We were discussing the fact that I'm the girl that everyone falls for before they find the one. Because Mason found Bee after meeting me. Rob found Daphne. Tyler found Hails. And now apparently Matt has a crush on me."

"What is this about Matt having a crush on you?"

"Nothing. It's all nonsense. I just...what if someone else is your one?" My tears started falling again.

He shook his head as he wiped my tears away with his thumbs again. "Do you remember what you said to me in your vows?"

"Which part? I feel like I rambled."

He smiled. "This is all consuming, terrifying, heart stopping love. It's the greatest kind of love." He let one of his hands fall from my cheek and he pressed it against my chest. "You put words to my own thoughts when you said that. You're my one, baby." He pressed his forehead against mine. "My everything. There is no moving on after you. There is no me without you."

I closed my eyes and breathed in his exhales. "Scarlett keeps saying a snake is going to get me."

"I'll talk to her about it tomorrow. You won't hear another mention of snakes." He didn't move away from me. It was like my breaths were the oxygen his lungs needed.

"I'm sorry I freaked out."

"I'm just glad you gave me an excuse to come see you. But can we please back up for a second to the thing about Matt being in love with you?"

"It's really nothing. My friends are insane."

He was quiet for a moment. "Let's get our own room tonight." He ran the tip of his nose down the length of mine. "Let me help calm you down."

God that was tempting. "You already have."

"And your ankles are okay?" He held me at arm's length as he inspected me. "Nothing hurts?"

"I'm okay. I think I just missed you. And as your sister so graciously mentioned, I have crazy pregnancy hormones." I shrugged my shoulders.

He pulled me back in and hugged me tight. "Maybe we can just pretend you're still upset for a few more minutes so I don't have to leave yet?"

"That sounds like a good idea." I listened to the constant thud of his heart beating. Yesterday I was upset that he claimed his heart only beat for me. But today I didn't want it any other way. I didn't care how selfish that was. He was mine and I was his.

CHAPTER 22

Saturday

I cringed. All morning long, the baby had been kicking me. It was like he was eager to start dancing at the reception. *Calm down.*

"Are you nervous?" Matt asked.

"What?"

He smiled down at me. "You look really nervous."

"Ask me that again before I give my speech," I said. "Right now, my baby is just kicking me nonstop."

"May I?"

I nodded. I didn't care what my friends said. Matt wasn't in love with the idea of me. And he certainly wasn't in love with me.

Matt placed his hand on my stomach. "Maybe he's going to be a soccer star."

I laughed. "Definitely a striker."

"Does it hurt? When he kicks?"

"A little."

"Sorry, Penny." His eyes met mine again.

There was something so warm in them. He wasn't an unemotional brick wall. He was kind and sweet. Jen was just wrong about him. Maybe she made her whole story up.

"You really are going to be a great father one day," I said.

"Why do you keep saying that to me?"

"Because I think it's true."

"Penny, I'm not even dating anyone. That seems like a long way off."

"You should go on one of those dating sites."

He laughed. "I don't think so."

"Why not?"

"Because I'm happy the way things are."

"Can I steal my wife for a second?" James asked and pulled me away from Matt.

I hadn't even heard him approach us. "James, we're walking down the aisle in a minute. Justin is going to be pissed that we're out of formation."

He pulled me across the corridor. "He was touching you."

I laughed. "He wanted to feel the baby kick. Our baby." I gestured back and forth between us. "You're being ridiculous."

"Well, I also caught the end of your conversation. He said he was happy the way things were. With his hands on you."

"Seriously, James? You're jealous of Matt? There's nothing to be upset about. He's one of your best friends."

"Exactly. He's one of my best friends. So what the fuck is he doing hitting on you?"

I shook my head. "James?"

He didn't acknowledge me. Instead he was staring daggers at Matt.

"James. Hey." I grabbed his face and turned it back to me. "If you want to assume the worst about him, fine. I can't change your mind. But that doesn't mean there's anything to worry about. You know that my heart is yours."

"Don't hang out with him while I'm gone."

I laughed. "He's going to be at the brunch tomorrow. Do you seriously want me to ignore him?"

"Yes."

"You're impossible."

"And stop letting him feel the baby kick. If he touches your stomach one more time I'm going to punch him in the face." He put his hand on my belly. "This is mine."

"Of course it's yours. Every piece of me is yours."

"Then don't let anyone else touch what's mine."

It had been a long time since James had been jealous of anyone. Really, the last person he was jealous of was probably Tyler. Or maybe it was of one of my fellow interns when I had my brief stint at Hunter Tech.

"Okay. I'll try to be better about people being excited about our child's birth."

James smiled. "You're making fun of me?"

"Just a little. You're walking down the aisle with Marie. She's married. Should I be worried about you hitting on her?"

He put his hand on the back of my neck and pulled me in for a kiss. And not just a peck. His tongue parted my lips. His free hand dipped slightly below my lower back. He was kissing me like he was about to fuck me against the wall behind us. I knew it was a show. A show for Matt and anyone else watching. A reminder that I was his. But I loved it despite the message. I was swept up in him.

"Places, people!" Justin yelled. "Please go stand where you belong, love birds." He snapped his fingers at us.

"You're mine, Penny," James whispered as our lips parted.

I nodded because that was all I seemed capable of doing.

He walked me back over to Matt, kissed my cheek, and joined Marie behind me.

Matt was quiet as we stood there. It was like he could tell that James was mad at him. The atmosphere was tense. It didn't fit the mood of the wedding.

"Matron of honor and best man are up!" Justin said. "Remember, walk slow. And smile," he said to Matt. "It's a wedding." He grabbed my arm, draped it over Matt's, and gently pushed us forward.

Matt glanced behind him and then turned back to me. "Is James mad at me?"

I laughed awkwardly. "No. Why would you think that?"

"Last night he kept punching me in the arm really hard whenever he made a joke. There's a bruise on my bicep. And now he's staring at me like he wants to aim those punches at my face."

"What? That's ridiculous."

He put his hand on top of mine. "Penny. You're the worst liar in the history of liars. Just tell me."

"Honestly?" We stepped out onto the roof and slowly began walking down the aisle.

"Yes, honestly."

I shrugged my shoulders. I was hoping he'd drop it when we started walking down the aisle. "Jen was talking last night about how I'm the girl that people fall for before they find the one. Or, they fall in love with the idea of me or something. Mason, Tyler, Rob..." I let my voice trail off. "It's silly really. Forget I said anything."

"James thinks that I'm in love with you?"

We were nearing the end of the aisle. "I told you it was silly."

He didn't say anything.

"Right?"

He squeezed my hand before dropping his arm. "Right."

I awkwardly stood there for a moment before walking over to Bee's side of the arch. I glanced at him standing on the opposite side. He smiled and I immediately looked away. His answer hadn't really seemed sincere. But I had a feeling he was messing with me. He probably thought it would be fun to tease me forever now. I had certainly given him ammo. Why had I told him I thought he had a crush on me?

James was walking down the aisle now, Marie's hand on his arm. I didn't question the two of them together. Why did everyone have to put weird ideas in my head about Matt? Now I was starting to feel uncomfortable around him.

Ow. I put my hand on my stomach. *We'll be dancing soon enough, sweet boy.*

James lowered his eyebrows slightly as they drew closer.

I gave him an encouraging smile. There was no need for him to worry. I watched as he parted from Marie. My eyes automatically gravitated to his butt. God, I loved his ass in a tuxedo. The sight practically made me drool.

He winked at me when he turned to stand alongside Matt. As if he knew that I had been inappropriately staring. I blushed and looked away.

Axel confidently walked down the aisle after Hailey and Tyler, who were lucky enough to be paired together. Maybe he wasn't nervous because his parents were in eyesight. Everyone smiled at him and he smiled back. He even stopped and waved at people with the pillow he was holding. Luckily the rings were tied down to it. Scarlett and Sophie both skipped down the aisle behind him, throwing petals mostly at the guests instead of on the ground. But everyone seemed to enjoy it. She really was adorable. Of course, I was biased, but it wasn't just her cute little face that made her so wonderful. She had the carefree attitude I never had as a child.

The music changed and everyone stood as Bee appeared. Her parents were divorced and her father and mother had both opted to walk her down the aisle. Bee's eyes were already filled with tears. This wedding had been a long time coming. Damn it, she was going to make me cry too. She looked absolutely gorgeous. She had gone for a ball gown dress that accentuated her small waist. Her long, loose curls blew in the wind. And the backdrop of the city sunset made her blonde hair almost glow like a halo. I glanced at Mason. It looked like he might even cry. They truly were perfect together.

I let my eyes wander back to James. He was staring at me so intently. I swallowed hard. Suddenly, it felt like it was us. Like we were back at our wedding. His eyes didn't stray from mine for even a second. In a lot of ways we had been robbed of our fairytale wedding. At least, the wedding night and honeymoon. But I wasn't bitter at all. I was just grateful that he was here with me.

I dropped his gaze as Bee handed me her bouquet. When I looked back up at him, his expression had changed. It wasn't one of love anymore. He was looking at me in *that* way. The way that made my knees weak. The way he looked at me right before he fucked me hard.

It was difficult to pay attention to Bee and Mason's vows. It was hard to pay attention to anything when he looked at me like that. Before I even realized it, the ceremony was over, and James was grabbing my hand, pulling me away from the rest of the bridal party.

"I love you, Penny. I love you with everything that I am." His lips crashed against mine.

I love you. I loved that carnal need of his. I loved that it matched my own.

"Ow, ow!" Rob said from behind us. "You'd think you two were the ones that just got hitched."

James laughed and released me from his grip. "Don't you have a wife you can go bother?"

Rob waved his hand through the air. "Nothing I do bothers Daphne."

"Is that so?" Daphne said and caught his hand. "You guys, they want to take a few pictures back up at the altar."

James looped his arm behind my back. "Once the dancing starts, do you think we could sneak away for a few minutes?"

I smiled up at him. "Did you think I'd let you fly across the Atlantic without a proper sendoff?"

"I hoped that would be your answer."

"Daddy!" Scarlett called and ran over to us.

He leaned down and picked her up.

She giggled as he peppered her face with kisses.

"You were perfect, pumpkin," he said.

"I know."

She was also way more confident than I was at her age. Hell, maybe she was more confident than I was now.

CHAPTER 23

Saturday

I cleared my throat for the second time. My hands were shaking so badly, I knew it must look like I was about to drop the mic. Matt had killed his speech. He had the whole place in fits of laughter. How was I supposed to top that? James put his hand on my knee. I swallowed down the lump in my throat. Somehow knowing that he was beside me calmed me down. I took a deep breath. *You can do this.* "Bee, you were the first real friend I made in New York. Well, besides for James' friends, which included your new husband. I never thought someone would be able to tame him."

A few people laughed, including Mason and Bee.

"But seriously, Bee. I struggled moving to New York, leaving everyone I knew back home. But you made me feel like I was accepted here. The big bad city terrified me. Moving here from a small town in Delaware was quite the adjustment. And you understood that too. You were a piece of home. You were open and kind and warm. Unlike most of the people here."

More people seemed to laugh at that joke. My hand stopped shaking so dramatically.

"You were basically me except that you were totally killing it."

"That's so not true, Penny!" Bee said with a laugh.

"It is true! You made me realize that I could belong here too." I put my hand on my chest. "And I'm so, so grateful to you for that."

Bee gave me a tight-lipped smile. It looked like she might start crying again.

"I love you, Bee. I love you both. You're two of my best friends. I can't believe two of the nicest people I've ever met were able to find love with one another. I think you're perfect together. And I truly believe that you can make it through anything. Your love is timeless. You're timeless." I held up my glass. "To the happy couple."

There was a smattering of applause. Not nearly as loud as what Matt had gotten, but I'd take it. I quickly sat back down.

James put his arm around my shoulders. "You were amazing."

I laughed. "I wasn't." I turned my head toward his. "But thank you. I still can't believe how nervous I get when I have to speak in front of a crowd. You were a terrible Comm professor."

He pulled me a little closer. "If I recall, you never finished my class. Maybe if you had focused a little more on my lectures and less on my body..."

I elbowed him in the side and he laughed. "You're so full of yourself. I did pay attention. I took excellent notes."

He kissed my temple as he reached for his glass of champagne. He raised it slightly. "Cheers to you actually not paying attention at all." He brought the glass to his lips.

I laughed. "You know, if you read my book, you'd know I paid attention. Mostly."

"I'll read it as soon as I'm back from London."

I rested my head on his shoulder. "I can't wait for you to get back."

"Baby, I haven't even left yet." He set down his glass. "Come with me." He was about to stand up but I put my hand on his knee.

"It's the middle of dinner."

"Your point is?" He raised his left eyebrow.

"We have to watch Scarlett. And everyone would notice if we were missing from our table for a lengthy period of time."

"My father is currently watching Scarlett." James nodded to the table next to ours. Scar was perched on James' father's knee, making her chicken nuggets walk through his fancy entree. "And no one gives a shit what we do. Except me. Because I want to be doing you."

"How eloquent, professor."

He smiled and leaned forward slightly so that his lips brushed against my ear. "Now come with me. It's not a request, Miss Taylor." He stood up and put his hand out for me.

Not a request. I gulped. I had been right about his stare earlier. He did want to fuck me. I glanced back at the newlyweds. They seemed perfectly content. I slipped my hand into James' and let him help me to my feet. Why he desired to fuck me when I looked like an elephant didn't really matter. I wanted him to.

"I thought we could visit your hotel room for the evening," James said as we walked out of the ballroom. "That way the sheets will smell like me."

I smiled up at him. He knew how much I hated sleeping without him. Especially when I was away from home. Normally I'd snuggle up with one of his t-shirts and finally be able to drift to sleep. But that wasn't exactly possible in a hotel room. He was so thoughtful. He held my hand a little tighter as we walked over to the elevators.

"Actually, James, do you mind if I use the restroom real quick?" We had just started to walk past the women's room.

"Can't you wait until we get to the room?"

I put my free hand on my stomach. "Not really. I think he's kicking my bladder. I'll just be a sec."

He smiled and dropped my hand. "I'll be waiting."

I pushed open the door to the restroom. It was almost as elegant as the ballroom. It was all gold, marble, and mirrors galore. I walked into one of the stalls. I was just smoothing my dress back into place when I heard someone else walk into the restroom. Some women were talkative around strangers. But I definitely wasn't one of those women. I kept my head down as I stepped out of the stall. My eyes stayed focused on washing my hands. I turned off the faucet.

"Penny."

I nearly jumped out of my skin. "James what are you doing in here?" I hissed.

"You're acting like we've never had sex in a bathroom before." He kissed the side of my neck.

"Well, we haven't in a place like The Plaza."

"Good. It'll be that much more memorable." He pushed down one of the straps on my dress and kissed my shoulder.

I laughed. "We can't." I grabbed his wandering hands. "It's the women's restroom. There will be a line in a matter of seconds if we don't get out of here." I tried to step around him.

He caught my wrist. "Fair point."

Really? I was surprised when he pulled me toward the exit. I was almost disappointed as we walked back into the hall. Normally he'd tell me I was wrong. And then fuck me even harder for going against his word. I remembered the last few months that I had been pregnant with Scar, though. James had been more careful with me. Not less passionate, just less domineering. Were we already to that point in this pregnancy? I wasn't sure I wanted to be. I loved making love to him. But I liked when he was rough with me too.

"The men's bathroom is a much better option," he said with a grin and pulled us through the next door in the hall.

"James!" I laughed as he locked the door. "And there won't be a line for the men?"

"I don't really care." He pushed my back against the door. "Let them wait." He grabbed the hem of my dress and pulled it up my thighs. "Let them hear you scream my name." He gripped the side of my thong.

I squealed as the elastic bit my hip when he tore the fabric in two.

"Let them know you're mine." He thrust his finger inside of me.

Oh God. I guess he wasn't being gentle with me yet. My fingertips dug into the back of his tuxedo jacket as his thumb slowly circled my clit. "James, I need you inside of me."

He kissed the side of my neck. "Baby, I am inside of you." He slipped another finger in beside his first and began pumping his hand faster.

Fuck. "That's not...I want more."

He kissed my neck harder, gently sucking. I knew he was giving me a hickey. I knew and I didn't care. Sometimes he did that before he had to leave on business. It was like he was branding me. Leaving his mark for the world to see. Like my pregnant stomach wasn't enough evidence. But I didn't mind. I liked when he was territorial. I liked that he wanted the world to know I was his and his alone.

"I need you." My voice was desperate and needy. "Please."

His fingers slid out of me and he put them into his mouth. "The sweetest taste on earth."

"James." God, why was he torturing me?

He stared at me as he unhooked his belt. "Get on your knees, Penny."

No, he definitely wasn't done being rough with me yet. I looked down at the ground. Normally I wouldn't want to kneel in a public restroom, but we were in The Plaza for goodness sakes. If there was ever a restroom to fuck in, this was the one.

"Now."

I slowly got to my knees.

"I'm going to tell you exactly what I want. Exactly what I want to remember when I'm away. Exactly what

I'm going to jerk off to in my hotel room when I'm missing you."

I swallowed hard.

"And then you can tell me exactly what you want. Deal?"

He didn't have to ask. I wanted exactly the same thing he did. "Deal."

He reached out and lowered my bottom lip with his thumb. "I want to picture myself fucking your beautiful face when we're apart. Now put those perfect lips around my cock."

I leaned forward and brought his tip to my mouth. He didn't ask me to lick it. He didn't really ask for any foreplay. So I put my lips around him and took him all the way to the back of my throat.

"Fuck," he said with a groan.

I heard him press his palm against the door above me. I moaned as he gripped my hair in his fist.

"Fuck, just like that, baby."

Even though his hand was in my hair, he wasn't taking control. He wasn't guiding me at all. I knew what he liked. I knew what made him lose control.

"Are you ready to tell me what you want?" he asked through gritted teeth. "Because I'm about ten seconds away from ending this way too soon."

I knew what I wanted. And I wanted to taste him. I wanted to swallow every ounce of his cum. I quickened my pace.

He gripped my hair a little tighter and pulled his dick out of my mouth. "I asked what you wanted, baby." He pulled me to my feet. "Do you want my fingers again? My tongue? My cock?"

I watched his chest rise and fall. "I want the same thing you want." I turned away from him, put my hands on the bathroom door, and arched my back. He was right. I didn't want to taste him. I wanted to feel him. I wanted him to fill me. That was the feeling I wanted to think about while he was gone.

"This feels a lot more like something I'd ask for." He ran his fingers up the backs of my thighs and cupped my ass cheeks in his hands.

He'd start being gentle with me soon enough. Right now, I just wanted everything he'd give me. "Use me for your pleasure. Fuck me so hard that I can't walk."

"God, how did I get so lucky?" He grabbed my hips and thrust into me hard.

Yes.

"You're so fucking tight, baby. It's like your pussy was made for my cock."

My hands pressed harder against the wooden door. "James."

He gripped my hips even tighter as he picked up his pace. "Tell me if I'm hurting you."

Technically he was hurting me. But God, it was a good kind of hurt. The kind of hurt that had toppled into pleasure. It was my favorite feeling in the world. And I wanted more of it. "Harder."

His fingertips dug into my skin as he fucked me just the way I liked. His hipbones slammed into my ass. I wouldn't have been surprised if the repeated impact left a bruise.

"Baby, I need to feel you come around my cock." He let one hand wander off my hip as he tangled his fingers in my hair. "Now." He pulled on my hair, making me arch my back. Just the slightest change of angle made me completely lose control.

"James!"

"Fuck," he groaned. He continued to thrust into me harder, if that was possible.

"God! James!" I probably left nail indents in the wooden door as I felt his warmth spread up into me. Completion. Pure and utter completion.

He pulled my back against his chest for his last few strokes. They were slow and loving, completely different from what he had just done to me. He slowly pulled out with another groan.

I turned to look at him.

He was standing there in all his glory. His tuxedo pants around his ankles. His cock somehow still at full attention. "Now we can go upstairs," he said and leaned down to pull his pants back up.

I laughed. "We have to get back to the reception."

"No. The only thing we need to do right now is make love. As nice as that was, it wasn't actually how I wanted to leave things."

I smiled. "James, we did just make love." I put my hand on the side of his face as he buttoned his pants.

He lifted his gaze to mine. "Penny, I just fucked you against the door of the men's restroom. It was hardly making love."

I stood up on my tiptoes and kissed him. "Well I certainly feel loved."

He smiled.

"Come on, James," I said and grabbed his hand. "I want to dance. As long as I look okay?" I tried to smooth my hair back into place.

He leaned down and grabbed my ripped thong from the ground and slipped it into his pocket. "It looks like we just had wild raunchy sex," he said.

We both laughed as we walked out of the bathroom.

Matt was standing there with his arms folded across his chest and a smile on his face. "Can't a guy take a piss around here?"

"There's a bathroom down the other hall," James said as he straightened his bowtie.

"Also occupied. Mason and Bee have been mysteriously missing since the end of dinner. It's probably them. Can I use the restroom now?"

"Sorry, Matt," I said and stepped out of the way. I was sure my face was crimson.

"No one should ever apologize for having an orgasm. That's what I always say." He pushed through the bathroom door. It closed behind him with a thud.

"How long do you think he was standing out here listening to us?" James asked and stared at the closed door. "I think I need to go talk to him."

"Nope." I grabbed James' arm and steered him back toward the ballroom. "He was waiting to use the bathroom. I warned you there'd be a line. You promised me a dance."

CHAPTER 24

Saturday

I smiled as I watched Scarlett and James dancing. At first she had been standing on his shoes, but she had found out that twirling was much more fun. I didn't understand how she hadn't gotten too dizzy to stand yet.

"May I have this dance?" Matt asked and put his hand out for me.

I laughed. "Honestly, my feet are killing me, Matt. And I'm exhausted."

"One dance." He smiled and kept his hand out.

"Fine, just one." I put my hand in his and he helped me to my feet.

It was a slow song I didn't recognize. Some old love ballad. I was glad that my stomach was in the way of us being able to dance any closer.

"So all of our friends, including James, think I'm in love with you," Matt said.

"I didn't say..."

"But what do you think?" He twirled me around and then pulled me back in close.

"I think that you're nice to me because you respect your friendship with me and with James. And that you wouldn't do anything to jeopardize either of those friendships."

He smiled. "So you do think I'm in love with you?"

"I didn't say that."

"If you want to put your mind at ease, I'm not in love with you."

"Good."

He smiled again. "Good." He twirled me around once more. "I'm the youngest of my friends. I'll eventually get married. I'll eventually have kids. But I'm not in any rush for either."

"Good," I said again. I wanted to roll my eyes at myself.

"So do you think maybe you could tell your husband to take that stick out of his ass?"

I laughed. "I can try. I don't get it though, Matt. What happened with Jen? And Kendra? Why do they all think you're an unemotional brick wall? You're always so nice to me."

"Let's make a deal. How about you stay out of my relationship issues and I'll stay out of yours."

"What relationship issues?"

He laughed. "Penny."

"Matthew."

"You know I hate being called Matthew," he said and gave me an exaggerated frown.

I couldn't help but laugh. "Then tell me what you meant."

He shrugged.

I punched him in the same spot that James had apparently been punching him."

"Ow."

"Tell me."

"James has a huge list of problems. I don't think you need me to name them all. I love him like a brother, but that doesn't mean he's perfect. I've never really understood why you chose him."

Harsh. "It's simple. I love him."

"Right, I get that. But there are plenty of guys out there with their shit together that would love to be with you."

Every word out of his mouth was making me more and more pissed. "What, like you?"

He smiled. "Yeah, like me."

"You just said you didn't like me." I punched his arm again.

"No, I didn't say that. I said I wasn't in love with you. There's a pretty big difference between like and love."

"I know. There's a huge difference. But I don't think you understand the difference, Matt. I love James with everything that I am. He's my husband, the father of my kids. He's everything to me."

He stared at me blankly.

"I'd take a bullet for him."

"Would he for you?"

"Of course he would."

"You never saw what he was like before he met you."

I swallowed hard. "I know. But he's not that way any-more." The song had stopped, but we were both still standing in the middle of the dance floor. "What was he like?" I don't know why I asked it. Matt's ulterior motives were pretty clear tonight. But he had been drinking since this afternoon. And every person here without a date was probably a little lonely. Being single and going to a wedding was never the best mix. He probably wouldn't re-member this conversation in the morning. I wanted the information, though. I wanted to understand that part of James that I never knew.

"He was a dead man walking," Matt said. "I'm not an unemotional brick wall. But he sure as hell was."

Another song had started. He grabbed my hand and pulled me back in close.

"You're drunk," I said.

"Maybe. But I meant what I said."

"Which part?"

He smiled. "All of it."

I punched him in the arm again.

"Jesus, Penny." He released his hand on my waist to grab his arm. "Would you cut that out?"

"If you stop hitting on me I'll stop hitting you. I hate you for making James right about this. It's bad enough I lose arguments without putting my neck out for a friend."

Matt laughed. "I'm not hitting on you. You're so full of yourself. Which is a good quality. Guys like girls who embody confidence."

I punched him again. "There are plenty of single girls here who would love to be with you."

"Good," he said.

"Well, good then."

He smiled down at me.

"Stop smiling at me."

"I'm not allowed to smile at you now? Penny, we're friends. What I think about in my free time is really none of your business." He winked at me.

So I punched him again.

I jumped when James put his arm around my waist.

"Can I steal my wife for this dance," James said. It was phrased as a question, but there wasn't a hint of a question in his tone. And he didn't wait for Matt to answer. He just pulled me into his arms.

"Why did you just punch him?" he asked. There was a hint of humor in his eyes.

"He was making me mad."

"Okay, I'll rephrase the question." He tucked a loose strand of hair behind my ear. "What were you two talking about?"

"Nothing important." I put my hands behind his neck. Maybe I'd tell him when he got back from his trip. But there was no reason to make him worry. I didn't care if Matt liked me. I only had eyes for James. "I'm pretty sure Matt is drunk."

James laughed. "He's young. He's in his prime to make mistakes."

"Like when you were his age?"

"If I'm being honest, I can't really see them as mistakes anymore. How can anything I've done be a mistake if it's lead me to this moment?"

I smiled. "You can't."

He leaned down, pressing his forehead against mine. "I have to get going."

No. "Don't leave tonight."

"I'll be back before you know it."

I frowned and pulled my face away from his. I didn't understand why I felt like crying. He had gone away on business countless times.

"Is something else bothering you? I'm only going to be gone for a few days. You'll barely notice I'm not home."

"Oh, I'll definitely notice." I bit the inside of my lip. "Did you have a chance to talk to Scar? The whole snake thing has been getting to me."

"I talked to her. I don't think she'll be mentioning it anymore. She even claimed she wanted to watch the movie again. She was insisting actually. Don't worry, though, I shut that down right away. But I thought it was a good sign. It probably means she's not as scared anymore."

"Well that's good. What exactly did you say to her to calm her down? Every time I told her the snake was just in the movie, it seemed to make her more upset."

"I told her that she was scaring you."

I laughed. "You did not."

"I absolutely did. I told her she needed to stop talking about snakes because it was scaring Mommy."

"I'm supposed to be able to protect her. I don't want her to think I'm easily terrified."

"She doesn't. Besides, I'm the protector of the house. And I'll be back before you know it. I really have to get going, though."

I had a feeling in the pit of my stomach that I couldn't quite place. I wanted to protest. I wanted to beg him to stay. Instead, I just nodded my head and tried to ignore the imminent tears pricking the corners of my eyes.

He placed a gentle kiss against my lips.

I grabbed the lapels of his tuxedo to deepen the kiss, but he pulled away far too soon.

"Feel free to keep punching Matt as long as he keeps flirting with you," James said and placed a kiss on my cheek. "I'm going to have a little chat with him before I head out."

Before I could say anything, James had dropped me from his embrace and was stalking over toward Matt. He grabbed him by the arm and pulled him off the dance floor.

Bye, James. I put my hand on my stomach. What was this feeling? All I knew was that it wasn't just a chill down my spine. It was like my whole body felt cold.

CHAPTER 25

Sunday

Maybe I was wrong about Axel weighing more than Scarlett. Tonight she felt like she weighed a ton. It was almost tempting to wake her up so that she could walk. Instead, I adjusted her on my hip and pressed the button for the elevator. James had been gone less than an hour and I already missed him terribly. I carried Scarlett onto the elevator and leaned against the wall as the doors closed.

Ow. I slouched forward as a pain rippled through my side. *Are you doing cartwheels now too?* I put my free hand on my stomach. *I need you to behave while your father is gone. Okay?* Another sharp pain made me wince.

When the elevator doors opened, I slowly stepped out. I glanced at the sign posted on the wall, signaling that our room was to the right. I adjusted Scar again and made my way down the hall. My hand rummaged around in my purse, searching for the keycard. *Damn it, where did I put it?* This was why I didn't like when James left. I wasn't good at handling more than one thing at a time. I was exhausted. My stomach hurt. It felt like I was holding a bag of concrete in my arms. And I couldn't find my fucking keycard. I knew it was just my hormones that made me start crying. I wasn't even sure why I had agreed to spend the night in the hotel. All I wanted to do was curl up on James' side of the bed at home and breathe in his smell. I was always a mess when he wasn't around.

The sound of a door opening and laughter made me turn my head in the opposite direction. I'd recognize Tyler's laugh anywhere. I didn't want anyone to see me in my current state, whether I knew them or not. *Come on, you stupid keycard.*

"Penny? Are you okay?"

I could smell the alcohol on him. But his appearance was evidence enough that he was drunk. His tie was hanging loosely around his neck. Half the buttons were undone from his dress shirt and his tuxedo jacket had long ago been abandoned downstairs in the ballroom. He was holding an ice bucket in one hand and was awkwardly trying to button his shirt back up with the other.

I turned away. "Yeah, I'm just trying to find my keycard. Goodnight, Tyler."

"Let me help you," he said and reached for Scarlett.

The relief of having her weight off of me made me sigh.

"You're not really supposed to be lifting anything, are you?"

"No, not really, but she's not that heavy." Now that I could actually see into my purse better, I was easily able to find the keycard. "Found it." I lifted it up and smiled at Tyler. "Thanks." I put my arm out for Scarlett, but he kept her on his hip.

"I'll put her down for you." He nodded to the door.

"Oh, that's not necessary. I can do it."

"You're not really supposed to be lifting anything," he repeated.

I rolled my eyes and he laughed.

"Fine." I put my keycard in the door and it beeped open.

Tyler followed me in, hitting the lights as he made his way through the room. He set his ice bucket on the nightstand and easily pushed back the sheets while still balancing Scarlett in his arms. He gently laid her down and pulled the covers up, tucking them under her chin.

I leaned against the wall as I stared at them.

He pushed her hair off her face. "She looks just like you."

"She has James' eyes."

Tyler nodded and looked up at me. The smile seemed to evaporate from his face. "Have you been crying?"

I quickly shook my head. "No. I'm just tired."

"Why do you like to pretend that I can't tell when you're lying?"

I didn't know what to say. That I missed James desperately? That my baby wouldn't stop kicking me? That I was worried a snake was going to kill me in my sleep?

"Okay, you don't have to tell me." He pulled the covers off of Scarlett and lifted her back in his arms. "But you don't have to sit here moping all night." He grabbed the ice bucket off the nightstand and walked past me.

"Where are you going?"

"To get ice. And then all three of us are going to go watch a movie."

"Tyler, I'm not going to interrupt your night with Hailey." I tried to grab Scarlett, but he shifted her away from me.

"You're not. We were renting a movie to watch with Axel. Unlike Scarlett, the kid is completely wired. I think he got more cake when we weren't looking."

I laughed. "I don't want to ruin your night."

He started walking backwards. "When have you ever ruined my night?"

"Oh, I don't know. Maybe that time I kneed you in the junk?"

He laughed. "I'm pretty sure I deserved that one. You coming or not?" He somehow managed to open the door even though his hands were full.

I looked back at the empty bed. He was right. I didn't want to spend the night alone. I followed him out of the door and grabbed the ice bucket out of his hand. "I can at least get the ice for you." We had passed it on the way to our room.

"You really don't want to talk about what's wrong?" Tyler asked.

He was a good designated uncle. He was a great dad. But none of that surprised me. Tyler was good at everything he did. "Does Axel ever say anything that scares you?"

"What do you mean? Like how he wants to grow up and be a football player? Because I have issues with that. I'm pretty sure their concussion protocol scares every parent now."

I laughed and tried to let my thoughts disappear with the churning of the ice machine. I picked up the full ice bucket. "You're right. You shouldn't let him be a football player."

Tyler grabbed the ice bucket from me.

"I can carry a little ice," I said.

"You can do anything. But it doesn't mean you should." He smiled at me.

We were quiet the rest of the way back to his room. I was pretty sure he was waiting for me to tell him what Scarlett said that scared me. But I didn't feel like talking about it. A movie to distract me actually sounded kind of perfect.

"Scar!" Axel yelled when we entered the room.

Scarlett immediately opened her eyes. She looked over Tyler's shoulder at me. "Slumber party?" she asked and yawned.

I nodded.

Tyler set her down on their king-sized bed and she plopped herself next to Axel in the middle. Tyler walked to the other side of the bed and climbed over Hailey to the empty spot that he had apparently abandoned on his ice expedition. He put his arm around Hailey's shoulders. "What are we watching?"

"We agreed on Trolls," Hailey said. "Does that sound alright, girls?" She reached over and tickled Scarlett.

I smiled and sat down in the chair in the corner. "That sounds great."

"Mhm," Scar said. "But, Mommy, you sit here." She patted the bed beside her.

"Oh, no. I'm okay right here."

"That chair is like a rock," Hailey said. "Get up here, Penny!"

I laughed. It really was uncomfortable. I was so glad that Hails wasn't mad at me anymore. "Okay." I climbed up on the bed beside my daughter. I thought she might snuggle up next to me, but instead she put her head on Axel's shoulder, mimicking the way that Hailey and Tyler were sitting.

I had walked into this room knowing I'd feel like the third wheel to Hailey and Tyler. But I didn't expect to feel like the fifth wheel.

***

"Are you sure you don't want to talk about it?" Tyler asked.

I glanced over at him. Everyone seemed to be asleep but us. Somehow watching trolls singing on the screen had calmed me down. And Tyler had always been good at listening to me.

"Scar said a snake was going to get me," I said. "And that she was worried about James not being a good dad when I was gone."

"Well, that's not creepy at all." Tyler smiled. "Sometimes Axel says weird stuff, but it's usually from something he heard."

"We let her watch Harry Potter and the Chamber of Secrets. You know, the one with that huge snake? She started saying it after that."

"So that's it. She's just scared of the movie."

"I guess. I don't know why she's projecting the snake on me though."

"We're all worried about you, Penny. Kids are smart. They can pick up on stuff like that."

"Yeah, I know." I ran my fingers through Scarlett's hair. "James worries all the time about being a bad father. Yet, I'm the one terrifying our daughter."

"Penny, you're a great mom. Right up there with Hailey and my own mother."

I smiled. "Thanks, Tyler. It's late, I should probably get us to bed." I scooted off the side of the bed.

"You can spend the night if you want," he said. "The bed is certainly big enough."

I laughed. "I appreciate the offer, but we paid for a perfectly good room down the hall." I leaned over the bed to reach for Scarlett.

"Do you want me to carry her for you?"

"No, I've got her." I lifted her up into my arms.

She moaned lightly in her sleep.

"Thanks for tonight, Tyler. It was just what I needed."

"Any time, Penny." He yawned and switched off the television. "Goodnight."

"Goodnight." I walked out into the hall. This time I had no trouble finding my keycard. I carried Scarlett into our hotel room and switched on the lights so I wouldn't trip on the way to the bed.

But that made Scarlett open her eyes. She looked around for a moment, slightly disoriented.

"Can't we sleep in Axel's room?" she said. "It's slumber party."

I laid her down in the bed. "We're going to sleep in here tonight." I pushed her bangs off her forehead and pulled the covers up around her.

"But, Mommy, I'm scared."

"There's nothing to be scared of." I leaned over and kissed her forehead.

"I miss Daddy. The snake never comes when Daddy is here."

I swallowed hard. "Scar, there is no snake. Didn't Daddy tell you that earlier today?"

"No, he said you were scared of him and that I shouldn't talk about him coming anymore. But I'm scared of him too."

She blinked up at me in the most innocent way. But the words she said weren't innocent. They were haunting.

What was I supposed to say in response to her words? I took a deep breath and grabbed her hand. "Baby girl, there are no snake monsters. And there's nothing coming for us. Now, I'm going to go get ready for bed. And then we can have snuggles, okay?"

She let go of my hand and gripped the top of the sheets in her fists. "Okay, Mommy. But we could sleep with Uncle Tyler. Or Uncle Rob. Or Uncle Matt. Or Uncle Mason..."

"Scar, I can take care of us. There's absolutely nothing to worry about."

She pressed her lips together, like she was considering the possibility. "Can you look under the bed?"

I smiled. "Of course." I slowly got down on my hands and knees and looked under the bed. "Nothing there," I said and got back to my feet. "I'll be right back." I kissed her forehead and made my way over to my suitcase.

I almost started crying when I opened it up. There was one of James' t-shirts sitting on the top of the rest of the items, with a note. I picked up the slip of paper.

My beautiful wife,

In case you can't sleep without feeling close to me. I'll be back before you know it. Call me when you wake up. I miss you already.

Love always,

James

I quickly got ready for bed and then pulled his shirt over my head. James' cologne immediately surrounded me. It calmed me better than anything else in the world.

But a clicking noise disrupted any calming effect the shirt had. "Scar?" I opened up the bathroom door and walked out when there was no response. "Scar?" I turned toward the bed and froze when she wasn't lying where I had left her. "Scarlett?!" I glanced around the room, but it was completely empty.

"Scarlett!" Fear gripped my heart as I ran to the door. *Oh God. Oh God.* I ran out into the hall and stared at my daughter wreaking havoc on a whole floor of The Plaza Hotel.

Scarlett was at the opposite end of the hall, banging on a door. "Uncle Mason!" she screamed at the top of her lungs.

"Scar, what are you doing?" I hissed.

She turned toward me. But then immediately ran to another door, farther away from me. "Uncle Tyler!" she yelled and banged on the door.

"Scarlett, stop it." I started walking toward her. "You're going to wake up everyone on the floor." *Ow. Not right now, baby boy.* I stopped and placed my hand on the wall. A searing pain hit my chest right after another kick in the ribs. I closed my eyes for a second.

"Uncle Matt!" Scarlett screamed as she banged on another door.

"Scarlett Hunter, stop that right now," I said sternly and opened my eyes. "Come over here."

She just ran to another door. "Uncle Rooooob!"

Damn it, Scar. I put my hand on the center of my chest and pushed myself off the wall. *Ow.* I knew she had scared me. That's why my chest hurt. *It's just in my head.*

Scarlett started banging on another door.

"Scar, please stop. Please stop for Mommy." She hadn't listened to my demand. Maybe she'd listen to me begging.

Matt walked out of one of the rooms she had banged on earlier, wearing nothing but a pair of boxers.

"Uncle Matt!" Scarlett said and ran over to him. She jumped into his arms as he leaned down to talk to her.

I slowly hobbled over to them. "Scar, you can't run off like that. We just talked about this the other day. What were you thinking?"

"It's okay," Matt said. "I got her."

"And what if it hadn't been you? What if it had been some stranger that just snatched her up?"

"But it was me." He said it slowly.

I knew he was trying to calm me, but I didn't think anything could calm me down. "You promised you wouldn't leave without a grown-up, Scarlett. Get over here, right now."

"I said I wouldn't leave the house," Scarlett said and hugged Matt's torso even tighter. "We're not in our house, Mommy."

For God's sake. When had my daughter become a smart ass?

"And we need Uncle Matt to sleep with us," she said before I could respond.

Matt laughed.

"We don't need anyone else, Scar. I told you I'd take care of you."

"Yes we do!" she yelled. "Because the snake is going to get you and you can't stop it. And then I'll be alone. We need Uncle Matt. We'll sleep in his room tonight." Scarlett pointed to his door.

"Actually, kiddo, you can't go in there right this second." He awkwardly ran his hand through his hair.

Not only had we most likely awakened half the floor, we had interrupted Matt in the middle of whatever normal single people did at weddings. Which was clearly sex. There was no doubt in my mind that he had a naked woman lying on his bed, waiting for him to return.

"Come on, Scar. We're going back to our room. I'm so sorry, Matt."

She gripped Matt even tighter and turned to face him. "But the snake is going to kill my mommy."

My chest hurt. And I thought someone had kidnapped my daughter. And I missed James. And I was seven months pregnant with a son who wouldn't stop kicking me. And I didn't want to die. God, I didn't want to even think about death. It was like her words had pushed me over the tipping point. I couldn't even help it. I burst into tears.

"Mommy?" Scarlett said.

I turned away. "Can you just...can you hold her for a second, Matt?" I tried to wipe away my tears as fast as possible. I tried so hard to be strong in front of Scarlett. I never, ever wanted her to see me cry. And I had just ruined everything. Now she'd know that I wasn't invincible. But clearly she already knew that if she thought a snake would be the end of me. *Fuck, stop crying.*

"Mommy?" she said again.

I tried to take a deep breath. *Ow.*

"Let's get you girls back to your room," Matt said and put his hand in mine.

I should have pulled my hand out of his. I should have been able to tell Scarlett no and get her back into our room on my own. But my chest still hurt. My stomach still hurt. Everything just hurt. And Matt's hand was comforting. The fact that Scarlett was comforted by him was also a huge plus.

"But you'll stay the night?" Scarlett asked as he walked us down the hall.

"Yeah, sure," he said.

I knew he just said it to calm her down. But the thought of Matt coming into my room in nothing but boxers made me cringe. James was jealous enough as it was. This wasn't going to help. I wiped away the remaining tears on my cheeks. "I can take her now," I said when we reached our door.

"No!" she yelled at the top of her lungs. "I want Uncle Matt."

She was a little terror. When had she become impossible for me to handle alone? I guess daddy's girls wreaked havoc whenever their fathers weren't around.

"It's fine," Matt said. "Key?" He nodded to the door.

Shit. I hadn't grabbed the key when I had run out looking for her. I reached out and turned the handle, but it was locked. "It's in the room." I leaned my back against the door. *Why me?*

"You're going to sit with your Mom while I go get another room key, okay, Scar?" he said.

"No," she replied and hugged him even tighter.

He gave me a tight-lipped smile.

"I'll go get it," I said.

"No you're..." his voice trailed off. "You're only wearing a shirt."

I completely forgot that I was inappropriately dressed. Normally James' t-shirts covered me pretty well, but with my pregnant stomach they barely covered my panties. I awkwardly tugged on the hem of the shirt. "But you're just wearing boxers."

He laughed. "It won't be my first time making a scene in a hotel lobby." He adjusted Scarlett on his hip. "We'll be right back." He winked at me and made his way to the elevator.

Scarlett didn't yell to stay with me. Or cry for being taken away. She clung to him like she loved him more than anyone else in the world. As they disappeared onto the elevator, I let my back slide down the door, until my butt hit the hallway carpet. And I cried. I cried and I couldn't seem to stop.

CHAPTER 26

Sunday

"Do you want to talk about it?" Matt asked.

I opened my eyes and looked up at him. "Where is Scarlett?"

"With Rob and Daphne. She seemed perfectly content in his arms. Wasn't anything special about me except that I was a man, I guess."

I laughed. "Well whatever it was, she wanted you more than she wanted me."

"Do you want to talk about it?" he asked again.

"Not really."

"I got your keycard." He put his hand out for me and helped me get to my feet.

"Thank you. Is the little monster that used to be my daughter spending the rest of the night with Rob and Daphne?"

"Yup. It's just us." He put my keycard in the door and pushed it open for me.

I stared at him apprehensively. "Thank you for coming to my rescue tonight with Scar. And for getting my key. I really appreciate it. But it's the middle of the night. And you're practically naked." I gestured to the chiseled abs staring back at me.

"So are you."

I tugged on the bottom of my shirt again. "Goodnight, Matt," I said.

He crossed his arms as he leaned against the door-jamb. "Look, it's true, I think you're beautiful. And sweet and kind."

"Matt..."

"Let me finish," he said with a laugh. "I like pushing your buttons because you get all flustered." He smiled. "Sure, if you were single, I would have tried to sleep with you years ago. But I promise I'm not trying to steal you away from James. I just like messing with you."

Rob used to say something similar to me. Like he enjoyed seeing me blush or something. "Am I really so fun to mess with?"

"Absolutely. So will you let your guard down for two seconds and tell me why your daughter is insisting that a snake is going to murder you in your sleep?"

"Is that what she said to you?"

"Something along those lines."

"God." I walked past him into the room. "She just saw a scary movie. It's nothing."

"So the tears..."

"What would you do if your kid wouldn't stop talking about your impending death? How am I supposed to comfort her when I don't..." I let my voice trail off. "I'm too young to die." My eyes started to get watery again.

"There it is." He opened his arms like he wanted to hug me.

"I'm not hugging you when you're only wearing boxers."

He lifted up his arm and sniffed his armpit. "What? I smell fine, I swear."

"Matt."

"I just told you I didn't love you. What's the big deal? All our friends can screw themselves. You know I love you, but just as a friend. Come on." He gestured to his chest. When I didn't move, he sighed. "If the pregnant stomach wasn't enough to remind me that you're off limits, the hickey James left you with would be."

I put my hand on the side of my neck. I had forgotten that James' kisses had probably left a mark.

"Or the fact that I heard you two fucking in that restroom a few hours ago and you very much enjoying it. Or that he threatened to kill me if I hit on you."

"He did not." My words were meaningless. I had seen James pull Matt off the dance floor. Of course he had threatened him. I didn't doubt it for a second.

Matt shrugged. "Regardless, I'm not hitting on you. I'm being a good friend. You know that, Penny." He gave me the signature Caldwell smile.

"Fine. I'll take that hug now." I didn't care that it was inappropriate to be hugging Matt in his boxers. I didn't care that James would probably be upset. Because right now, I just needed a hug.

He laughed and wrapped his arms around me.

And for just a second, I didn't feel so alone. Was that really what was bothering me? Did I feel abandoned? I tried to shake away the thought. Scarlett loved me. She was just scared. And James would be back soon enough.

"You're not going to die, Penny. I'm sure James has you going to the best doctors."

I didn't respond. "You should probably get back to your room."

"There's no rush. Tiffany already fell asleep. Or was her name Stephanie?"

I laughed. "You're ridiculous."

"It was definitely Tiffany. Actually, I was thinking about it and maybe I should give that online dating thing a try."

"Really?"

He released me from his hug. "Yeah. Maybe you could help me sign up to one of those sites?"

"Um...yes!"

"I'm glad you're smiling, but I don't mean right this second. Why are you so excited about this anyway?"

"I met James when I was young. I know people who did the whole online dating thing, but I never experienced it. I think it'll be fun."

"Maybe for you. You won't have to go on the dates."

"Right. I just get to catfish a bunch of people for you."

"What? No. I meant you could help me set up a profile. Not respond to people. I don't want you to pretend to be me."

"We'll see."

He shook his head.

"And what about Tiffany? You don't want to date her?"

He shrugged. "I want a woman who cries when I leave. Not snores and rolls over."

"Someone needy? Got it."

"Not needy, Penny. Just someone who needs me."

"I get that."

"But I probably should get back to the snorer. If you're good?"

"I'm good."

He smiled. "Night, Penny."

"Hey, Matt?"

He turned around before he reached the door.

"All that stuff you said about James. About why I chose him. And that I didn't know what he was like before I met him..."

"I was joking." He smiled. "Just wanted to see how flustered I could get you."

"Oh. Right."

He laughed. "You know where my room is if you need anything else."

"Mhm. Goodnight, Matt." I watched the door close behind him. I turned and looked at the bed. Despite my brain telling me not to, I got down on my hands and knees and looked under it. I shook my head. *There are no snakes in The Plaza Hotel.* I climbed into bed and turned the light off. But instead of closing my eyes, I just stared at the ceiling. James wouldn't land for another several hours. I bit the inside of my lip. A voicemail would be a nice thing to land to, though. Besides, I really just needed to hear his voice. I grabbed my phone off the nightstand and clicked on James' name. His voicemail switched on automatically.

"You've reached James. Leave your name and number, and I'll get back to you as soon as I can."

I smiled at the sound of his voice. "Hey, James," I said after the beep. "I know you're probably a hundred miles from home by now. And you can't answer your phone until you land. I think I can actually feel the distance. Is that crazy?" I laughed. It sounded sad in the empty room. I rolled onto my side and stared at the empty spot beside me. "I can't fall asleep because the bed is too empty without you. Try to finish up and get back to us as fast as you can, okay? I miss you. Scar misses you. Liam misses you." I put my hand on my stomach and smiled. "And we can't wait to see you when you get back. I love you." Suddenly I thought I might cry. I was desperate for his touch. We had only been apart for a few hours. How could I feel his absence so completely? I cleared my throat. "I just wanted to warn you that I'll probably sleep on your side of the bed when I get home tomorrow night. Thanks for leaving the shirt, but I feel like your scent has already disappeared." I laughed, but it sounded forced. "Have a safe trip, James. I'll see you in a few days." I hung up before my tears could start falling.

CHAPTER 27

Sunday

"Looks like you two had fun last night," I said as I sat down at the table where Jen and Ian were seated.

Jen put her hand on her forehead. "Ugh. It feels like a dump truck ran over my face."

Ian laughed.

"Don't laugh at me," she said and put her head on his shoulder. "You're not allowed to laugh at your fiancée. It's like...a rule."

He kissed her forehead. "Noted. Do you want me to get you some water or something?"

She sighed and lifted her head. "No, I've got it. If I don't move I'm going to fall asleep." She slowly stood up. "Be right back. Don't talk about me when I'm gone," she said and pointed back and forth between Ian and me.

"We won't," I said and started to pick at my eggs. I wasn't planning on talking about her. But I was planning on bringing up something she didn't want me to. As soon as she was out of earshot, I set down my fork. "Are you really moving back to New York?"

Ian smiled. "That's the plan."

"It'll be nice to have you back."

"It'll be nice to be back."

I glanced over at the buffet table where Jen was chatting with someone. The time to ask Ian was now or never. "I know Jen said you wouldn't want to, but I have to ask...because I miss you and our new driver is so formal and I feel like he doesn't like me..." I let my voice trail off.

"Are you asking if I want my old job back?" He took a sip of his orange juice. It looked like he was studying me.

"Yes. God, Ian, we'd love to have you back. But obviously if you and Jen..."

"I've been waiting for the offer ever since we landed." He set down his cup and his familiar smile spread over his face. "Maybe Jen doesn't want me to work for you and James, but I've been on a few terrible interviews this week, and honestly, I couldn't imagine working for anyone else. I'd love to come back."

I tried not to squeal. "You have no idea how excited I am. Although, breaking the news to William won't be very fun." I bit the inside of my lip. I had never fired someone before.

"Hell, I'll break the news to him," Ian said with a laugh.

I smiled. "Let's just let James do it when he gets back."

"Let James do what?" Jen asked as she sat back down.

"I'm going to let you two talk," I said and picked up my plate. I had a feeling Jen was going to be mad at me for offering Ian his old job back. They needed to talk it out between themselves without me butting in.

I glanced around the restaurant to find another seat. Most of the people at the brunch looked as hungover as Jen. My eyes landed on Scarlett. She hadn't left Rob's side since last night. She was currently sitting on his lap, making it almost impossible for him to eat. *Geez, Scar.* I started to make my way toward them.

"Hey, Penny!" Matt said, before I reached Rob's table. "I saved a seat for you." He patted the chair beside his.

I turned my head toward my daughter. Now she was grabbing food out of Rob's hand. "I think I need to go save Rob from Scarlett."

Matt laughed. "It doesn't look like he minds. Sit."

I watched Rob laugh and try to steal his food back from Scarlett. Maybe Matt was right. "Okay." I hadn't really had a chance to eat anything. But that wasn't why I sat down. "When do you want to set up your online dating profile? We could do it today."

He rolled his eyes. "I didn't mean right this second. Just like...soon."

"You have no idea how excited I am about this."

"Don't you have any other hobbies besides being a pain in my ass?"

I laughed and lightly shoved his shoulder.

"Are you going to eat those?" he asked and pointed his fork at my eggs.

I slid my plate toward him. "They're all yours."

"Aren't pregnant women supposed to eat tons?"

"Yes. But we're not hungry this morning." I put my hand on my stomach. "No, that's a lie. We're hungry, but we want ice cream, not breakfast food."

He laughed and shook his head. "Are you feeling better this morning?"

"You know, I actually feel really good. I didn't sleep very well last night, but I still feel full of energy. It's weird. For the past several weeks I've actually felt kind of awful.

But I'm good today. I feel like I could run around Central Park. And you know how much I hate to run."

"You probably just needed a break from that," he said and pointed at Scarlett.

I laughed. "No. Even when she's being a terror, I don't want a break from her."

"Do you want me to come over today? I can entertain Scar while you get some rest."

"No, that's okay. I want to have a girls day with her. I'm trying to trick her into liking me again."

"She likes you," Matt said with a laugh. "She's just going through a phase."

"You're just saying that because she prefers you over me. When she's a moody teenager and wants nothing to do with either of us, you'll see how I feel. I'm going to get going."

"Call me if you want some company later." He leaned over and gave me a hug.

"I will." I left him with my plate of food and made my way over to Scarlett. "Hey, Scar. You ready to get going? We have a fun day planned."

"No, Mommy." She animatedly shook her head. "We're going to Uncle Rob's for a slumber party!"

"We can take her if you want," he said.

"That's okay, Rob. Scar, come with me. It's time to go." I put my hand out for her.

"No," she said and stuck out her lower lip.

I folded my arms across my chest and tried to give her a stern look. "Scarlett, you have to the count of five to come here." It was something James did with her when she was being stubborn.

"No, Mommy, we have to go with Uncle Rob."

I sighed. It worked when James did it. Clearly I didn't have the same air of authority.

"We really don't mind taking her," Daphne said. "When was the last time you had a night all to yourself?"

I hated nights all to myself.

"I'll bring her by in the morning before work," Rob said. "It's fine."

"Well, okay then. Are you sure, Scar? I had a fun day planned for us."

"I'm sure. Mommy, you should come with us. It's safer."

Rob raised both his eyebrows at me.

I decided it was best to not acknowledge her comment. I leaned down and kissed her forehead. "Have a fun day, baby girl."

"I will."

And that was it. She turned away from me and started playing with the food on Rob's plate. "Thanks," I said to Rob and Daphne.

Daphne was giving me that look. The one that meant she was concerned about me. But like I had said to Matt, there was nothing to be concerned about. I felt better than I had in days. Yes, my daughter didn't want to spend time with just me. But I was okay. I swallowed down the lump in my throat.

I wandered over to Mason and Bee's table. "I'm going to get going," I said and leaned down to hug Bee.

"So soon?" she asked. "We'll be here for at least another hour. Our flight isn't until noon."

"Yeah, I need to get going." I didn't need to. But being here alone made me realize just how much weddings sucked when you were single. I didn't want to hang out anymore. I missed James. I just wanted to call him. "Have fun on your honeymoon, you two." I reached over and patted Mason's shoulder.

"Oh, we will," Mason said.

"Thanks for everything, Penny," Bee said. "Are you still going to grab my dress..."

"I've got it all taken care of. Don't worry about a thing. See you guys when you get back. I can't wait to hear all about it." They were finally taking that trip to Italy. Originally Mason had planned to propose there. They were going to meet us on our honeymoon so that we'd all be able to celebrate together. But Isabella had foiled those plans. They had been sitting in a hospital on the day that Mason had planned out for months, waiting to see if James would come back to us. I was happy that they were finally taking the trip. Maybe one day James and I would finally get to go. We had never talked about recreating our honeymoon itinerary. Instead, we had gone to the Bahamas for a late honeymoon once he recovered. Italy was still highest on my list of places I wanted to see. But there was plenty of time. I truly did feel good. Healthy. My chest didn't hurt at all.

I stepped outside of the restaurant and took a deep breath.

"Penny!"

I turned around to see the Caldwell brothers' father pushing through the doors. "Hi, Mr. Caldwell. Did I forget something? Bee's dress is already in the car. I was going to take it to get it preserved."

"No, dear. You didn't forget anything." He reached into his pants pocket and pulled out his wallet. "I didn't know when the best time to bring this up would be, but I wanted to catch you before you left. Mason told me about your heart condition."

That explained the look of pity he had given James at the rehearsal dinner. It had still been bothering me in the back of my head. Now it made sense. I thought maybe some business deal had gone south. I hated that people knew about my heart. But at least James hadn't told him. He promised he wouldn't tell anyone else.

"I wouldn't call it a condition. I'm fine. I was actually just thinking about how great I feel."

"Good. But either way, I wanted to give you this." He pulled out a business card from his wallet and handed it to me. "I'm sure you're seeing a great doctor. But this is the number for my cardiologist. I can't recommend him enough. The man saved my life. I wouldn't be standing here today if it wasn't for him."

I looked down at the card. "Thanks, Mr. Caldwell. But I really am good. There's nothing to worry about."

"It never hurts to get a second opinion. Just think about it." He gave me the signature Caldwell wink that Mason and Matt did so often.

I smiled. "Thanks. I will."

"I should get back to the festivities. Take care, Penny." He gave me a quick hug and then disappeared back into the building.

THE LIGHT TO MY DARKNESS

I looked down at the card again. Normally, thinking about my heart would make it hurt. But it didn't ache at all today. I stuffed the card into my purse and started walking home.

CHAPTER 28

Sunday

I sighed and leaned back in my chair. The words weren't flowing today. All I could seem to do was stare at my clicking cursor. I turned off my computer and checked my phone for what felt like the hundredth time. James still hadn't called me back. His plane must have landed hours ago. I had called him a few more times this morning, but hadn't left any more messages. What was taking him so long to call me?

My eyes wandered to the camera mounted in the corner of the room. It used to make me uncomfortable, knowing that our security detail could see me at all times. But James assured me that they didn't watch us when we shed our clothes. The cameras were just a precaution. After everything that had happened to us, James didn't want to take any unnecessary risks. And that meant putting cameras in every room, despite my insistence that I didn't want them. I begged him to at least not put them in the bathrooms or our bedroom. James' response to my request was that we had sex just as often outside our bedroom. Which was true.

I clicked on Porter's name in my phone and held it to my ear.

He answered after one ring. "Yes, Mrs. Hunter?"

"Cole?" I knew he still preferred when I called him by his last name. But sometimes I just needed that sense of familiarity. And whenever I called him Cole instead, he knew something was bothering me.

"Is everything alright, Penny?"

I smiled at him calling me by my first name. "When did James' plane land?" I heard the shuffling of papers.

"At 8:51."

I bit the inside of my lip. That was hours ago. "Do you know what his itinerary is?"

"He just said it was business."

"Could you call Briggs and see if James is available for a call?"

Porter cleared his throat. "Briggs is with me."

"Briggs didn't go with James?" For some reason, I was starting to feel uneasy. James knew how I felt about him traveling without a member of our security detail.

"Despite my requests, no. You know how Mr. Hunter is."

I sighed. I did know. He worried about his family when he went away on business. He wanted to keep Scarlett and me safe, even though it put him at risk. "Do you think maybe we should hire one more person?"

"I think that's a great idea. I'll pull some resumes of recommendations and bring them to you tomorrow."

Over the past few years, the members of our staff had gotten used to catering to my requests. I cringed at the fact that I had used the term staff. They didn't feel like staff to me. They felt like family. I relied on them endlessly. Originally, I hadn't been able to ask them questions without them skirting around the answers. Apparently because of

James' high standards and odd rules about what I was allowed to know. But now they let me make decisions as if I was an extension of James.

"Do you want me to try to call him?" Porter asked.

"No, I'll just keep trying."

"Alright. Is there anything else you need?"

I looked up at the camera and then quickly turned away. I was embarrassed by what I was about to ask. "Actually, yes. Could you maybe check Scarlett's room for snakes?" A part of me thought that maybe that was why I couldn't focus on writing. I was worried a snake was going to come out of nowhere and bite me.

"Snakes?"

"She's been obsessed with them after seeing this Harry Potter movie. And I knew we shouldn't have let her see it. But now she won't stop talking about snakes."

"Snakes huh? I thought she'd be more of a bunny collector if anything."

I laughed. "I know. But she has this strange fascination with them. And she keeps saying they're going to take me away."

"What do you mean by that?" There was suddenly a sense of urgency in his voice.

"That they're going to kill me, I guess? I don't know. She keeps saying stuff like that to me and it's freaking me out."

There was a knock on the front door. I slowly stood up and ended the call. I knew it was Porter. A few seconds later, I opened up the door for him, even though I knew perfectly well that he had a key.

"I'm sure she doesn't have any hidden snakes in her room. Kids and their imaginations." He winked at me. "But let me check it out just in case." He had winked. And he had smiled. But his expression was serious even though his tone wasn't. He was suddenly ready to get down to business. And that made a world of difference to me. He didn't laugh at me or call me crazy. He took the threat seriously. Because it was his job to keep my family safe. If he said that the upstairs was all clear, I'd believe him.

I wandered into the kitchen while Porter checked Scarlett's room. It was easy to get lost in writing about memories like they were currently happening. And even though I wasn't being as productive as usual, I had completely lost track of time. It hadn't just been hours since James had landed. It had been almost exactly eight hours.

I tried not to let myself worry. Worrying never helped anything. He was probably just in meetings all day. "I know I promised you ice cream, little man," I said and opened up the freezer, trying to distract myself. I pushed a few things aside and frowned. No ice cream? How was that possible? I shoved a few more things to the side and sighed. Now that it wasn't an option, I was desperately craving it. *Sorry, baby boy.* I stared at the contents of the fridge, but nothing else looked appealing. Maybe I was just thirsty. I opened up the cabinet to grab a glass and saw a note from Ellen on the counter, sitting in front of my bottle of vitamins.

Penny,

When I unpacked your suitcase, I didn't see your pill holder. I'm so sorry, but I must have accidentally put it in

James' suitcase. It was a careless mistake and I'm very sorry. It won't happen again. I do hope you two had fun at the wedding.

My apologies,

-Ellen

I shook my head as I poured myself a glass of water. Did she really think I'd be upset with her? I had forgotten them too. I unscrewed the cap and took six instead of two, to make up for the missed days, and swallowed them down with a huge gulp of water. *Ugh.* I hated these pills. I couldn't wait until I was allowed to go back to my daily gummy vitamin. Scarlett had gotten me hooked on them. They were fruity and delicious and probably everything a vitamin shouldn't be. But it got her to take them.

"If she's hiding snakes it must be under the floorboards," Porter said.

I jumped. I hadn't even heard him walk down the stairs, let alone into the room. "Thanks for looking."

"I'll call an exterminator in the morning just in case. They can probably check it out better than I can. I really don't know a thing about snakes."

I breathed a sigh of relief. I'm glad he was taking me seriously. "That would be great."

"Where is Scarlett right now?" he asked.

"She's spending the night at Rob and Daphne's. Apparently she didn't think I was capable of protecting her from the snakes." I laughed awkwardly.

He gave me a tight-lipped smile. The same kind of smile that Mr. Caldwell had given James. The same smile that people gave me when they found out about my heart murmur.

"Maybe that's for the best. I know she usually sleeps in your bed when James is away, and I was just about to advise you against it."

Whenever James was away on business, I always forced our daughter to sleep in his spot. I didn't need to be embarrassed. Porter had cameras everywhere. He knew I didn't like to sleep alone. But I still felt a blush cross my cheeks. "Why were you going to advise against it?"

"In case she's planning something."

I laughed. "Planning something?"

"It would have just been a precaution. But we don't have to worry about it now."

Now. Because my daughter refused to be alone with me because she was scared I couldn't protect her. I pressed my lips together. "Okay. But she gets scared when James isn't home. She's probably going to call in the middle of the night for me to come get her. And then she's going to try to crawl in my bed regardless."

"So, we'll lock her door."

"Lock her up?" I laughed again. "She's not a criminal. Besides, you know how good she is at opening locked doors."

Porter shrugged. "Just be careful until the exterminators come. And let me know if she does call tonight. I'll escort you to Rob's to get her. Is there anything else you need tonight?"

This conversation was ridiculous. But not because of the snake part. Because there was literally no chance Scarlett would call me in the middle of the night if she was scared. I needed to hear James' voice. He always knew exactly the right thing to say to me. "Could you maybe call James real quick? To see if he answers? I've been trying to call him all day."

"Of course." Porter pulled out his phone, clicked on a few buttons and put it to his ear. "Good evening, Mr. Hunter." Silence. "Yes, everything is fine." He gave me a smile. "Mrs. Hunter just wants to talk to you." Silence. "Very well. Goodnight, Mr. Hunter."

I reached out for the phone, but Porter pulled it from his ear and then hung up. I blinked. "Did he not realize I was standing right here?"

"He's in a meeting. He said he'll call you as soon as it's finished."

I went through the time difference in my head. "It's after 10 o'clock in London. What meeting would he have so late?"

"I'm not sure. But he said he'd call you once it adjourns. I should get started on those resumes. And I'll schedule the appointment with the exterminator as well. Anything else on your mind?"

"No. Thank you, Porter."

"Have a good evening," he said with a nod. He closed the front door behind him. I heard the click of the lock, knowing perfectly well that Porter would stop anyone unlocking that door if it wasn't someone who was allowed to come in.

CHAPTER 29
Sunday

I stared at the T.V. screen, but I wasn't really focused on the show. I glanced down at my phone again. It had been an hour since Porter had called James. Yet James still hadn't called me back. Which meant it was now past 11 o'clock in London. Much too late for a business meeting. I looked down at the t-shirt I was wearing. I had pulled it out of the hamper, so it still smelled like him. Here I was, missing him like crazy. What on earth was he doing?

I was tempted to Google him on my phone. Paparazzi loved to follow James. There were probably photos of him from this evening. Instead, I picked up my phone and clicked on Melissa's name. It had been far too long since I had called her.

"Penny!"

I smiled and leaned back on the couch. "Hey, Melissa. How's Texas treating you?"

"It's hot. No one told me how hot it would be."

I laughed. "Trust me, it's hot here too."

"I've actually been meaning to call you. I know I talked about it a ton, but I officially took a week off of work when the baby is due. I figured I needed to ingrain in the baby's head that I'm the favorite aunt right off the bat."

I laughed. "God, I miss you so much."

"I miss you too, Penny. And Josh has never even seen your place. He thinks his mansion down here is as nice as your apartment in the city. It's great and everything, but it's no Manhattan penthouse."

"Josh is coming too?"

"Mhm."

I smiled. "That's going to be so much fun. I mean...minus the fact that I'm going to be exhausted and no fun at all." I looked down at my huge tummy.

"Nonsense. You were so fun after you gave birth to Scarlett. Or maybe I was just too obsessed with your beautiful baby to notice you were being a total bore."

I laughed. "Thanks."

"Two months and we'll be hanging out just like old times. Except with your children cramping our style. I'm so excited!"

"Me too." A beeping noise made me pull my phone away from my ear. "I'm sorry, Melissa, but James is on the other line and I've been waiting for his call all day..."

"Say no more. I need to finish getting ready for dinner. It's our one year anniversary. Well, new one year. If you don't count when we dated in college."

"I bet he's going to take you some place glamorous."

"Always. I love you, Penny. Call me more often."

"I will, I promise." I clicked on the incoming call. "James! I was starting to think something happened to you."

"No, baby. I've just had tons of meetings today. I only just got back to the hotel."

Hearing his voice calmed me. "Meetings that last until 11?"

He laughed. "London is just as electric as New York. You know how business dinners go."

"I do. I just missed you. And then I found out you didn't take Briggs and you know how I worry."

"I left two girls at home that need our security detail more than I do," he said. "Speaking of which, put our beautiful daughter on the phone for me."

"Your beautiful daughter has been a terror since you left. She's spending the night at Rob's. You've created a monster."

"Me?" He laughed.

I smiled and pressed the phone harder against my ear. "I love your laugh. I miss you so much when you're gone."

"I miss you too, Penny."

There were some static noises on the line and then a long pause.

I moved the phone to my other ear. "James? Are you still there?"

"I'm here."

"I was thinking that we should hire another person for our security detail. So you don't have to travel alone."

"Spread your legs, baby."

I laughed. "What?"

"You're all alone. Spread your legs for me."

I looked up at the camera in the corner of the family room. I didn't think I'd ever be comfortable knowing that either Porter or Briggs could be watching. James' assurance that they didn't watch us when our clothes were off wasn't that convincing. He said they were required to check the cameras every five minutes to verify that everything was in order, but that was it. To me, that just verified the fact that they looked, regardless of whatever we were doing. And that meant that they had seen us in very compromising positions. Quite often. It also meant they were watching me now. I swallowed hard. "James, the cameras. You know, it's been over three years since our wedding night. Not a single bad thing has happened to us since. Not one. We're safe. We need to discuss the cameras again."

"I was actually just starting to like the cameras. Did you know that you could access them remotely?"

I frowned and stared at the camera in the corner. "You're watching me?"

"I want to see you touch yourself."

My heart raced at his words. "But Porter and Briggs can see."

"I can see. And right now, I need to see you trail your fingers up the inside of your thigh."

We'd had phone sex before. When he was away on business. But not like this. Not with him watching me. "James, I don't think..."

"Baby, I need you. I'm so fucking hard."

I pressed my lips together.

"Let me hear you," he said. "Let me see you."

I closed my eyes, blocking out the camera, trying not to think about the fact that James might not be the only one watching. I leaned back on the couch and slowly traced my hand up my thigh.

James groaned. "Just like that, baby."

I knew he was jerking off to this. I could easily picture him with his hand wrapped around his erection, staring at me through his computer screen.

"Touch yourself."

I grabbed the sides of my thong to lower it.

"No. Push the fabric to the side. Like we don't have much time. Like I'm about to fuck you hard and fast. Just the way you like it."

I pushed the fabric to the side and let my fingers slip between my legs. I was so fucking wet.

"Imagine it's my tongue."

And I moaned, because I knew exactly what that would feel like.

"Fuck. Penny." His voice sounded strained. "Pump your hand faster."

I followed his instructions.

"Rub your clit with your thumb. Imagine it's me fucking you hard."

"James," I moaned.

"Harder."

I moved my hand faster.

"You're soaking wet for me, aren't you?"

"Yes," I said breathlessly.

"You like when I watch you touch yourself."

It wasn't a question. He knew I liked it. He could see how much I liked it. "James."

"You're so fucking sexy, baby. You're gonna make me cum so hard."

I liked when he talked to me like this.

"Open your eyes and look at the camera. Look at me when you come."

I slowly opened my eyes.

"I wish it was my cock. My fingers. My tongue. God, I love the taste of you. Baby, let me taste you. Lose control.

Show me how much you love my tongue. Show me how much your pussy needs me. Show me, baby."

Jesus, that dirty mouth. I felt myself start to pulse around my fingertips. "James," I moaned.

"Fuck," he hissed. By the way he was breathing, I knew he was losing control too. "Fuck," he said again and sighed. "You're so beautiful."

I pulled my fingers out of myself and awkwardly wiped them off on my shirt. I immediately closed my legs and looked away from the camera.

"Baby, look at me."

I glanced back at the camera.

"You're perfect. So fucking perfect." His voice was heavy with lust.

"James, I'm seven months pregnant."

"You are. And just as beautiful as ever. Let me talk to the one on the way."

I smiled. "I'll put you on speaker."

"No, just...just put the phone up to your stomach. I need to have a private conversation with her."

Her. I shook my head. "He'll be happy to hear from you. One sec." I pulled the phone away from my ear and put it up to my stomach.

I turned away from the camera again. I was seven months pregnant and Porter and Briggs were probably watching. They probably saw me looking at the camera. I could feel my face turning red. Would they know James was looking too? Or would they think I was looking at the camera for them? God, I was so embarrassed. It had already been several seconds. James was probably done talking to our baby. I clicked on the speakerphone just to check.

"Your mother has the biggest heart in the world," he said. "Please don't break it. Please don't break mine. And don't come a week late like your sister. We need you to come right around your due date, alright? We're excited to meet you."

Tears formed in the corners of my eyes. I should have taken the phone off speaker. He hadn't wanted me to hear him talking. He didn't want me to know he was begging our baby not to hurt me.

The line was silent. I hit it off speaker and pulled the phone back to my ear. "James?"

There was a long pause. "Why are you crying?"

I looked up at the camera. I forgot that he could see me. Did he know I had hit speaker phone? I'm sure the camera was the best quality. But it was just a small button. He probably didn't know. "I miss you so much. And I'm...hungry."

He laughed. "Then eat something."

"There's nothing to eat. I'm out of ice cream."

"Put it on the list for Ellen tomorrow. And I'm flying back tomorrow afternoon. Just a few meetings early and then I'm done."

I didn't try to hold back my smile. I beamed up at the camera. "You should have started the conversation with that."

"It would have been harder to convince you to have phone sex if you knew I'd be back tomorrow."

I shook my head. "Were they watching?"

There was another awkward pause. "I told you that they don't watch. They just...glance."

"Maybe it's time to get rid of the cameras altogether? I'd feel so much more comfortable if they were gone."

"We can talk about it when I get back."

"I should let you get some sleep."

"I love you, Penny. So much. And you're still feeling okay? No swollen ankles or..."

"I actually feel really great. No chest pains at all today. I'm good."

He exhaled slowly, like he had been holding his breath. "I'll be back before you know it."

"And I'll be waiting. Goodnight, James." I looked up at the camera.

"I love you with all my heart. I'll finally be able to smile again when you're back in my arms. Goodnight, Penny."

Smile again? "James." But no response came. He had already hung up.

CHAPTER 30

Sunday

I remembered James' proposal like it happened yesterday. I hated being away from him. And most of all, I hated having to sleep without him. I was terrible at sleeping alone, constantly reaching out for him, being jarred awake by my hand touching empty sheets. So I had skipped ahead in the book I was writing. To one of my favorite moments. Him proposing. But now I felt as jarred as when I touched empty sheets.

"Because life without this feeling, the feeling that you give me, isn't a life that I'm interested in at all."

I leaned back in my chair and stared at the line. Maybe I remembered it wrong. Maybe I was paraphrasing and missed some important aspect of that sentence. I bit the inside of my lip. *Smile again.* That's what he had said to me on the phone earlier. Like he had been walking around London in a foul mood because I wasn't beside him. This line fit with that. Really, everything he did fit with that.

It was tempting to call him. I glanced at the time in the corner of my computer and quickly calculated the time difference. It was 4 a.m. in London. If I called, he'd be worried something had happened. And although I hadn't been hungry for anything but ice cream, and therefore hadn't eaten all night, I felt fine. I still felt better than I had a few weeks ago. There was no reason for him to worry.

I reached for my mouse, with the intent of shutting my computer down. Instead, I opened up a new document. Ever since I had found out about my heart murmur, I had meant to write a will. And now that I didn't feel sick, it didn't seem as horrid of a task. It didn't seem final. It just felt like something I needed to check off a to-do list.

Nothing in this house really belonged to me. Maybe you could say our wedding presents were technically half mine. But besides those and a few things I had kept from college, everything was James'. I didn't have anything to leave anyone. Staring at the blank screen made me realize exactly what I wanted. And it had nothing to do with divvying up material things. I took a deep breath and let my fingers fly over the keys.

James,

If you're reading this, we both know what happened. I don't need to say it. And all I can say is that I understand what you're feeling. Like your heart hurts. Like you don't know if you'll ever smile again. Like the world has stopped. Like the only thing you can see for miles is darkness.

You see, I almost lost you once. I know that feeling. My mother found me falling apart in a bathroom stall at the hospital. And she told me something that really stuck with me. She told me that you have to keep living in order to keep the memory of those you love alive. And I'm asking you to do that for me. Remind Scarlett of who I was.

Tell stories to our son. Don't let me disappear to our children. Don't let them forget how much I loved them.

Maybe that seems like the hardest thing in the world. But what I'm about to ask you to do, it may just be harder. I need you to keep the memory of me alive to our children. But I need you to let the memories of me with you fade. Because I need you to keep your heart open. Keep loving. Keep living. I need you to let me go.

All I've ever wanted was for you to be happy. And even though it feels like the world has stopped, it hasn't. Because despite what you think, there is so much light in this world. There's so much light in you.

Remind Scarlett that I love her. Tell our son I wished I could have met him. And find a new love for yourself. You've always been stronger than you realized. But it's okay to lean on your family and friends. Let them help you. Let them in. Don't shut out everyone who cares about you. Because despite how it feels, you are not alone. You're strong. You're good. You're whole. You're loved. You are so loved, James.

Now smile,

Penny

I wiped away the tears on my cheeks and pressed the print button. The printer whirred to life. And then I was left with one sheet. One sheet that felt like it held the weight of the world. My family's future and wellbeing all depending on James listening to this. I folded the paper, put it in an envelope, and sealed it. I wrote James on the front and set it back down on my desk.

I had asked him to keep living once. He had denied my request. Then I had begged him to not move on. He had accepted my request. I just hoped that him reading this would nullify anything else we had talked about. That he'd be able to read this and know it's what I truly wanted. He had to know.

I stood up from my computer and stretched. Tomorrow, I'd deliver the letter to our lawyer. He could file it away. And hopefully James would never have to read it. I wandered out of my office and up the stairs, exhausted, yet knowing that sleep wouldn't come. I struggled when James was gone. It was hard to sleep without his arms around me. Without him whispering he loved me before bed. I tried not to think about the roles being reversed. And how hard it would be to keep living without him. Because, honestly, I had given up on life when he almost died. I thought my heart would stop beating the moment his did. Even though I was pregnant. Even though I wanted to keep the memory of him alive. I just hoped to God that he was stronger than me.

I crawled into bed, pulled the covers up to my chin, and stared at the ceiling. The smell of James on the shirt I was wearing just made me more aware of the fact that he wasn't beside me. I rolled over onto my side. My son immediately started kicking my ribcage. *Ow.* The time on the alarm clock stared back, mocking me. Sleep wasn't going to come like this. I pushed the covers off of myself and made my way back downstairs.

A shiver ran down my spine as I stepped off the bottom stair. For some reason the image of Rob lying unconscious at the base of the staircase popped into my head. The pool of blood. Isabella holding the gun. I swallowed hard and made my way into the kitchen. Maybe Axel was right. Maybe it was scary down here. Or maybe my mind was too preoccupied by killer snakes.

"What's wrong? Are you hungry?" I said into the nothingness. "Is that why you won't let me sleep?"

I opened up the fridge and stared at the contents. But I wasn't hungry. *Ow.* I put my hand on the center of my chest. *No, not this again.* I closed the refrigerator door. *It's just in my head.* I made my way back up the stairs, clutching the handrail whenever the sharp pain returned. *I'm okay.* When I finally reached the bed, I curled up on James' side.

"We're okay," I said into the silence, even though pools of tears were forming in my eyes. It felt like it had the night James and I had fought about dishes. When I had fallen asleep on the floor because it hurt too much to reach the bed. *It's just in my head.* I curled into a ball. *We're okay.*

CHAPTER 31

Monday

"Scar's at Hunter Tech?" I asked as I poured myself a glass of orange juice.

"She refused to go home," Daphne said through the phone. "She wanted to go to the office with Rob."

I set my glass down on the counter and sighed. "I'll go get her now."

"It's fine. Rob said it was a light day at the office anyway. He'll bring her by around lunchtime."

"Are you sure? I don't want her ruining his day." And I strongly doubted that it was a light day. If it was, he probably would have accompanied James to London.

"Scarlett's a doll. She doesn't ruin anyone's day."

A doll? I wasn't so sure about that. I could picture her spilling coffee all over Rob's desk and throwing papers around for fun. "I think I'm going to go get her."

"You're supposed to be on bed rest," Daphne said.

"You sound like a mother."

"I guess that's what happens when you become a mother yourself. Is James coming home soon?"

"Mhm. His flight is supposed to arrive this afternoon. So I'll have my whole family back soon."

Daphne laughed. "You didn't enjoy your night off?"

I thought about the will sitting on my desk. "Not really. This place is a little big for one person."

"Well, the whole gang will be back soon. Now go get in bed."

"Okay, geez. Thanks for watching Scar last night."

"It was my pleasure. Do you want to do lunch tomorrow?"

"Yeah, that would be great. See you tomorrow."

"Bye, Penny."

I hung up the phone and looked down at the omelet Ellen had made me. My stomach seemed to churn.

"Hon, is everything alright?" Ellen asked. "You haven't touched your breakfast. I made your favorite."

"I know, I'm sorry. I'm just not hungry this morning."

"Penny, you're supposed to be eating for two. You're not even feeding one."

I laughed. "Trust me, if he wanted food, he'd be kicking me mercilessly." I pushed the plate away.

She sighed and picked it up from the counter. "Do you want anything else? I'll make you whatever you want. You're not really supposed to take those on an empty stomach." She nodded at the pill bottle next to my glass.

I wanted ice cream. But I wasn't going to ask her to make a special trip for me. I had put it on the grocery list and she usually went in the afternoons. I'd have it soon enough. "I'm fine. Everyone is making such a fuss this morning."

"Of course I'm making a fuss. Exterminators are here, tromping mud all through the house. Throwing off my whole cleaning schedule." She seemed truly flustered.

"I'm sorry, Ellen."

"Oh, no, it's fine, dear. I'm just on edge this morning. Do you really think there are snakes in the house?"

"Honestly? No. I have no idea how Scar could sneak a snake into the house. I'm just being paranoid."

She smiled. "No, you're just being a mother." She turned off the faucet. "Are you sure you don't want anything else to eat?"

"I'm sure."

"Well, I'm going to go follow those men around with a broom."

I shook my head as she exited the kitchen. I shouldn't have gone through with the exterminators coming. It was completely ridiculous. *Ow.* I put my hand on the center of my chest. Maybe I should get that second opinion that Mr. Caldwell had advised. I stood up and walked over to my purse on the counter. My hand rummaged through my purse until my fingers found the card. I pulled it out and looked down at the information. A second opinion never hurt.

"Mrs. Hunter, we have the all clear."

I looked up at Porter and dropped the card back in my purse. "They checked everywhere?"

"It's their job to."

"So...nothing?"

Porter nodded. "Nothing. I had them check for everything while they were out here. No rats or anything either."

"Well, that's good."

He smiled. "Scarlett is cleared to come back in the house now. Did you want me to go pick her up from Rob and Daphne's?"

"No. She insisted on going to work with Rob. He's bringing her by at lunch."

"Thanks for keeping her at bay."

"I didn't." I walked back over to my glass of orange juice. "She didn't want to come home." I took a sip of the sweet juice. "Are you sure there was nothing?"

"I'm positive."

"Then what is she so scared of? Why can't I comfort her?"

"Kids." Porter shrugged his shoulders. "You know how they are."

"Porter, you don't have any kids."

"Yeah, but I certainly hang out with Briggs' kid enough."

I laughed. "She's an angel. Whereas my daughter thinks something possessed by the devil is residing in our home."

"That's not true."

I suddenly wished my orange juice was something stronger. "I already know what's going to happen this afternoon. Rob's going to try to drop her off and she's going to put up a fight and scream at the top of her lungs. God, I hate that noise. When does James' flight arrive?"

"His plane should touch down around 2. William will be waiting for him at the terminal."

I bit the inside of my lip. *William.* My stomach seemed to churn again. I was starting to feel guilty that we were going to have to let William go. How was he going to take it?

"Before I forget, I have those resumes you requested," Porter said and handed me a stack of folders.

"Wow. I didn't realize there'd be so many."

"And those are just the vetted ones. A lot of good men in there. Lots of ex military."

"So tons of serious men like you that want me to call them by their last names?"

"Exactly." He gave me a smile.

"Well, let's find one with a soft side like you." I opened the top folder.

"A soft side?" Porter laughed. "I'd beg to differ."

I looked up at him. "You just had my home searched for snakes on a whim of mine. You're a sweet guy."

He shook his head. "Check out folder twelve. I have a feeling you'll like him the most. I should get back to my post."

"Thanks for everything, Porter." I picked up the stack of resumes and walked into my office. I had a few hours before Scar came home. Hopefully I could get a little writing done first. I dropped the stack of folders down on my desk and switched on my computer.

***

My eyes kept glancing at the time instead of focusing on the words I was writing. My ability to concentrate was officially gone. Besides, Rob would be here any minute, depending on when he was able to get away.

I pulled out the folder labeled with a twelve. I could at least get started on sorting through these. I opened up the folder. A picture of Ian stared back at me. *What?* I flipped to the write-up Porter had made and scanned the information. Ian had served in Iraq for three years. He was honorably discharged after a gunshot wound. He passed the written admissions test for Quantico, but failed the physical examination due to the damage in his left knee from the previously mentioned gunshot wound in Iraq. And last, he was a former member of Mr. Hunter's security detail.

Security detail. Ian wasn't a driver at all. How had I not known that? He had served our country and gotten injured. And he couldn't follow his passion of being an FBI agent because of his injury. I felt a pang of guilt. I should have known this. Why hadn't James told me?

I picked up my phone and clicked on Porter's name. He answered in one ring.

"Read the file?" Porter asked.

"Ian was one of you."

"Technically, he was my boss."

Ow. Why was this conversation making my chest hurt? "And William?"

"Also a member of your security detail. James asked me not to divulge this information to you. He didn't want you to know how much the security detail had implemented themselves in your everyday life. But I can't help it if you requested the files."

"Why did you want me to know?"

"Because you should know that Ian isn't just a driver. He's overqualified for the position, really."

"I can see that." I flipped back to the picture of him. "And what about William?"

"What about him?"

"Is he ex military too?"

"He was in the navy."

I put my forehead in my hand. No wonder he was so serious. He was younger than Ian. He had probably seen terrible things more recently. "Can we transfer him to a position like yours instead?"

"Certainly. Or Ian could be in our office instead of on the line of duty. That's up to you and James."

I looked up at the camera in the corner of the room. I thought about the things that Porter and Briggs could see. "I don't want him to have to watch me. I'd rather him be out in the field."

There was an awkward pause on his end. "Of course." He cleared his throat. "I'll draw up the necessary paperwork for William's transfer. And for rehiring Ian. I'll run through it with James when he returns."

"That sounds perfect." I bit the inside of my lip. Exactly how far had they implemented themselves in my life?

"Is there something else?" he asked. He could probably see my expression through the camera.

"What about Ellen? Is she..."

Porter laughed, cutting me off. "Ellen is the best housekeeper and chef I know. But no, she is not a member of your security detail."

I laughed. "I just had to check."

"Rob and Scarlett have entered the building. He'll be knocking in about a minute."

"Okay. And Cole?"

"Yes, Penny?"

I could hear the smile in his voice. "I appreciate everything you do for us. I hope you know that."

"I do. Have a good afternoon, Penny. I'll call you when Mr. Hunter lands."

"Thanks." I hung up the phone and slowly got up. I was comforted by the fact that William and Ian were both members of the security detail. But now it made even less sense that James hadn't taken Briggs with him. Maybe it wasn't the reason I thought it was, though. Maybe James knew how hard it was to be away from his family. And he didn't want Briggs to be away from his own daughter. I smiled as I walked over to the door.

"Ow," I said out loud and put my hand on the wall. "What are you doing in there?" I stared down at my stomach. My son kicked me again. It felt like he was doing cartwheels in my belly. The pain seemed to grow, spreading into my chest. I took a deep breath and told myself that the pain wasn't real. That it was all in my head.

CHAPTER 32

Monday

I opened the door and smiled down at my daughter.

"Hi, Mommy." She looked up at me in a strange way. As if she were studying me.

"Hi, Scar, I missed you." I bent down to hug her but she ran past me.

"Ellie!" she screamed.

I tried not to show the disappointment on my face. I had told myself that she wanted to hang out with Rob because she missed her father and wanted to hang out with another male in James' absence. But that wasn't the case. She seemed perfectly content as Ellen picked her up.

"Hi, sweet girl," Ellen said. "Did you have fun at the office?"

"Yes! I got to play with the copy machine."

I glanced at Rob.

He shrugged his shoulders.

"Come in," I said. "I hope she wasn't a nuisance."

"Nah, it was fun. Soph never wants to come to work with me. Everyone doted on her all morning. They couldn't stop talking about her beautiful red hair."

"Mhm." I looked over at Scar. Ellen was taking her upstairs to play. Ellen could entertain her for hours, yet she didn't want to spend one minute alone with me.

"James called last night to say goodnight to Scarlett. And he may have mentioned that you needed this."

I smiled and grabbed the grocery bag that I hadn't noticed. "I love you so much, Rob." I pulled out the pint of Ben and Jerry's Chunky Monkey ice cream. "Do you want some?"

"I've never turned down ice cream before."

We walked into the kitchen and I grabbed two spoons. "Did you already have lunch? I'm sure we have something more substantial to go with this."

"We grabbed hot dogs on the way here. Scarlett insisted."

"Of course she did." We made our way into the family room. I took the top off the ice cream container as I sat down on the couch, and then I took a huge bite. "God, it's everything I've been craving and more."

Rob laughed as he took a bite. "It's good, but it's not orgasmic, Penny."

I shook my head and laughed. "It's all I've been craving since the wedding." I put my hand on the center of my chest.

"Hey, are you okay?"

"I'm fine." I immediately removed my hand and took another bite. "I just have indigestion or something." I frowned at my own words. I had barely eaten anything in the past two days. What would I be having indigestion from? "Being pregnant sucks."

Rob laughed. "Daphne's getting into that phase too. Pregnant women. Ugh."

I lightly shoved his shoulder and tried not to wince at the pain that had now shifted to my stomach.

"Seriously, are you okay? You look really pale."

"Nothing a little ice cream can't fix." I took another bite and forced myself to swallow. Now I felt incredibly nauseous. "So what deal was James trying to land?"

Rob laughed. "How should I know?"

I set the pint of ice cream down on the coffee table. "Rob, you're the CEO. Shouldn't you know everything that's going on?" I smiled at him.

"Yeah, and I do." He said it a little defensively.

"Okay, so what deal is James trying to get for Hunter Tech in London?"

"I have no idea what you're talking about."

Another pain shot through my stomach and I leaned forward slightly. "You asked him to go to London."

"What? No, I didn't. He's not there for Hunter Tech."

Ow. "What do you mean? Why else would he go to London?"

"I don't know. I thought it was for the university."

"He's not teaching an abroad program." I laughed awkwardly. "Seriously, Rob, why was he in London?"

"I don't know. But the paparazzi probably do." He picked up his phone and typed something in. He lowered both his eyebrows.

"What?" I asked.

"Nothing." He tried to move his phone away from me but I grabbed it.

He had done a Google image search. There were tons of images of James dining with some woman at an outdoor restaurant. Some gorgeous woman with long, brunette hair and skin that was too tan for London's dreary climate. "Who is this woman?" I asked.

"I don't know, I've never seen her before."

I laughed. "Is this some kind of weird joke, Rob? One of your pranks?" I stared at him hopefully and tried to ignore the pain in my chest. *What the fuck was James doing with some beautiful woman in London? And why had he lied to me about it?*

"I'm sure there's an innocent explanation," Rob said. "He should be back pretty soon, right?"

I glanced at the clock. "In about an hour."

"I should probably get back to work." Rob abruptly stood up.

"Rob."

He seemed to cringe.

"Is he cheating on me?"

Rob laughed. "No, of course not. He wouldn't." But there was doubt in his voice. Suspicion. And maybe, just maybe, a small hint of anger. I just didn't know if it was directed at me or his brother.

"Rob? If you know something you have to tell me." I stood up and immediately hunched forward.

"Penny?"

I felt his hands on my shoulders. "Ow." I put my hand on my stomach. I didn't realize I had said it out loud. But by the look on Rob's face, I definitely had.

"Penny, are you alright?"

"No." I shook my head. "I'm going to be sick."

"Okay...just..." his voice trailed off as he ran into the kitchen.

Fuck. I grabbed my stomach.

Rob came back just in time with a bowl.

I sat down on the carpet and threw up. Every little bit that was left in my stomach barely covered the bottom of the bowl.

He ran his hand up and down my back. "Do you want me to get Ellen?"

I shook my head. "No. I don't want Scar to see me like this." I leaned over the bowl again. My stomach still ached, but nothing else seemed to want to come up.

Rob handed me a paper towel.

"I'm so sorry." I wiped my mouth off.

"I'm the one that should be apologizing. The ice cream I brought made you sick."

"No, it's probably just really late morning sickness. I'm fine." *Fuck, it hurts.*

"I think I should take you to the doctor."

I shook my head. "Rob," I said and looked up at him. "Is James having an affair? Tell me he's not. Please." It felt like my heart was ripping in two. Something was wrong. Something was terribly wrong.

"No." He said it firmly this time. The doubt was gone.

And then I felt it. A wetness surrounding me. It was too soon. Panic started to weigh on top of the searing pain in my stomach. "My water broke," I croaked. Two months too early. I felt tears welling in my eyes.

"Shit," Rob said. "I'll get Ellen."

"No. Scar can't see me like this." I grabbed his leg. "Help me up. William will take me to the hospital."

"Penny..."

"Please, Rob. Scar already thinks I'm weak. She can't see me like this." I tried to blink away the tears. "I don't want her to see me like this."

I leaned over in pain.

Rob pulled out his cell phone. "My sister-in-law's water just broke," he said into the cell phone. "Twenty minutes, are you fucking kidding me?" He hung up the phone. "Okay, I'm going to help you up." He leaned down and grabbed my hands.

I grimaced in pain. "Something's wrong. It's too soon." It didn't feel the way it had when my water broke when I was pregnant with Scarlett. Everything felt wrong.

"It's okay," Rob said as he slowly helped me to my feet. But then something in his face changed. Horror. Dread. Agony. They swept over his features in a flash.

I suddenly felt faint and I teetered forward slightly.

"Ellen!" he yelled at the top of his lungs. "Ellen, call William and tell him to get the car started!"

I winced in pain. Why was he calling for her? I had just asked him not to.

Ellen came running down the stairs and gasped. The look of horror on her face matched Rob's.

I followed her trail of vision and stared down at the pool of blood at my feet. Seeping into the carpet. Dripping down my legs. The blood was everywhere.

"You're okay," Rob said as he scooped me up into his arms and started running. "You're going to be okay."

But I wasn't. I just knew I wasn't. Because the pain in my stomach was growing worse by the second. And my son wasn't kicking me. He wasn't fucking kicking me.

"Christ!" Rob yelled as he slammed his fist against the elevator button.

Porter and Briggs ran out of their office down the hall.

"What happened?" Porter asked. He reached out to take me from Rob.

I grabbed the collar of Rob's shirt. I didn't want him to let me go.

"I've got her," Rob said.

"This way then," Porter said and ran toward the staircase.

"I'll call James," Briggs said and ran back to their office.

I closed my eyes. Each step downwards on the stairs made my stomach ache more.

I heard a car door open and close. I heard the squeal of the tires. Cursing. I had never felt more weak. It felt like the life was draining out of my body. And not just my son's. My own. My heartbeat seemed to slow. A chill entered my bloodstream. It felt like the coolness was pulsing through my whole body.

"It's okay," Rob said. "We're almost there."

I was vaguely aware of the fact that he hadn't set me down in the back seat. That he was cradling me in his arms. Like he knew if he let go, I'd be gone.

"Take care of him," I said.

"Penny." His hand on my cheek felt scalding hot.

"Promise me you'll take care of him."

"You're going to be alright. Everything's okay."

I looked up at his face. It was wet with tears. I had seen him cry once before. When James had gotten shot. When we thought we might lose him. And I knew it then. He thought I was going to die. I thought I was going to die. And I felt the death in my stomach. I felt it rip my heart in two.

"Promise me." My voice came out as a whisper.

He shook his head.

"Take care of Scarlett."

"Penny..."

"Take care of my family."

"We're almost there," he said.

"I'm scared." I tried to grab his hand, but my grip was too weak. The pain was easing as the feeling of ice spread. It was peaceful. Like my body was trying to comfort me as I slipped. As it became harder to breathe. "I'm so scared," I whispered.

"Penny, open your eyes."

I tried, but I couldn't.

"Penny, you're not allowed to leave us. Do you hear me? Open your eyes, okay?"

But I couldn't. I couldn't do it.

"Please."

The desperation in his voice pained me. But I couldn't frown. I couldn't move at all.

"Fucking open your eyes!"

PART 3

James

CHAPTER 33

Monday

I read through the contract once more. My lawyer had already gone over it. Now all it needed was Penny's signature. I took a sip of my drink. Hopefully she'd be so excited that she'd forgive me for having been reading her book ever since she started writing it three years ago.

I had tried not to. I had tried to respect her decision for me to wait. But I couldn't stop once I had started. Her account was linked to mine. I was able to see every word she typed as she typed it. Sometimes I'd sit in my office and stare at the screen, watching her create a scene. Watching her pull our memories out of her head and paint a picture on the page. To see her version of us unfold. To see her feelings grow.

No, I couldn't stop. I couldn't look away. It was brilliant. A perfect mix of fiction and reality. A one-sided tale of grief and love and hope. She deserved the publishing deal I had just landed her. And I couldn't wait to surprise her. I couldn't wait to kiss her perfect stomach and hug the beautiful daughter she had given us. I missed her so much that it physically hurt. I took another sip of my drink.

It had only taken two meetings. The second publishing house I met with showed immediate interest. The negotiation process was easy. As far as I could tell, I had landed

Penny a deal that was better than many authors who had been writing for years. Hopefully that would also be enough to get Penny to forgive me for butting into the publishing process. And for lying about the reason for my trip in the first place.

"We'll be landing in a few minutes, if you could buckle your seatbelt," the flight attendant said.

I looked up and nodded. For a second, I had wondered if she was talking to me. But I was the only one on the plane. "Of course." I reached over and fastened the buckle in place as she removed my drink. I stared out the window as the city came into view. *Home.* But it wasn't the place that was home. It was her. Wherever she was, that was home to me.

I lifted up the contract and put it into my satchel. Before she had given birth to Scarlett, I had read that you should give your wife a gift before the baby arrived. I had transformed the library into her office and filled it with books that she loved. She had been so excited. This publishing contract was my gift this time. She had been writing ever since she found out she was pregnant the first time. This was the perfect gift. She deserved this. It didn't matter how she got it.

But the closer we got to the airport, the more unsettled I felt. What if she didn't want this? What if I had overstepped again? I hated that look she gave me. The one where her eyebrows pinched together in disappointment. She had to forgive me for reading her book without her permission. For inserting myself in the publication process. For lying to her about the trip. That was a lot of forgiveness. *Maybe I should buy her something too.* I shook my head. She never appreciated gifts like that as much. It was one of the many reasons why I fell for her in the first place.

And there were a lot of reasons. The way her hair shimmered in the sun. The way her smile could light up a room. The way her laughter vibrated through me. The way she melted at my touch. The way her breasts fit perfectly in my hands. The way she moaned my name in need. God, I was lucky. Every day I counted my blessings. The life she had given me. The fresh start I didn't deserve. I owed everything to my beautiful wife. Every single thing.

Recently, I wasn't sure if she was happy. I saw the frowns when she thought I wasn't looking. The tears that pooled in the corner of her eyes when she got a rejection letter. No one should have been allowed to make her feel like she wasn't good enough. She was perfect. Everything about her was pure perfection. She wanted more out of life. And I didn't blame her. I loved being her husband. I loved being a father. But I loved teaching too. She was allowed to have it all. I could give it all to her.

The plane started to descend. I missed my daughter terribly, but I needed some alone time with Penny. To tell her the good news. To make love to her. Maybe Ellen could take Scarlett to the park and Penny and I could meet up with them later. I pulled out my phone when the wheels touched the ground. As soon as it turned on, it started buzzing. The unread messages icon popped up and started flashing, signaling more and more coming in. Followed by the voicemail icon. Flashing. Flashing. Buzzing.

I was unbuckling my seat belt before we even started moving toward the terminal.

"Mr. Hunter, if you could please remain seated..."

I ignored the flight attendant and clicked on the first voicemail.

"Mr. Hunter, it's Briggs. There's been an incident. Penny is on her way to the hospital. William will drive to the airport as soon as he's dropped her off. You need to come straight to the hospital."

An incident? What kind of incident? "Stop the plane!" I yelled. I tried to call him back, but my phone wasn't working properly yet. Instead, I clicked on another voicemail.

"James, it's Ellen. Scarlett is with me at the house. I didn't know if you'd want me to take her to the hospital. Please call me when you land. If we don't hear from you soon, we're going to head over. She won't stop crying. I don't know what to do."

I started pulling on the handles of the door.

"We can't stop the plane," the flight attendant said.

I clicked on another message as I continued to fumble with the lock.

"James, it's your father. You need to come to the hospital. They just took Penny into surgery. You need to hurry."

No. No, no, no. I slammed my fist against the door.

"I will not ask you again," the flight attendant said. "You need to take your seat."

"My wife is in the hospital. I need to go." It felt like someone was strangling me.

She gave me a sympathetic look. "You can't exit on the landing strip. The sooner you take a seat, the sooner we can pull up to a terminal.

"Fuck!" I slammed my fist against the door again.

"Mr. Hunter!"

I brushed past her to my seat as I clicked on another message.

"Answer your fucking messages!" Rob yelled. "She needs you. Where the fuck were you, man? Why were you in London? She needed you here."

I buried my face in my hands. *Please be okay, baby. Please be okay.*

The plane slowly started to roll toward the terminal.

I clicked on another message.

"James, is she okay?" Mrs. Taylor's concerned voice filled my ear. "We're driving up now. I received a voicemail at work." It sounded liked she had started to cry. "Tell me my baby is okay. Please call me back."

It felt like I was choking. "Stop the plane! Stop the fucking plane."

"We're pulling up now," the flight attendant said calmly.

I stood up, grabbed my satchel, and ran back over to the door as I clicked on another message.

"James." It was Rob again. "No one is here to sign off on anything. I don't have any authority to make decisions. They're delivering the baby. That's too soon, right? Seven months is too soon. I tried to tell them that..." Rob cleared his throat. "She's still unconscious. I don't know if she's going to make it. What if she doesn't make it?" The message ended.

Two months was too soon. I was supposed to be there for the birth. I needed to be there. We were going to grow old and gray together. All of this was too soon. I wiped the tears off my cheeks. I couldn't lose her. I couldn't.

The door slowly opened and I started running.

"You forgot the rest of your luggage!" the flight attendant called after me.

I didn't need my luggage. All I needed was her. All I had ever needed was her.

CHAPTER 34

Monday

I clicked on Ian's number. *Fuck. Not Ian.* I bumped into someone.

"Watch where you're going," he growled.

Fuck off. Fuck everything. God, I can't lose her. I picked up my pace, trying to avoid the people absentmindedly going through their days. How could everyone be acting normal when it felt like my whole world was caving in around me?

I scrolled through my phone until I saw William's name. But I didn't need to call. As soon as I pushed through the doors to the airport, I saw my car. William had parked it on the curb and he was arguing with an airport traffic policeman.

I started to run over to them.

"You have to keep moving," the police officer said. "I'm not going to ask you again."

"Or what? It's an emergency!" William looked like he was a few seconds away from punching the policeman in the face.

"Everyone has an emergency. Move along."

"I'm here, I'm here," I said as I ran up to them.

"Front seat," William said to me as he ran around to the other side of the car.

"Have a nice day too," the police officer mumbled.

I climbed into the passenger's side, ignoring him. I had barely closed the door when William hit the gas. "What happened? Is she okay?" Part of me didn't want to know the answer. If I didn't know, she was fine. She was still breathing. She was still with me.

William shook his head. "I don't know. She lost a lot of blood on the way to the hospital."

I turned around to look at the back seat. The leather upholstery was covered in blood. Her blood. My wife's blood. I shook my head. "But is she okay?"

"I don't know." He swerved to avoid another car.

Someone honked at him and he cursed under his breath.

"She lost consciousness before we arrived," William added.

I looked at the back seat again. "Was someone with her?"

"Your brother was with her."

I nodded. If she had been alone, I wouldn't have been able to forgive myself. But she had Rob. Rob would have taken care of her. She would have felt safe with him. *She would have felt safer with you.* I tried to shake the thought out of my head. *Damn it. Why now?* Of all the times for this to happen, why did it have to happen the one day I was out of town? I clenched my hand into a fist. I wanted to go back in time.

The image of her asking me to stay at the wedding popped into my head. She had asked me not to go. Why hadn't I listened? What the fuck was wrong with me? I wanted to surprise her, but why hadn't I realized she was begging me to stay? Did she know something was wrong then? Had she been in pain? The thought made me feel paralyzed. She didn't want a surprise. She just wanted to spend time with me.

I looked at the back seat again. She was in pain now. And it didn't matter that Rob had been with her. Rob wasn't me. She needed me and I wasn't there. I vowed to catch her every time she fell. I promised her. I had failed her.

"Is Scarlett still at the apartment?" I asked.

"Yes. No one could get a hold of you to ask you what to do. Apparently she won't stop crying."

I tried to take a deep breath. My daughter needed reassurance. I pulled out my phone to call Ellen, but stopped myself. *Fuck.* I needed reassurance. I couldn't call them to calm them down when I could barely breathe. "Go a different way," I said as William started to approach stopped traffic.

"I'll try, Mr. Hunter."

Another car honked at us as William cut them off.

"Was Penny asking for me?" I didn't really want to know the answer. Even if she hadn't been asking for me, I knew she needed me. I let her down.

William didn't respond as he slammed on the brakes, unable to avoid the stopped cars.

"Was she asking for me?" I repeated.

"She asked Rob to take care of her family. She kept saying she was scared."

I shook my head and unbuckled my seatbelt. She was thinking about me even though she was in pain. She was selfless. She was perfect. God, she had to be okay.

"It's three miles away, Mr. Hunter."

I ignored him as I pushed opened the door. I slammed it closed and started running. Normally the summer heat in the middle of the day would bother me. Running in a suit would bother me. But all I could feel was my heart. It fucking hurt. I let her down. She needed me and I wasn't there. *Please be okay, baby.*

***

I pushed through the doors of the hospital, gasping for air. "Penny Hunter!" I said before I even approached the front desk. "Penny Hunter," I said a little louder as I ran over to the woman who looked bored out of her mind. Again, I found it jarring that the whole world wasn't in pain like me. Everyone should have been breaking. Everyone. Yet no one seemed to understand the extent of what was happening.

"Penny Hunter," the woman said as she typed the name into her computer. "Third floor. She's still in surgery."

"What happened?"

She shrugged her shoulders. "I don't know, sir. Are you related to the patient?"

"I'm her husband."

"Okay, great. If you could just sign in and we'll give you a wristband."

I didn't have time for this nonsense. My wife was in surgery. She had just said that. Didn't she realize how ridiculous her request was after what she had just told me? I ran over to the elevators and slammed my fist against the arrow pointing up.

"You need a wristband, sir!" she called after me.

Fuck you. I ignored her. When the doors didn't immediately open, I looked around for the staircase. I sprinted over to it and took the stairs two at a time. I burst through the door and into a waiting room. Familiar faces turned toward me. My father. Daphne. But Rob didn't look up. He was sitting with his elbows on his knees. Daphne was rubbing his back.

"Is she okay?" I asked. But I knew she wasn't. By the way they were looking at me, I just knew the love of my life was dying. I could feel my body turning cold. It was like I could feel her pain. And the weight of it was unbearable.

Mascara was smudged under Daphne's eyes, tears dried on her cheeks. She pressed her lips together, unable to answer me. But I could read her expression pretty clearly. It was one of loss. Insufferable loss. The kind of loss that I knew would kill me.

God, Penny. Someone fucking say something!

Rob shook his head as he slowly looked up at me. "I don't know. They won't tell us anything. All I know is that they said they were trying to deliver the baby. But that was half an hour ago. We haven't heard anything else."

The baby. I looked down at his dress shirt and pants. He was covered in blood. My wife's blood. I didn't care about the baby. Why were they talking about the baby? It didn't matter. I wanted to know how my wife was. "I didn't ask about the baby, I asked about her. Someone fucking say something!" I was losing it. The side of my face started twitching with agitation. A feeling I hadn't experienced since meeting Penny. A nervous tick that made me aware of just how quickly I was losing control. A feeling I used to numb.

"Why don't you sit down," Daphne said. "I'll go talk to the nurse at the front desk again."

I shook my head and stepped back from them. Why weren't they telling me? God, how bad was it?

"Son, take a seat," my dad said, placing his hand on my shoulder. "I'm sure the doctor will be out in a moment. We just have to wait. We've told you everything we know."

Fuck that. "I need to know if she's okay."

"She's not okay," Rob said. "She died in my arms and you weren't there. She stopped breathing. They're not saying anything because they're trying to deliver the baby before it dies too. Because her body is no longer supporting it."

"Robert," my dad said sternly. "That's enough."

She can't be dead. I shook my head. I put my hand on the side of my face where my eye wouldn't stop twitching. It felt like my feet were melting into the floor.

"Where were you, James?" Rob said as he abruptly stood up. He walked toward me. "You piece of shit!" He shoved me hard.

"Robert!" my dad said more sternly and grabbed the back of Rob's collar. "Sit down." He pushed him away from me.

"Rob," Daphne said and grabbed his arm. "This isn't the time or place for this."

But Rob was right. He should shove me. I had nothing to say. I felt like shit. I let Penny down. "She can't be dead." I shook my head. "She can't be." I shook my head again. I wanted Rob to shove me again. I wanted him to hit me. I needed to feel the pain. I clenched my hand into a fist. I needed to feel the pain she was feeling.

My dad grabbed my arm and pulled me to the front desk. "Her husband is here now. Can't you give updates to him?"

The nurse looked up at us. "She's in surgery. As soon as she's out, a doctor will come to talk to you. It shouldn't be much longer."

"I need to talk to someone now," I said.

"I'm sorry, sir, that's just not possible."

I glanced to my right where there was a door marked hospital personnel only. I started walking toward it.

"Sir!" she called after me. "Sir, you can't go back there!"

I pushed open the doors, ignoring her. "Penny!" I called at the top of my lungs. "Penny!" It felt like I couldn't breathe.

An orderly rushed out of a door down the hall. "You're not allowed in here," he said as he hurried toward me.

"Penny!" I yelled again. I turned my head toward one of the glass partitions. *Not her.* I kept walking.

"You really can't be back here," the orderly said and grabbed my shoulder.

I pushed him off of me.

"Penny!" The desperation in my voice made me feel crazy. Was I losing my mind? Was any of this really happening?

The orderly tugged on my arm and I shoved him again.

I needed to find her. I needed to see that she was okay.

"We need security up here," he said into a walkie talkie. "Now."

And that's when I saw her. I was looking through a glass, like I was watching something that couldn't possibly be happening. Her face was pale. There was a tube down her throat. She no longer looked like my wife. She looked empty. Like a shell of who she once was. I put my hand against the glass partition. "Baby." And a piece of me died.

CHAPTER 35

Monday

"Get off of me!" I yelled as the security guards pulled me back through the doors. "She needs me! My wife needs me." I tried to fight them off.

"Daddy!"

I stopped fighting when I saw my daughter running toward me. And I fell to my knees. Because the sight of her pained me. Her mouth. Her nose. Her hair. They weren't hers. They were her mother's. She was a living, breathing mini-replica of my wife. I closed my eyes as she launched herself into my arms. I tried to hold back my tears.

"Daddy, the snake came. You weren't here, and the snake came for Mommy."

She didn't understand what was happening. But she was right about one thing. This was all my fault.

"Daddy, is Mommy okay?" she asked.

I buried my face in her hair. How was I supposed to answer her? How was I supposed to look at her? How was I supposed to console her when I couldn't even look at her? "She's okay, pumpkin," I said into her hair and held her tighter. "She's going to be fine," I lied.

"I want Mommy."

Me too. God, me too. The image of Penny's pale face seared through my mind. It was haunting.

"Sir, you need to come with us," one of the security guards said.

"He's not going to go through the doors again," my father said.

An argument pursued, but I blocked it out.

"Daddy, I want Mommy," Scarlett mumbled into my neck.

"I know, pumpkin." I tried to keep my voice even. "But we have to wait a little bit."

"No, I want Mommy."

Her words made the reality settle around me. What if she never got to see her mother again? What if I never got to? Scarlett no longer felt comforting in my arms. She felt heavy. Suddenly she seemed more like a burden than a blessing. Why couldn't I look at her? The side of my face twitched again.

"He needs a wristband if he's staying," the security guard said. "It'll just take a minute, but he needs to come with me."

I couldn't keep holding Scarlett. I couldn't keep pretending I knew how to comfort her when my world was dark. I opened my eyes and looked up at the ceiling. "I need you to go sit with Ellen, okay?"

"No." She gripped me tighter.

"Dad, can you take her?" I asked.

"Of course." My father reached down and lifted her out of my arms.

"No! Daddy!" she screamed and started crying.

I turned away without looking at her.

"Daddy!" she cried as I quickly followed the security guard out of the waiting room.

I usually couldn't stand to hear her cry. I doted on her all the time. I spoiled her, just like Penny said. But right now, I could barely hear her cries. They sounded muffled. And I was very aware of the fact that it felt like the world was becoming blurry. My chest hurt when I took a breath. Penny always made it easy to breathe.

I winced at Scarlett screaming for me, but I didn't turn back. I needed a minute. I just needed one fucking minute.

**

I blinked as a hospital bracelet was fastened to my wrist. I stared at the man who was warning me I wouldn't get another chance. But I didn't seem to be able to process his words.

"You can go now," he said, irritably, like it wasn't the first time he had spoken the words.

I slowly walked back toward the stairs. Everything felt methodical. Like I wasn't really there. Like it wasn't real. But then I took a deep breath before I pushed through the doors back into the waiting room. And suddenly it felt real. It felt like I'd never get to see Penny again.

I dropped my hands from the door, sat down on the stairs, and cried. I cried because I had a beautiful daughter. I had family. I had friends. But I wanted none of it. I'd trade it all for one more moment with Penny. One more kiss. One more fucking breath.

Because, God, I couldn't breathe. I put my hand on the side of my face, trying to stop the twitching. How was I supposed to breathe without her?

CHAPTER 36

Monday

My hands were shaking as I splashed water on my face. I gripped the sides of the sink and stared at my reflection in the mirror. I was whole when I left for London. But there was a broken man staring back at me now. I knew what this looked like. I was all too familiar with it.

It had always been my fear. The darkest one. The one I didn't know how to let go of. The one that no amount of goodness could erase. I closed my eyes so that I wouldn't see the twitch of my eye. Because the truth was, my supply had just run out. And I needed a fix. I needed to kiss her lips. I needed to smell her hair. I needed to feel her skin against mine. I gripped the sink even harder. Penny had always been my drug. Taste. Touch. Smell. Sight. Sound. She was everything. Without her, I had nothing left.

I kept my eyes closed as the restroom door opened.

"Where were you?" Rob asked.

I didn't say anything. Where was I? Where had I been when my wife was dying? In the air? At a meeting? How long had she been in surgery? How long had I been standing in this fucking bathroom, hiding from the world?

"She needed you," Rob said and shoved my shoulder.

I didn't move, I was gripping the sink so tight.

"You were in London screwing some random girl when your wife was seven months pregnant with your child." He grabbed the back of my shirt, pulling me away from the mirrors. "Fuck you." He pushed me, slamming my lower back against the sink.

It was the first thing I had felt besides my twitch in too long. *Fire.* I used to love getting into fights when I was young. When I had nothing to lose. The feeling of my knuckles against someone's jaw was thrilling. I tried to shake away the thought. This wasn't some random guy in a bar. This was my brother. I tried to focus on what he had just said. *Screwing some random girl?* "What the hell are you even talking about?"

He shoved my chest. "You fucking prick."

Fire.

"I lied to her for you. That's the last thing I'll ever say to her. Covering for your cheating ass."

Fire. I clenched my hand into a fist. "I didn't cheat on Penny."

"This happened right after she saw pictures of you with some slut. This is your fault."

Crack. That sound. The one of bone hitting flesh. My fist against his jaw. That was the sound I had always loved so much. *Fire.*

Rob put his hand on his jaw where I had punched him. He shook his head. "I wanted to kick your ass anyway," he said. He launched himself at me, knocking us both to the floor.

I tasted blood in my mouth as Rob's fisted landed against the side of my face. And I felt something besides the twitch. Bone against flesh. Blood. My heart started beating again for just a second as I unsuccessfully tried to break my brother's nose.

He punched me again, knocking my head back against the cold tile floor. And a strangled sob escaped my throat. Not because it hurt. But because I imagined Penny's skin being as cold as that disgusting floor beneath me. Like ice. She was so pale. The fire I had felt had evaporated as quickly as it had come. And all I could feel was pain. My chest ached. I couldn't breathe.

"Jesus." Rob climbed off of me.

The only noise in the room was the stifled sound of me holding back my sobs.

Rob wiped the blood dribbling down his chin with the back of his hand. "You cheated on her," he said. "How could you?"

"I don't know what you're talking about. I love my wife." The word "wife" sounded as broken as I felt. *Please, baby. Please still be breathing.* I pulled myself to a seated position.

"Then what the hell were you doing with that side-piece in London?!" He took a step toward me, but stopped. I stared at his hands forming into fists. He was showing restraint. But I wished he wouldn't. I wanted to feel the pain of his fist against my jaw again. It was better than the numbness. It was better than craving something that I wasn't sure I'd ever be able to have again.

"I wanted to surprise her." I shook my head, realizing how dumb it was now. "I got her a publishing deal." It was all empty. I was in London for something Penny didn't want. At least, she didn't want it from me. *I should have fucking been here.*

Rob wiped his hand off on his jeans, which were already covered in blood. I couldn't stop staring at the red stains on his clothes. Penny's blood. I should have been holding my wife instead of a contract that meant nothing. She needed me.

"Who was the woman?" Rob asked.

I stared at him blankly. And then shook my head, trying to think of anything but the blood. "A literary agent." I finally realized the extent of what my brother was saying. "Penny thought I was cheating on her?" It was getting harder and harder to breathe.

"What would you think if you were in her shoes?"

"I just wanted to surprise her. I wanted her to feel..." I let my voice trail off. *What? Happy?* Her frowns killed me. I didn't understand why she needed more than what I could give her, why she felt unfulfilled in our lives. Because the truth was, I'd still be happy if I stopped teaching. As long as I had her, I didn't need anything else. So why wasn't I fucking enough for her? I took a deep breath, but it didn't feel like anything filled my lungs.

"Worthy of you instead of just lucky," Rob said.

"What?"

"That's what Penny wanted. She thought writing a book and making a name for herself would make her worthy of you. Instead of just lucky that you chose her. That's why she wanted it. That's why she didn't want your help with it."

"Did she tell you that?"

"She didn't have to, man." He sat down on the floor next to me.

"I fucked everything up. I don't know what I was thinking."

"You were thinking you wanted to make her happy. It's not like that's some fatal flaw. But yeah...it looked bad. I may have been projecting though."

I looked up at him.

"She started throwing up after I brought her ice cream. Then she started bleeding." He looked down at the floor. "All of this is actually my fault."

I shook my head. "No, I'll tell you whose fucking fault it is. Her last OB-GYN who didn't tell us about her heart condition in the first place. I need to go talk to my lawyer."

"I don't know if this had anything to do with her heart. She was having stomach pains."

"It has everything to do with it." I slowly stood up. "I'll be back."

"You can't leave. Scar won't stop crying. She needs you."

"I can't..." I shook my head. "I can't look at her right now." I walked over to the door.

"Penny needs you here. You have a kid that needs you. And any minute now, you'll have another one. The lawsuit can wait. You need to be here."

I pushed open the door.

"Penny never left your hospital bed after you got shot," he said to my back. "Never."

"That's the thing, Rob. I was never worthy of Penny, not the other way around." The door closed behind me with a thud. If Rob was expecting me to feel guilty, that wasn't going to work. I couldn't feel anything but the numbness creeping into my bones.

CHAPTER 37

Monday

"He withheld information!" I slammed my fist down on the desk.

The man sitting across the desk from me jumped. A small man. One I had talked to only a few times. One that hadn't earned my trust yet. Not that any lawyer could. Not after the one I had trusted ended up being in bed with Isabella. I stared at him, pleased that he quavered under my gaze.

"James," he said in a voice that didn't demand an ounce of respect. "We don't know if that's what caused the incident. Malpractice isn't a petty lawsuit. You'll ruin his reputation. We'll need more proof."

I cringed at the word incident. Why did everyone keep saying that? It diminished the situation. This wasn't just some random event. This was my whole fucking life. I wanted to reach across the desk and wrap my hands around his throat.

"Penny called me this morning," he continued. "She wanted to deliver her will to the office. Well, an amendment to the will you had made for her. But I didn't have any appointments open until this afternoon. She was supposed to come in right around now, actually."

The side of my face twitched. I looked away so he couldn't see it. "What the fuck are you talking about?"

"She said she wanted to add to it. But based on that phone call, is there any possibility at all that this could have been planned?"

I turned back toward him and leaned forward. "My pregnant wife bleeding out in the back seat of a car? You think that was planned?"

"Signs of suicide..."

I stood up. The chair squeaked behind me against the wooden floorboards. "You don't know my wife. You know nothing about us. So I'll forgive you this once. But if the next words out of your mouth aren't, 'I'm filing the suit,' then you're fired."

"James." He sounded exasperated. "Why else would she want to update her will hours before this happened? I understand that suicide isn't..."

"Stop saying suicide." I slammed my fist against his desk again.

He flinched, but I found no joy in it.

"We have a daughter. She was pregnant with our second child." *She has me.* "She didn't try to kill herself. You'll be hearing from my new lawyer about this slander."

"No lawsuit is going to fix this, James. Go be with your family in their time of need."

"Their need?" My voice cracked. I walked over to the door so I wouldn't strangle him. "It's *my* need. She's my wife." She's my everything. "Go fuck yourself." I slammed the door to his office as I walked out.

The receptionist looked up at me. "Mr. Hunter," she said, "your brother has called for you several times..."

But I was already out the door. The city air was stale. *Their need?* It felt like my heart was slamming against my ribcage. My eyes landed on a bar down the street.

I felt the familiar twitch, and immediately turned away from it. Alcohol wasn't going to fix this. Nothing could fill this void. I put my hands on my knees. *Fuck, I couldn't breathe.*

A car screeched to a halt in front of me.

"Jesus, there you are," my dad said as he stepped out. "Get in the car, James."

I shook my head, my hands still on my knees. "I can't."

"Penny's parents just arrived at the hospital. How do you think that looks? You not being there?"

"I don't care how it looks." I stood up, my eyes wandering back to the bar. *Twitch.*

"I didn't raise you..."

"You didn't raise me at all!" My blood was boiling. I was slowly slipping into the darkness. "You don't get to suddenly show up in my life and pretend you've been a father to me for the past thirty years. You're a fucking hypocrite."

"You're hurting. I understand that," he said through a clenched jaw. "But this isn't about me being a shitty dad. This is about you being one."

I laughed and ran my hands through my hair. "Give me a break. I'm nothing like you."

"Your daughter is terrified. She needs you to comfort her."

"She's fine. Rob's there. Ellen's there."

"She needs you, James! What don't you understand about that?"

I shook my head.

"Get in the car."

"I can't." I looked longingly at the bar down the street.

"You have to."

"I can't! I can't look at her. She's the spitting image of Penny. I can't." The sob in my throat escaped. I put the back of my hand against my mouth, trying to hide the pain on my face.

And my dad did something I don't remember him ever doing. He hugged me. And then I did something I don't think I had ever done. I cried on my dad's shoulder.

"What if I lose her, Dad?"

"Then you'll grieve for however long it takes. But then you keep living this life that you two created together. Because you have a family now. It's more than just you and your feelings."

I shook my head. "You don't understand. I'm not...I can't do it without her. How am I supposed to raise a kid without her?"

"Kids."

"What?" I lifted my head off his shoulder.

"You have a son, James."

A son. That was supposed to be exciting news. It was exactly what Penny wanted. I wanted to smile. I wanted to be happy. But the corners of my lips wouldn't rise.

CHAPTER 38

Monday

We used a different entrance to the hospital to avoid the waiting room full of people I couldn't face. I followed my dad through the maternity ward full of crying babies, until we stopped in front of a window.

I peered into the room. It wasn't like where Scarlett had been kept. She had been healthy, born a week after her due date. These were tiny babies hooked up to tubes and wires. They were all so small. One of them was mine. But I still couldn't feel anything. I looked up at the sign above the window. Neonatal Intensive Care Unit. These newborns were sick. They were dying, just like my wife. *Twitch.*

"There," my dad said and pointed to a baby in the corner. I stared at my son through the glass. There were tubes attached to him everywhere. Tubes to help him breathe. Tubes to help him hold on. He had my dark hair. And my nose. But I felt nothing. Nothing except for a familiar itch in the back of my head. A feeling of emptiness. A desire to do anything to escape from numbness.

My son needed me. But I didn't need him. I took a step back from the glass. All I needed was my wife. And she was dying. I could almost feel it. Like a part of my own heart was failing. The side of my face twitched.

"He looks a lot like you," my dad said.

I shook my head. None of this felt real. The tubes and wires were the only things keeping him alive. He was so small. He'd probably fit in my hand. He was too young to be born. It wasn't right. None of this was right. He needed to be in his mother's arms. Not shut off from the world. *Like me.*

"What did they say when they told you about the baby?" I asked.

"That he has to stay in the NICU for awhile. He has anemia and they've already done one blood transfusion. But his lungs are fairly strong so he doesn't need a ventilator. Just that little machine over his mouth. A CPAP I believe they said. They also mentioned that skin to skin contact is good for preemies, if you want to hold him."

Preemies. I still felt nothing. "Is he going to live?"

"The doctors seem optimistic."

I nodded and turned away from the window. "What did they say about Penny?"

"That she's still in surgery."

"That's it?"

"And that they had to do an emergency C-section. That's all they said. Come say hello to her parents. They could use a familiar face."

I nodded and walked away from the window without looking back at my son.

"Daddy!" Scarlett yelled as she scrambled out of Mrs. Taylor's lap.

I lifted her into my arms without really looking at her.

Mrs. Taylor's face was pinched, like she had been crying and willed herself to stop. I didn't know what to say to her. Or to Penny's dad, who had just stood up.

But I didn't have to say a word. He just gave me a nod, clapped me on the back, and sat back down next to his wife.

I couldn't sit here with them. I couldn't comfort them in any way. My daughter squirmed in my arms. It was like she could sense I didn't want her there. Like she felt like a dead weight. Like she no longer belonged in my arms. I needed to be out of the hospital. What I really needed was a drink. I tried to hide the twitch of my eye.

Someone clearing their throat made me turn my head. A doctor I didn't recognize had just walked through the swinging doors. He looked exhausted. Like it was his own life hanging in the balance.

I put Scarlett down, even though she started to cry. "Someone take her," I snapped as I walked over to him.

The doctor eyed me curiously. "James Hunter?" he asked.

"Is my wife okay?" The desperation in my tone didn't even make him flinch. He was the complete opposite of my lawyer. Composed. Used to delivering bad news to families.

He looked over my shoulder at the whole waiting room coming over toward us. "We had no choice but to put her on life support." His eyes met mine again.

I heard Penny's mom start to cry.

"Mr. Hunter, we need to have a word in private." He nodded down the hall.

"What does that mean exactly?" I asked as I followed him. "Did some of her organs shut down? Is she breathing on her own?"

"There is no easy way to put this, so I'll be frank with you, Mr. Hunter," he said as he came to a stop, out of earshot of my family. "There were high levels of poison in her blood. We pumped her stomach, but we're not sure how long it's been in her system, or what the extent of the damage is. We sent some lab samples out. We should hear back shortly."

"Poison? What are you talking about? Did someone poison my wife? Why aren't the police here? Why aren't you telling them this?"

"Mr. Hunter," he said and put his hand on my shoulder. "Nine times out of ten this is an intentional thing."

I stared at him. "Exactly. Someone intentionally poisoned my wife. We need to call the police."

The doctors eyes softened. "I meant intentional on her part. Suicide," he added, when I had no reaction. "There's no reason to suspect foul play."

I shook my head.

"Have you noticed any signs of depression or..."

"No." I shrugged his hand off my shoulder. "I need to see my wife."

"She's unresponsive. She's not awake, let alone speaking, and..."

"I need to see my wife," I said again, cutting him off.

He nodded. "We just moved her to room 502 of the ICU. She can only have one visitor at a time."

"When is she going to wake up?" I had already started walking toward the elevators.

"It's not a question of when, Mr. Hunter. It's a question of if. And I don't have an answer for you."

I slammed my fist against the button with an up arrow.

"Mr. Hunter?"

I tried to ignore him and hit the button again. The doors slowly opened.

"Some of the damage is irreversible. We had to re-move..."

I stepped on. The dinging of the doors closing blocked out the rest of the sentence. I didn't care what they had to remove. I didn't care if they amputated her fucking leg. I just needed her heart to still be beating. I needed her to be in my arms.

As soon as the elevator doors opened, I ran down the hall. "Room 502," I said to a nurse standing at a desk.

She pointed down the hall.

I continued to run until I saw the room marked 502. I pushed through the door and froze. *Penny.* Her face was pale. She had as many tubes and wires as my son had. But this time I felt something. Agony. An ache in my chest. I closed my eyes. *This isn't happening.*

Suicide, my lawyer had said. *Intentional,* the doctor said.

I walked over and put my hand on top of hers.

Ice.

The side of my face twitched. My wife had always been so warm. Her skin. Her soul. *Come back to me.* My tears stung my eyes and I dropped her hand.

"Is it true?" I said into the silence. "Did you want to leave me? Did you hate our life that much?"

I needed to hear her voice. I needed to see her smile. I placed my forehead on her hand. She didn't even smell like my wife. She smelled like hand sanitizer and death.

I stepped away from her.

She wanted to die.

I buried my hands in my hair.

She hated her life.

I backed up, bumping into one of the machines.

She didn't want me.

"Why, Penny? Why was this life not enough? Why wasn't I enough?" I realized I was shouting and no one could hear me. What the fuck was I doing? Why would I believe the word of some incompetent lawyer? And a doctor that probably couldn't even distinguish my wife from any other patient?

I stepped forward and knelt by Penny's hospital bed. "I'm sorry. Baby, please forgive me." I grabbed her hand again and tried to ignore the feeling of ice. "I know you didn't do this. I'm sorry." I touched the side of her cold face. "We have a son. Wake up." I slid my hand to the side of her neck. "You have to wake up now. We need you."

She lay there, frozen in time.

"I need you." I closed my eyes. I couldn't look at her like this. "Baby. You know I can't do this alone."

"Please be gentle," a nurse said from behind me.

I didn't realize how hard I was holding on to her. I let go of the side of her neck and winced at the white spots I had left on her skin. I quickly stood up. The worst part was that Penny didn't even look peaceful. She looked like she was in pain. I slowly backed out of the room. I couldn't be here. I couldn't breathe in this fucking hospital.

CHAPTER 39

Monday

"We're going home," I said and pulled Scarlett off the floor where she was coloring.

"Is Mommy going to be at home?"

"No, pumpkin."

"But I want Mommy."

"I can go fetch whatever you need," Ellen said and bustled over to us. "Let me be of some use."

"No, that's okay. Scarlett's tired. I'm taking her home."

"I'm not tired, Daddy."

"We'll be back later," I said to everyone without looking at them.

"No! I want Mommy!" She squirmed out of my grip and plopped back down on the floor with her arms folded across her chest.

"We're leaving," I said more sternly.

"I want my Mommy!" She started crying. "Where's Mommy?"

Rob and Daphne were staring at me. My dad was staring at me. Penny's parents were staring at me. I took a step back. I couldn't do this. I couldn't comfort them. I was barely holding on.

Twitch.

I turned around and pushed through the doors to the stairs.

"James!" Rob called after me.

I started running.

Twitch.

God, I needed something to hold on to.

With each step, I knew I should turn around. I knew everything that mattered was back in that hospital. But for some reason, I couldn't hold on to my family and friends. I needed air. I tried to breathe in the stale air of the city, but it was stifling.

***

"How is she?" Porter asked as soon as I stepped out of the elevator in our apartment building.

"I need you to bring me the surveillance footage from when I was away."

"Okay. But, James, how is she?"

Could I trust him?

Twitch.

No. Someone had poisoned my wife. I had no idea who it was. "She's on life support."

Porter pressed his lips together and shook his head. "And what about the baby?"

What about the baby? That baby was part of the reason why my wife was lying in the hospital unresponsive. "Just get me the footage." I brushed past him and opened the door to our apartment.

I closed my eyes as soon as the door closed and breathed in the smell of our home. I could imagine Penny lifting her head from the book she was reading in the kitchen. A smile spreading over her face as she dropped it on the counter. Me pushing her back, taking her against the granite.

My eyes flashed open and I quickly walked through the foyer, kitchen, and hall. I pushed open the door to her office and closed my eyes again. It smelled more like her than the rest of the house. It was almost like she was here with me. The memory came in a flash.

"James, I'm writing," Penny said and tried to swat me away.

I continued to kiss the side of her neck. I knew exactly what she had been writing about. I had been reading every word in the other room. She was writing about me fucking her against a tree in the middle of the golf course. It made me hard just thinking about it.

She hadn't started to show yet, pregnant with our second child. Her hair was in a knot on the top of her head and she was biting her lip as she concentrated. So fucking beautiful. *I kissed the side of her neck again.*

"James, I need to focus. I've barely written a thing today. And Scar will be home soon."

All of that was true. But she had just written about my cock fucking her sweet pussy. And reading about it didn't do it justice. I needed to feel her. I wanted to reminisce too.

"Baby, I'm so fucking hard for you."

She laughed. "Can't you wait a few hours until we've put Scarlett to sleep?"

I ran my hand down the front of her tank top and hooked my fingers around her waistband.

She tried to slap me away again.

"Baby, I don't want to wait." I moved my hand lower, brushing my fingers against her clit. "And it doesn't really feel like you want to either."

She moaned.

"What exactly are you writing about? You're so fucking wet." I bit her earlobe.

"James."

I slid a finger inside of her.

"Fine, you win." She tilted her head back and gave me that smile that always seemed to stop my heart. "Scar's going to be home any minute, though. You better get busy."

I laughed. "I'm five seconds ahead of you." I pushed the papers off her desk, grabbed her waist, and placed her on top of the desk. I pulled her shorts and thong down to her knees, not bothering to drag them all the way off, and thrust inside of her.

"God!" She spread her legs and leaned back slightly, knowing perfectly well what angle I liked best.

I reached my hand under her tank-top, pushed aside her bra, and grabbed a handful of her perky breast. "Baby, you have no idea what you do to me."

She wrapped her legs around my waist, pulling me closer. "I think I have some idea."

I pinched her nipple and she moaned again. I had been in the mood to fuck her. But now that I was buried to the hilt, I wished we had more time. I wanted to kiss every inch of her. I wanted to show her how much I loved her.

I groaned as she tightened around me.

"I love you," she whispered, as if she could sense my change of mood.

I leaned down and kissed her.

She ran her fingernails down the back of my neck, deepening the kiss.

I wanted to freeze time.

But I knew that wasn't possible. Time seemed to be speeding by. Our daughter was already two. But I could make this moment a little more memorable. I lifted Penny off the desk, carried her over to the wall, and pressed her back against it.

And I fucked her. Just like I had against that tree on that golf course so many years ago. Just like I had when we were first falling for each other. Back when we were wrong. Back when nothing we did made sense.

"James!"

"I love you, baby." Time changed us. It brought us closer together. We were a family now.

"I love you too," she said against my lips.

I grabbed her perfect ass firmly in my hands and slammed into her hard.

She screamed my name again as she came.

And I relished the feeling of her tightening around me. The feeling of being whole. The feeling that I knew was love. I exploded inside of her, a slew of curses leaving my lips. "Fuck, Penny."

She laughed, tightening around me again.

"God, you know how much I like when you do that."

"What?" she asked innocently, running her fingers through my hair.

"This," I said and tickled her side.

She squealed, trying to wiggle out of my grip, but I was still buried inside of her. And I had no intention of moving.

"We need to get dressed," she protested through her laughter.

"Or we could just stay like this." I dropped my fingers from her skin, knowing she was right. We were running out of time.

She sighed and pressed her forehead against mine. "James Hunter, you're impossible. Our daughter is going to run in here and see you with your pants around your ankles."

"She's three. She'll forget."

"Time is flying by too fast."

I gently eased her off the wall and placed her on her feet. "Then let's make sure to steal more moments like this."

She smiled. "Promise?"

"I promise."

I opened my eyes and stared at the empty chair.

Twitch.

That was the thing about time. It could change everything in the blink of an eye. She had been my student once. Then she became my wife. I opened up my eyes. Now she was slipping away.

I ran my palm along the back of my neck, remembering her fingernails digging into my skin. The room felt empty without her. Much more like a lonely library than her office.

I walked toward her desk like I was in a trance and sat down in her chair. I wasn't sure what I was looking for exactly. A sign that my lawyer was full of shit? That the doctor was wrong to point blame at her? She wouldn't try to kill herself. She just...wouldn't. We had come so far together. She wouldn't leave me, or Scar, or the new baby. I turned on the computer as I tried to ignore the image of my son that popped into my head.

A Word document was open. I stared at the last line she had written:

"Because life without this feeling, the feeling that you give me, isn't a life that I'm interested in at all."

I blinked, staring at the screen. I had said that to her when I proposed. And I had this awful feeling that maybe this was how she was feeling right before she started bleeding. Except, not in the optimistic way I had said it.

I made her feel loved. But if she thought I was cheating, she wouldn't feel that way anymore. Was she not interested in living her life because she thought I didn't want her anymore? Was this the fucking proof that my lawyer was right? That the doctor was right?

No. She was just writing about us. Remembering. *Right?* I put my elbow on her desk and placed my forehead in my hand. Just before I closed my eyes, I saw that my elbow was placed on an envelope. An envelope with my name on it.

My hands shook as I picked it up. This couldn't be the amendment to the will that my lawyer had talked about. That whole conversation was ridiculous. Everyone was just trying to mess with my head.

So why did it have my name on it? Why was it sealed? I tore it open and unfolded the page. It wasn't a will. I sighed. It was just a letter. She had probably written it and was going to mail it to me in London. But then I told her I was coming back. She wouldn't have had time to send it. I started reading her words.

James,

If you're reading this, we both know what happened. I don't need to say it. And all I can say is that I understand what you're feeling. Like your heart hurts. Like you don't know if you'll ever smile again. Like the world has stopped. Like the only thing you can see for miles is darkness.

You see, I almost lost you once. I know that feeling. My mother found me falling apart in a bathroom stall at the hospital. And she told me something that really stuck with me. She told me that you have to keep living in order to keep the memory of those you love alive. And I'm asking you to do that for me. Remind Scarlett of who I was. Tell stories to our son. Don't let me disappear to our children. Don't let them forget how much I loved them.

Maybe that seems like the hardest thing in the world. But what I'm about to ask you to do, it may just be harder. I need you to keep the memory of me alive to our children. But I need you to let the memories of me with you fade. Because I need you to keep your heart open. Keep loving. Keep living. I need you to let me go.

All I've ever wanted was for you to be happy. And even though it feels like the world has stopped, it hasn't. Because despite what you think, there is so much light in this world. There's so much light in you.

Remind Scarlett that I love her. Tell our son I wished I could have met him. And find a new love for yourself. You've always been stronger than you realized. But it's okay to lean on your family and friends. Let them help you. Let them in. Don't shut out everyone who cares about you. Because despite how it feels, you are not alone. You're strong. You're good. You're whole. You're loved. You are so loved, James.

Now smile,

Penny

I couldn't breathe. Smile? Are you fucking kidding me? I crumpled the piece of paper in my fist.

I hated that it felt like tears were threatening to fall from my eyes. How dare she compare this to what happened to me? How dare she pretend to understand what I was feeling? I got shot. That was an accident. She did this on purpose. This letter put all the pieces together. *Suicide. Intentional.* I stood up and shoved the piece of crumpled paper into my pocket.

My wife had tried to kill herself. I didn't know if she had succeeded. I didn't know what the lab tests would show. Organ failure? Would they ask me to pull the plug?

Twitch.

Why would she fucking do this? My phone buzzed in my pocket. I pulled it out and put it up to my ear. "What?" I said as I walked out into the hall.

"I pulled the footage," Porter said. "I'm emailing it to your computer now."

I walked out into the hall, closing the door to Penny's office. I was furious with her. But I wanted to preserve the room. Her smell. Our memories. "Don't bother." I clenched my jaw.

"But it's all ready."

"I'm not going to sit here and watch my wife kill herself." There was no reason to hide the truth from him now. He hadn't poisoned Penny. She took her own life.

There was a pause on the other end. "What are you talking about?"

"Penny poisoned herself. There were traces of it in her bloodstream and in her stomach. I'm not going to watch the video footage leading up to her decision to take her own life. Delete the footage from the past two days. I don't want to ever see it."

"Mr. Hunter, Penny wasn't suicidal. And you use all organic products. There isn't even any poison in the house, she couldn't..." his voice trailed off.

I stepped into the foyer. "What were you going to say?"

"Exterminators were here this morning. Penny was worried about the snakes that Scarlett kept mentioning. They didn't find anything. But they had brought all their equipment in. " He let his sentence hang in the air between us.

"Is there poison in pesticide?" I asked. But I already knew the answer. Of course there was.

"I'm not sure." There was a brief pause and the sound of computer keys typing. "Yes. There are several different poisons in pesticides."

"Destroy the footage."

"But shouldn't I look to see if..."

"No one knows about this but us. Scarlett will never know that her mother tried to take her own life. My family and friends will never hear about this. Not even the other members of the security team. Do you understand?"

"Yes."

I hung up and slid my cell phone back into my pocket. My fingers brushed across the crumpled piece of paper. *Smile? Seriously? Fuck you too, Penny.*

CHAPTER 40

Monday

I pointed to my glass and the bartender topped me off.

One drink. That's what I told myself. I stared down at my third.

Twitch.

Why wasn't alcohol helping? This was the only way I knew how to cope. This was the only way I knew how to numb the pain. But my body was betraying me.

I pulled the crumpled piece of paper out of my pocket and smoothed it out against the bar. She wanted me to forget about her. Was that because she thought I already had? I pushed my hair off my forehead. Where had we gone wrong?

No, I wasn't a perfect husband. But I tried. I kept my vows to her. I loved her more each day. Hadn't I told her that? Sometimes I stayed out late with my friends. Sometimes I'd lose track of time grading papers and miss dinner.

But most days? Most days I was there with her. Loving her. Cherishing her.

I read the words she had written again. Suddenly my anger was gone. I didn't know where I went wrong, but I knew it was my fault. I knew she had tried to take her life because of me. Whether it was because she thought I was cheating or something else. I had let her down. She wouldn't have done it otherwise. She loved our daughter. She loved our family and friends. But she didn't always love me. We fought. I made her cry too many times to count. I had somehow broken my perfect wife.

Baby, you need to come back to me. Let me try harder. Give me another chance.

I pulled out my phone and sent a text to Porter. "If you haven't deleted it yet, find when she did it. I need to see it." I pressed send and downed my third glass.

It wasn't the same feeling that Penny gave me. She made me feel alive. The burn of alcohol down my throat made me feel like I was barely holding on. I put some bills down on the bar and made my way back outside.

The sign for the hospital was in the distance, glowing now that dusk was upon the city. I was hiding. The note burning a hole in my pocket told me exactly what I needed to do. Penny was worried I'd be a bad father if she died. It was my biggest fear too. Whether she knew it or not, she had validated it. She was fucking right. I had a son that I didn't want to hold. I had a daughter that wouldn't stop crying. And all I wanted to do was head back into the bar.

I willed my feet to take me back to the hospital. Through the other entrance. Up the stairs to the NICU. I stared at my son through the window.

A neonatal nurse was inside, checking something on one of the machines my son was hooked up to. She looked up at me and then walked to the door. "Do you want to hold him?" she asked as she peered her head out.

I immediately shook my head.

She stepped out and walked over to me. "He's going to make it. He's strong."

My throat felt dry.

"What's his name?"

"My wife liked the name Liam." *Why did I say "liked" instead of "likes"?*

"Ah. Strong-willed warrior."

I turned toward her. "What?"

"I hear so many names. I started looking up all their meanings. That's a good name for him. Because he has to be strong to get through this. Are you sure you don't want to hold him?"

I ran my fingers through my hair. "I'm sure."

"Do you have any other kids?"

I wasn't sure why she was pretending she didn't know who I was. She knew which son was mine. She clearly recognized me from tabloids. "A little girl. Scarlett."

"The one with the red hair?"

I smiled. "That's the one."

"She's very cute. She's already been in to see him. Some older siblings don't realize how gentle they need to be with a newborn. But she was very good at holding him."

My daughter had held him. Who else had? The question didn't matter. What mattered was the fact that I couldn't seem to make myself hold him. What happened to my wife wasn't the baby's fault. I was putting blame on him. But he was fighting for his life too.

I stared at his dark hair. And his nose. He definitely had my nose. God, he was so small. I stepped away from the window. "Is Dr. Nelson still here? I haven't gotten the complete update on my son's condition."

"I can page him if you want to go in the waiting room. He just finished a delivery so he'll need a few minutes."

She didn't point out a baby as proof. Dr. Nelson had probably just delivered a healthy baby. With a mother that could hold him. With a father that wanted to. A baby that wasn't in the NICU.

"Thank you. I'll be in the waiting room."

"James?"

She had finally admitted to knowing my name.

"I'm sorry about your wife. To try to take your own life when you're pregnant...I just can't imagine what your family is going through right now."

My whole body turned cold. "Who told you that?"

She opened her mouth and then closed it again. "Just...word travels around the hospital."

"That's a lie. My wife would never do that."

The paper in my pocket made it seem otherwise. The doctor made it seem otherwise. My lawyer made it seem otherwise.

"Oh, I'm sorry," she stammered. "I didn't mean..." her voice trailed off.

No one could know. No one could think less of her. Because I didn't want her memory to be tainted by this. I was angry, but I still loved her. I loved her with every fiber of my being. *Please don't let anyone else know.* I pushed through the doors to the waiting room. I needed to keep Penny's secret. I had to.

Rob looked up at me as I walked in. He wasn't looking at me like he hated at me. He was looking at me like he knew.

I stood frozen in the waiting room.

They all knew.

There was no running from this. I sat down in an empty seat and closed my eyes. I was going to follow Penny's instructions. I was going to be a good father. And that meant waiting here for a few minutes so I could talk to her OB-GYN. To find out what was wrong with my son.

"The night of Bee's wedding I found her crying outside her hotel room," Tyler said.

I opened my eyes and looked up at Tyler.

He sat down next to me. "I tried to talk to her, but she wouldn't tell me what was wrong. I should have pressed it. I should have..."

"Stop."

Tyler shook his head and looked up at the ceiling. "I didn't know that she was struggling. I just thought she missed you. I should have..." his voice trailed off but he kept staring at the ceiling. "I thought I could read her. But this? Why the hell would she do this?"

I didn't have anything to say.

"Look, I know the only reason we became friends was through Penny," said Tyler. "But you need to know that I think of you as a brother. I love your daughter like she's my own. If you need anything..."

"I just need her to wake up." My back stiffened when he hugged me.

I was pretty sure the only physical contact Tyler and I had ever had were handshakes and fists to the face. I awkwardly patted his back in return and then pulled away.

"Do you want me to take Scar for the night?" he asked. "I'm sure Axel would be able to help calm her down."

"No. I'm going to take her home in a few minutes. I'm just waiting to talk to the OB-GYN."

Tyler nodded. "I should get home too. Hailey still doesn't know. I can't believe this happened."

He stood up. I had nothing left to say. I couldn't believe it either. I watched him walk out of the waiting room. And a part of me wondered if he felt lucky. That he hadn't won Penny over. That he ended up with Hails instead. Hails was always smiling. Hails was still breathing on her own. Hails was still happy.

Dr. Nelson walked into the waiting room. His lips were pressed together, like he was dreading this conversation. "James," he said as he approached me and stuck out his hand.

I stood up and shook it. "My father told me that the baby already had a blood transfusion. Is he doing alright now?"

"Can we sit down?" he asked and nodded down at the chairs.

"Of course."

"It's been a long day for both of us." He sighed and sat down next to me. "We'll probably need to do another blood transfusion. It's common for preemies to have anemia. It's nothing to be too alarmed about. And his lungs are well developed for his size. We should be able to take him off the CPAP in several weeks."

"Several weeks? How long will he need to be in there?"

"It's standard to keep preemies in the NICU until their original due date. So about two months."

"Two months?" I hadn't realized how bad the situation really was. I thought I'd be taking him home soon. Alone. "Is there a possibility that he won't make it?"

"I'm not really a man of chance, James. I practice precision in everything I do."

"That doesn't answer my question."

"Eighty percent of babies born at 26 weeks live. The greater question is will he have a learning or developmental impairment. Because even though he will most likely live, eighty percent of the babies that do will have some sort developmental or physical problem in their lives."

I was familiar with the 80-20 principle in business. But I didn't like those odds for my son. That meant there was only a sixteen percent chance that he'd be healthy. Normal. *Fuck.*

"Even though we never want to see babies at 26 weeks out of the womb, he is technically a healthy weight for his size. So, that's a good sign. But with all the blood loss that Penny suffered, along with the poison she consumed, it does put your son at greater risks for more severe problems."

My dad hadn't mentioned any of this. Had Dr. Nelson told him? Or was he just adding more weight to my shoulders? "You said you're not a man of chance. So tell me. Do you think he'll be able to have a normal life?"

"No. I strongly doubt that he will."

Twitch.

I leaned back in my chair and sighed. The sounds of the hospital seemed to dull. It was like I could hear my heart beating. Why couldn't it beat for my wife? For my son? "I need some rest."

IVY SMOAK

"Of course," Dr. Nelson said and stood up. "We'll be monitoring the baby's vitals constantly. He's in good hands here. I'll keep a special eye on him. And I'll keep checking on your wife as well."

I nodded my head. "Thank you." I stood up too.

"I'm sorry about Penny," he said and placed his hand on my shoulder. "Sometimes these things are impossible to predict. I know I don't specialize in mental health, but I do apologize for not pressing the issue of her mood. When she kept wanting attention for a minor heart problem, I should have seen it as a sign." He shook his head.

I stared at him like he was an alien. Wanting attention for a minor heart problem? Was that a sign? To me it was a sign that she was scared of dying. Not that she wanted it.

"We're all hoping she and your son will pull through. But..." his voice trailed off. "No, never mind, you should go get some rest. I'm keeping you up."

"What were you going to say?" I asked.

"It can wait till another time. I don't want to add to this terrible day."

"Nothing you could say right now would be shocking, Dr. Nelson."

He nodded his head. "I know that we're still waiting for tests to come back. But the root cause of all of this goes back to her heart murmur. She was very worried about her diagnosis. It caused her extra stress. I'm not saying that's why she poisoned herself, but it is a possibility to consider. Her last OB-GYN was negligent. If you're filing a lawsuit, I'd be happy to testify on your behalf."

He was right. And it was exactly what I needed to hear after my pointless meeting with my lawyer. Someone was

- 332 -

going to pay for this. "Her last OB-GYN is an old friend of yours. Dr. Jones. Are you sure you'd be willing to be a witness?"

"Like I said before, James, I'm not a man of chance. Dr. Jones took a chance by not telling you about Penny's heart murmur. And as a fellow doctor, I can't uphold that decision. He was in the wrong. And even if he is done practicing medicine, he has a whole practice that was trained by him. We don't want something like this to happen again because of his negligence."

"Thank you," I said and stuck my hand out to him. "I needed someone on my side in this suit."

Dr. Nelson accepted my outstretched hand.

"Goodnight, doctor."

"Goodnight, James." He walked over to Penny's mom who had waved him down. Did she know that her grandson was going to have mental or physical issues? Was she learning about it now?

I needed to get out of here. I needed to be in my bed, with my face buried in Penny's pillow. I needed just a tiny bit of strength. My eyes wandered around the waiting room, looking for Scarlett. I almost started to panic, but then I spotted her, cowering behind a chair. She looked truly frightened.

And in that moment, it didn't matter that she looked just like Penny. If anything, it made me want to comfort her even more. I walked over to her and crouched down.

"Daddy." Her voice trembled slightly as she ran into my arms.

"Pumpkin, what's wrong?"

"He's a bad snake."

The hairs on the back of my neck rose. "What did you say, Scar?"

"Mr. Snake. From the movie." She pointed at Dr. Nelson.

I frowned as I turned around to look at Dr. Nelson. His hair was gray and always slightly long and disheveled looking. It almost looked greasy. He always wore the same color scrubs - black. It was a bit odd, since the rest of the doctors and nurses roaming about predominately wore light color tones of green, pink, and blue. But there was nothing snakelike about the man.

"Pumpkin, there are no evil snakes."

"Yes there are. He's evil snake. I want Mommy."

The side of my face twitched.

Scarlett buried her face in my neck. "Please, Daddy."

"We'll see her tomorrow, okay?" Tomorrow I'd be stronger. Tomorrow I'd sit with my wife. I'd hold her hand and will her to come back to us. I'd promise to be better.

"Can we at least hold baby before we go?"

I needed to do it. What if he died in the middle of the night? I'd regret not holding him my whole life. "Okay, let's go say goodnight to your brother."

"I thought I was getting a sister. But I like him."

"You and me both."

She ducked her head under my chin as if she was frightened again. I turned around to see Dr. Nelson staring at us. I waved before pushing through the doors.

CHAPTER 41

Monday

"She's good with him," Daphne said as she stepped up beside me at the window.

I stared at Scarlett gently holding my son in her arms. She was being careful not to touch any of the cords that helped him live. The nurse from earlier was helping her properly distribute the weight.

"I thought she might be jealous," I said. Or maybe I had been worried I would be. When Scarlett was born, I had been apprehensive. I liked having Penny's attention all to myself. But the transition with Scarlett was effortless. We both loved her. At least, I thought Penny loved her.

"James," Daphne said and waited until I turned to her. "It's not true."

"What?"

"Everything the doctor said. I know it isn't true. Penny would never try to kill herself."

"She wrote me a letter and wanted to add it to her will this morning. My lawyer brought up the possibility of suicide with only that information. And the doctor brought it up with just the poison. He didn't even know about the letter." I pulled it out of my pocket and handed it to her.

She quickly scanned the note. "James, she was scared because of her heart murmur. She wrote this in fear. Not in decisiveness."

"Daphne, there were exterminators at our house this morning. She had access to poison."

"I don't care about the poison. Or some letter." She put it back in my hands. "James, she didn't do this."

"That's what I thought at first too, but, Daphne, everything is pointing to that fact. How can you be so sure that she didn't want to die?" I truly wanted to know. Because I no longer knew what to believe. I loved my wife fiercely. And I was having trouble understanding why she didn't love me the same way.

"Because I know what it looks like. I know the signs. My brother..." she paused, her bottom lip trembling. "I beat myself up for not seeing that. But I know the signs now. And Penny was not depressed. She couldn't wait to give birth to her son. She couldn't wait for you to come back from London. She was fighting the news about her heart condition with strength, not fear. She was full of life and laughter and..."

"She thought I cheated on her, okay? Is that what you need to hear? She thought I didn't love her." I was raising my voice.

Daphne grabbed my hand. "Rob was with her when she thought that. There was no lapse of time where she could have ran off and guzzled poison, James. Your lawyer is wrong. The doctors are wrong. Everyone is just...wrong."

"But what if they're not?"

She shook her head. "What if they are? James, I know Penny. We share everything. She's my best friend. And she would never, ever do this. We both feel so lucky in our relationships. Not repressed or scared or upset. Lucky. She would never willingly leave this world. And you know that. I know you do."

I blinked away my tears.

"You know that." She squeezed my hand.

"Can you ask Rob to look into it? I'm tired and..."

"Drunk."

I stared at her. "I had a few drinks. I'm not drunk."

"You can go home and sleep it off. After you meet your son."

Scarlett had just come out.

"Aunt Daphne, isn't he the most beautiful baby?" she said and climbed into Daphne's arms.

"Yes, he is." Daphne smiled as she adjusted Scarlett away from her baby bump. "Go," she said to me.

I walked over to the door and opened it. The air was warmer in the small room. The nurse was just about to put my son back down when she saw me. "Do you want to hold him?"

He was even smaller close up. I nodded and put my arms out. He did fit in my hands. He was so light. His face scrunched up for a moment like he wanted to cry. But then his features softened.

And for the first time since my plane landed, I smiled. I smiled down at my son. Liam. Strong-willed warrior. "I need you to be strong for your mom. Because she's being strong for us."

I looked over to the window. Scarlett had her hand pressed against the glass, like she wished she was with us. And it felt like ice melted off my heart. My family wasn't broken. But it was breaking. Someone was trying to ruin us.

"I'll be back," I whispered to my son. "I promise I'll be back." I reluctantly gave him back to the nurse and stepped into the hall. "Can you watch her for one more minute? I'll be right back."

Daphne smiled and nodded, like she knew where I was going. But where else would I be fucking going? My wife was in the hospital. And it was about time I stopped doubting her. Right now she needed me. I wasn't going to let her down twice.

***

"Baby, you won the bet," I said, stroking my thumb along her palm. "It's a boy." I didn't know who else had visited her. I didn't know if she could hear me. "You won, but I'm the one that needs a wish. I need you to come back to me." I reached up and pushed her bangs off her forehead, trying not to cringe at the coolness of her skin. "Do you hear me, Penny? I need you. Scar needs you. Liam needs you."

I smiled at hearing his name out loud. "You were right. I wanted a son. But I was scared that I'd ruin him. I was scared he'd be too much like me." I looked down at the tube sticking out of her mouth. I wanted her to smile. I wanted her to tell me that everything was going to be okay. "I read your letter." I put my other hand on top of hers, sandwiching her small hand between mine, trying to warm her skin. "And I'm going to deny your request."

I could imagine her pouting.

"I'm going to be a terrible father from here on out. I'm going to ruin our son. I'm going to get high every night. I'm never going to smile. And I'm going to pine over you. Do you hear me?"

I imagined a line of worry appearing on her forehead.

"So you better wake up. Because our family's future depends on you. It always has. I know you want to wake up. Now you have an even better reason to."

She'd probably slap me right now if she was awake. Or tell me I was impossible. Or poke me in the middle of my chest and yell at me. And that's what I wanted. I wanted her to be feisty and strong and wake the fuck up. Our family needed her. I needed her.

"I'm going to find out what happened. I'm going to take care of it. You just focus on getting better, okay?" I leaned forward and kissed her forehead. The softness of her skin was the only thing that remained the same. "Fight for us, baby. Be as strong as I know you are."

I stared down at her. "You know, some people say another person shouldn't complete you. That you should be whole without having to rely on another soul. That you should just be happy the way you are. Do you know what I say to that? Fuck them. I don't care if no one understands us. I don't care if something like this isn't comprehensible to the average person. Because the average person hasn't experienced this love. Our love. Our story. A great love."

I swallowed hard. "Because I swear I can't breathe without you. I swear my heart will stop beating when yours does. And I swear I wouldn't want it any other way. So wake up. If the threat of me ruining our family isn't enough, think about that. Our children not having either of us. Not getting to experience growing up in a house full of love and laughter. Not getting to experience everything we could give them."

I ignored the twitch of my eye.

"I read your story and I'm sorry. I got you a publishing deal and I'm sorry. I lied to you about my trip and I'm sorry. And for five years I've believed that I'm addicted to you." I wasn't sure I would have said that if I thought she could hear me. But I needed her to know. That I had lived with that fear. "This whole time."

I ignored the twitch of my eye again.

"I'm not addicted to you," I lied. I needed to say it out loud, even though it wasn't true. I needed her to know I was trying to be strong too. I needed her to know that I did believe what we had was love. Even though I now had the proof that our love was infected by my problems. Even though I had always known in the back of my head. "I'm not addicted to you," I said again, more for myself than for her. "But I do love you. I love you with every-thing that I am. Come back to me, baby."

My words were greeted by the whirls and beeps of machines.

"Because this is love. Not addiction." I put my hand on the center of her chest and smiled at the feeling of her heartbeat. "You've always understood. You've always seen the truth."

THE LIGHT TO MY DARKNESS

I put my forehead against hers. "You've always been the light to my darkness. And, Penny, I can't survive without your light."

CHAPTER 42

Monday

"When is Mommy coming home?" Scarlett asked as we stepped into the apartment.

"Soon," I said. This time it didn't feel like a lie. When I was in my coma, I swore I knew she was beside me. I couldn't remember anything specific, but I just knew. And she'd know I was there today. She'd know that she couldn't give up. She'd hear my plea.

I placed Scarlett down when I heard a knock on the door. "Go upstairs and get ready for bed, pumpkin," I said and ruffled her hair. "I'll be up to read you a bedtime story in a minute."

"Can we watch a movie instead?"

I smiled down at her. She usually fell asleep with her head on my lap when we watched movies. I understood that she didn't want to be alone tonight. "Of course. Go pick one out. I'll be there in a minute."

She walked away. Not her usual skip. No giggle. *Don't change. Please don't let today hurt you.* I needed to stay strong for her. Despite what I had said to Penny, I would never. Ever. Forget that my first job in life was as a father.

I turned around and opened the door.

"Mr. Hunter," Porter said. "I went through the footage from the past two days. There was nothing there. She didn't do it."

Any remaining doubt I had dissipated. "Then watch the past several weeks. If she didn't do it, that means someone poisoned her."

"I already watched a few days back. No one's come in or out of the house." He stepped forward and dropped his voice. "Could it have been someone at the wedding?"

"No."

"Or Ellen?"

I shook my head. I was done doubting my gut. "Ellen didn't do it. It isn't someone from the family. Keep watching the tapes. It has to be something you missed. During the time in between scans of the house."

He nodded. "How far back?"

"Until you find something."

"I'll call you when I've found it." He closed the front door and I heard the familiar lock. Could someone really have gotten into our house? How long did it take to go from the entrance of the apartment, up the elevator, and perform a successful lock-pick? I ran my fingers through my hair. I had to be missing something.

My phone buzzed. At first I thought it was Porter already. I eagerly answered the call.

"James," Matt said. "How are you holding up?"

"Not great." I looked in the other room at my daughter playing with the remote control. She had turned on the same Harry Potter movie that had scared her the other night. I was about to go stop her when Matt continued.

"Daphne called me. She told me about the poison. I agree with her, man. Penny was happy."

I closed my eyes. For some reason, I needed to hear that from him. If he had been hitting on her, that meant she had turned him down. If she thought I was cheating on her, would she have? It just further validated what Daphne had said. Penny didn't even suspect anything until her conversation with Rob. "Where were you today?" Most of the day was a blur, but I didn't remember seeing him at the hospital.

"Rob was having me talk to an investigator. Look, I know you're probably exhausted. But I had a thought. Well, the investigator had a thought. I can't take the credit. What if her first OB-GYN, the retired one, didn't tell you that she had a heart murmur because it really did disappear after Scarlett was born? Apparently it usually does after a baby is delivered."

"But it didn't. It's just gotten worse."

"No, not necessarily," he said. "No one knows if she had one between her pregnancies. It may have actually gone away. What I'm saying is, what if someone's been poisoning her for a while? What if her heart condition is caused by it too?"

A chill ran down my spine.

"Yeah, but who, Matt? No one comes in or out of my apartment without my security alerting me."

A knock on the door made me jump.

I answered it and Matt was standing there.

I slowly lowered my phone from my ear.

"Not necessarily. I just snuck by them," Matt said. "Whoever did it must have hacked into the webcam of one of their computers. He must have watched them not watching the surveillance footage. Well, technically, he probably saw that they were just glancing at it every five minutes."

I frowned and looked up at the camera mounted in the corner.

"See. There's a chink in your armor." He closed the door behind him. "Someone could have snuck in here and poisoned her. Easily."

I shook my head. "They'd only have a few minutes to pull it off. And if your theory is correct, they would have had to be poisoning her for a long time. Not just this once."

"Right. So what does Penny eat a lot?"

"Ice cream."

Matt smiled. "Do you mind if the investigator comes up? He had some ideas of what it could be. He's waiting downstairs."

"Yeah, of course. Bring him up." If Matt was right, it had to be something that didn't spoil. No one would risk coming in here several times. Penny's cravings had been erratic.

"Daddy," Scarlett said and tugged on my pants leg.

"Not now, pumpkin."

"But, Daddy, it's the snake."

"Scarlett, I've told you so many times. There are no evil snakes."

"Yes there are. It's Mr. Snake." She pointed to the T.V. screen, where she was paused in the middle of the movie.

It was paused on an image of Professor Snape.

"Pumpkin that isn't..." my voice trailed off as I studied the image. The long greasy hair. The black robe. The actor that played Professor Snape looked uncannily like Dr. Nelson. A slightly younger version, but very similar.

"Bad Snake." She pointed at the T.V. screen again.

"Do you mean Professor Snape?"

"Yes! Snapes!" She looked so excited, like she had been trying to explain this to me for weeks. "Snapes," she said and nodded. "Bad Snapes. Snapes hurt Mommy."

"How did Snape hurt Mommy?"

Scarlett pretended to pop something into her mouth, tilted her head back, and made a gulping noise. "For healthy baby."

"Her pills," I said and turned around to Matt. I thought about Dr. Nelson prescribing them the first time. To take them instead of her usual prenatal vitamins. Penny had complained about being tired that day. He said they would help. Then he upped the dose once she started having chest pains. *Shit.*

I ran into the kitchen and opened up the cabinet where she kept them. But they weren't there.

"Here," Matt said and lifted them off the counter. "Oh, fuck." He picked up a note that had been sitting next to them. "Ellen accidentally sent them with you to London. Penny didn't take them all weekend. She must have taken a whole bunch last night when she got home to make up for it."

"Let me see it," someone said from behind us. I turned around as Matt tossed him the bottle. I recognized the investigator. Rob and I had used him on other occasions. He had actually helped me get my divorce papers signed.

He unscrewed the cap and bit one of the gel capsules in half. Then he immediately spit it out. "That's it. Taking these over time would do some serious damage."

I recognized the pills as soon as the investigator pulled one out. I had taken them while I was in London. Really, I had thought nothing of it. I assumed Ellen had just picked up a different brand of vitamins. The side of my face twitched again. And for the first time since the plane landed, I felt relieved. It wasn't withdrawal. There was poison in my bloodstream too. I wasn't addicted to my wife. It suddenly felt like I could breathe again. *I'm not addicted to her. I love her.*

"James?" Matt said, pulling me out of my stupor. "What do you want us to do?"

"Call the police." I knelt down to Scarlett. "Scarlett, how did you know this?"

"It was my fault." Her bottom lip trembled. "I opened the door when he knocked. Even though I knew I wasn't supposed to open doors. Even though I promised you I wouldn't. I was bad."

"It's okay, pumpkin. You're not bad. Just tell me what happened." I put my hands on her shoulders.

"He gave Mommy new healthy baby medicine. And said that she needed it. And he made me promise not to tell. He said he'd kill Mommy if I told. But I was scared." Tears were streaming down her cheeks. "So I told Mommy about snakes right away. But no one believed me. I tried to whisper, but I had to say it over and over and over again. He must have heard me." She pointed up to the cameras.

"He said he was watching. He said it would be fine and that everyone would think he was the best. But I knew it wasn't going to be fine. I tried to tell you." She started crying harder, unable to speak.

"Pumpkin." I pulled her into my arms, pressing her ear to the side of my face and covering her other one with my hand. "Get Porter to deactivate all the cameras," I said to Matt. "I need to get down to the hospital before he does something else."

Matt was still on the phone with the police, unable to listen to my request.

So I lifted Scarlett into my arms, ran out into the hallway, and down to the security office. I knocked on the door.

Porter looked alarmed when he opened it. Like he hadn't seen everything that just happened. Because he probably hadn't. Because I had told him to only glance every five minutes. Because Penny felt uncomfortable with them watching us. Because I didn't want them to see the curves of her body. Or me fucking her relentlessly. What had I been thinking?

Maybe I should have told him about the shooting pain in my left arm. Or the fact that I knew I had consumed some of the poison. But I was heading to the hospital anyway. So instead, I handed Scarlett to him. "Call the hospital. Dr. Nelson poisoned Penny. I should have seen it. He was the one that told us about the heart murmur in the first place. He made the whole thing up. He gave me the health records from her last OB-GYN. He probably fucking tampered with them!" How had I not seen any of the signs? "Him disagreeing with the doctors at the ER about Penny needing medicine for her elevated blood pressure and heart rate. His pretend sincerity for my family. Him saying he'd testify against Dr. Jones. Him pressing the fact that his rival practice was negligent. He wanted to ruin them. And what better than a public face like Penny's to do that? He was going to destroy Dr. Jones' practice with the tabloids, even without winning a lawsuit. He just wanted to be number one. And he said he was going to keep his eye on my son and Penny. I think he's planning to do something else." I winced at the pain.

"Are you alright?" Porter asked as he pulled Scarlett against his chest. She was still crying.

"I'm fine," I lied. "Scarlett?"

She looked up at me with her tear stained face.

"Tell Porter exactly what happened. Exactly when you saw Snape come, okay?"

Porter gave me an odd look.

"Okay, Daddy," she sniffled.

Twitch.

I ignored the twitch, just like I had the pain in my arm. "I'm going to the hospital. Make sure the police are there to meet me." I ran back out into the hall and down the staircase.

Three years ago, I had changed my life. I had started teaching again. I had stopped eating steak. And God, I fucking loved a good steak. I had started appreciating the little things more. My wife's laugh. My daughter's smile. With those changes, I had been able to lower my stress levels. I had been able to lower my blood pressure. I was healthy now. My last checkup verified that.

But I was tired. I told Daphne I wasn't drunk. But I wasn't exactly sober. The stress of the day had piled up. I felt physically sick with grief. With betrayal. I was angry. And heartbroken. And hopeful. It was too much.

So I shouldn't have been surprised by the sharp pain in my chest. I shouldn't have been surprised that my legs collapsed from underneath of me.

My shoulder landed hard on the step beneath me. My body continued to fall, and I couldn't seem to stop it. Finally the back of my head hit the floor at the bottom of the stairs. And it felt like all the life had just been sucked out of me. For a moment, I had the eerie feeling that Penny had just taken her last breath.

I tried to gasp for mine, sprawled at the bottom of the staircase. I tried to feel anything but the pain in my chest. My heart was failing. I had been so worried about Penny's that I had forgotten about the stress on my own.

I thought I was suffering from withdrawal, when in reality the twitch on the side of my face had been a sign of my body being attacked. The poison was killing me. And my heart was breaking because I was losing the love of my life.

Darkness. That was life without my light. Complete and utter darkness.

ABOUT THE AUTHOR

Ivy Smoak is an international bestselling author. When she's not writing, you can find her binge watching too many TV shows, taking long walks, playing outside, and generally refusing to act like an adult. She lives with her husband in Delaware.

Twitter: @IvySmoakAuthor
Facebook: IvySmoakAuthor
Goodreads: IvySmoak